when in
ROME

when in
ROME

Amabile Giusti

Translated by Sarah Christine Varney

Text copyright © 2014 Amabile Giusti
Translation copyright © 2016 Sarah Christine Varney

Previously published as *Trent'anni... e li dimostro* by Kindle Direct Publishing in 2014 in Italy. Translated from Italian by Sarah Christine Varney. First published in English by AmazonCrossing in 2016.

Published by AmazonCrossing, Seattle

www.apub.com

Amazon, the Amazon logo, and AmazonCrossing are trademarks of Amazon.com, Inc., or its affiliates.

ISBN-13: 9781503951273
ISBN-10: 1503951278

Cover design by Laura Klynstra

Printed in the United States of America

For those who know love . . . wherever you are.
"For you alone, I think and plan. Have you not seen
this? Can you fail to have understood my wishes?"

Jane Austen, Persuasion

ONE

The girl's got an hourglass figure, and she's wearing a polka-dotted piece of floss that she's trying to pass off as underwear. She's rummaging through my fridge, reaching past a hunk of lukewarm cheese and a bunch of tomatoes for a can of beer that's frosted to the back wall.

I stare at her, my eyelid twitching with rage. I should have just stayed in bed, but how am I supposed to sleep when the walls are shaking? All that noise—the slamming of the door, the coarse giggling, the creaking bedsprings, and of course, the moaning of the hungry lioness unleashed in the next room.

Of course, I didn't expect to find myself in the presence of the moaner herself, planted in front of the fridge. Ass and giraffe legs in plain sight, my pink hair tie in her hair, she's displaying all twenty-five years of her bold beauty as she grapples with the imprisoned can. She mutters something controversial about defrosting the goddamn ancient thing.

I'd like to tell this nosy tart that I'm the one who decides when and how to take care of my appliances. And since this is my home, my fridge, and my Strawberry Shortcake hair tie, I have every right to grab her by the collar and throw her out. Well, maybe not by her collar, as she seems to be wearing only a thong. But I swallow my profanity and stay silent, observing her as if she were made of organic manure. A deafening rage builds in my chest, but it's nothing compared to what's beneath: I'm so desperately jealous.

Suddenly, the young lady realizes she's not alone and turns around. Her boobs are so unbelievably perky that they almost touch her neck. Unfortunately for me, she's pretty. Her fiery red hair is shaped into a perfect bob. She has green eyes, plump lips, and teeth that are so white they belong in a whitening ad. So obviously, I hate her. I hate that she slept with Luca; I hate that she's criticizing my fridge and wandering naked through my house. But I especially hate Luca.

Not that I'm surprised he managed to seduce her. He's the kind of guy that women want and men detest. Unless they're gay, in which case, they want him, too. His shoulders look like they're cut from a mahogany tree trunk, his ass chiseled like a Greek statue's. He has cherry lips and eyes that are either green or black, depending on his mood and the light. When he laughs, he tilts his head back, gazing at the world from underneath his eyelashes as he runs his hands through thick, messy hair. Basically, Luca is gorgeous. At first, my friends were convinced that we must be secretly hooking up. But the truth is, in the six months that we've lived together, the most intimate moment we've shared was when I got sick of the dirty clothes piling up in his room and put his boxers in the washing machine—with salad tongs.

I catch the girl leering at my frizzy hair and my ridiculous red pajamas, a Christmas present from my aunt Porzia.

"So, do you have any more beer? This one's stuck," she says brazenly, gesturing to the iceberg in my fridge. She lisps the letter s.

"Nice to meet you, I'm Carlotta!" I blurt out, practically hysterical.

Luca comes in, naked except for a pair of excessively tight boxers. They don't leave much to the imagination. I think I deserve a little more consideration, and I stare pointedly at him, but he ignores me.

He smiles at the girl and gestures at her to come finish having fun. She cackles like a hen. No, like a hyena. She pretends to put up a fight and then puts her hand right *there*, like she's grabbing a microphone at karaoke night. If I had a bowling ball, I'd knock them both over. Strike!

I must be radiating hatred, as Luca suddenly turns to me, the redhead still firmly holding her microphone.

"What are you doing up?" he asks.

What kind of question is that? I actually contemplate slapping him and his thong-wearing mistress as he bends over to chip the can from the ice block, but I restrain myself. The girl loosens her grip and sits on the table; her legs dangle for miles. She stretches a foot to the place her hand just vacated, completely indifferent to my presence.

"The whole neighborhood heard you," I say through clenched teeth. "And you, would you mind getting your ass off my table? I eat off of that, and there's not enough rubbing alcohol in the world to disinfect it."

The lisping tramp just laughs again, still not stooping to acknowledge me and playing her inappropriate game of footsie. I envision using my own foot to punt her off the table. Luca hands her the can and rubs his cold hand.

"Poor Carlotta," he murmurs. "You've gotta get up early tomorrow, and we've kept you awake."

He gives me a little hug, as he usually does when he makes fun of me, and lifts me off the ground, which is pretty easy because I'm small. He has clearly forgotten that he's practically naked, and a shiver runs through my body as I feel him pressed up against my legs. But I don't let on; instead, I hide behind a horrified look and a punch that forces him to let me go. Luca gives me a friendly peck on the cheek, and the girl stiffens and murders me with a stare. I almost feel sorry for her now. I want to warn her that Luca is not her property, that after tonight, he'll shake her out of the house like a tablecloth full of crumbs. Luca's kind of disgusting that way. He never gives his conquests a second chance.

He won't even remember this girl's face tomorrow, and when she calls for round two, I'll be forced to answer and invent a bunch of lies. I guess you could call Luca a modern-day sex god. He's got a collection of condoms in every color and flavor in his nightstand, and he never sleeps with the same woman twice.

Now that he's put me down, I soften up. In all honesty, I'm in love with him. But that's one secret I'm not going to reveal. I just pretend that he's as intriguing as the marble cherub atop the fountain in my mother's garden—just something nice to look at. No one will ever know that I pretend my pillow is Luca, holding it like a child does a stuffed animal. While I may look furious because I've lost sleep, I'm actually furious because of the tormenting thought that the man of my dreams just rolled around in a twin bed with a woman he met tonight. I prefer to put on a brave face, but the harsh truth is that I want him the way a dehydrated plant wants a burst of fresh water. When he's around, I feel complete. He fills my life with his infernal mess, his laughter, the acrid smell of his cigars, the rhythmic clicking of his keyboard, and his spectacular body like carved granite, which he shows off without a second thought—as if I don't have eyes, hormones, or a heart. My anger tonight probably stems from sexual frustration. It's been ages since I've gotten laid.

My mother thinks I'm too dull and that I should hike up my skirt and put myself out there. Although, since she had a fling with her salsa dance instructor after twenty-five years of marriage, I'm not sure if she should be giving me advice. But can I help it if there just haven't been any sparks with the men I've gone out with? Can I help it if the only thing I can think about when they kiss me is whether or not I've paid the phone bill? Can I help it if when they touch me, my knee-jerk reaction is exactly that—to knee them in the balls?

Luca pats me on the cheek, but then the girl grabs him by the hips. He squirms like a dog shaking off the rain.

"I'll be good. Go back to bed, little butterfly," he tells me.

Obviously, he's in love with me. We just don't sleep together.

He walks away, leaving me with the rear view of his barely-there briefs. The girl must not be entirely stupid, because she has clearly noticed that something's up. She looks annoyed as she leaves hesitantly. I watch them disappear into the bedroom and, despite the fact that I know he'll keep his word, I am slammed with jealousy that makes me sour, like a bitter old maid. I rummage through the pantry, but all I can find is a Hershey bar. It's probably been here since I moved in five years ago, but whatever. I'd eat it even if it were moldy.

I lock myself in my room with my loot. I chew the chocolate angrily, as if punishing it, then swallow it spitefully, subjecting it to its digestive fate. Of course, in a couple hours, I too will probably be punished—by a formidable bout of intestinal unrest.

I sit on the edge of the bed, in front of the mirror, and observe myself. Here I am, Carlotta Lieti. Chronically insecure, sarcastic, and compulsive. Specializing in bad luck and all things related. I'll be thirty in a few months. I have no boyfriend. Not even a friend with benefits. I just lost a job that was actually less lucrative than begging on the street. Tomorrow I have an interview, and I have a zit on my nose.

I bite into another piece of chocolate. If zits are a symptom of youth, I'll gladly take a few more. Better that than crow's feet. I smile, and two dozen fine lines crowd my eyes. Damn. I haven't missed out on any of the symptoms of aging. My nose seems to have grown some hair. And is it just me, or are my ears bigger? They say that aging isn't graceful, that everything falls apart—my only consolation is that I have unripe apricots for boobs. They'll at least resist gravity a while longer. But along with my ass, they will droop to my ankles soon enough.

I'm not afraid of getting old—I've always thought that aging is simply an essential part of living a long life. What I *am* afraid of is time itself; I'm terrified of running out of it. I'm terrified of having nothing, of not having left my mark on this world. Especially considering that I'm almost thirty, clad in ridiculous pajamas, eating an expired chocolate bar, and watching my face break down while the man I love treats me like a houseplant.

My attempt at a smile fails. What if the same thing happens to my hair? The only advantage of the wild curls on top of my head—somewhere between brown and orange—is that they make me look taller. With a hat, I'm about as tall as Naomi Campbell's chin. I swallow the last square of chocolate and lick a finger. My stomach burns like I just swallowed lava. This is a terrible nightly habit.

I got only three responses to my roommate ad in the paper, so it's not like I had much to choose from. The first person to respond was a girl dressed like a flower child. Three seconds after coming inside, she had already criticized the shape of the furniture and the orientation of the bed, saying that they dangerously contradicted the principles of feng shui. She babbled on about green dragons, white tigers, red turtles, and phoenixes for the full half hour she was here. The second guy was about forty and smelled like grass. He didn't take his eyes off my ass the whole time as he talked about his passion for topiaries. I bet all his shrubbery is ass-shaped.

The third person was Luca. The beautiful, godforsaken morning he came into my life, it was summer, and the heat was invading my thoughts. My best friends were on vacation, as was the entire city, and I was the only person in Rome who spent her vacation languishing on a top-floor apartment and falling into depression as the sun beat in through the windows. I was broke, unemployed, and single—now that I think about it, not all that different from today. I vaguely remember thinking it was ironic that I was watching bikini-clad women on the television while sitting on the couch like boiled spinach. Some people drown their sorrows in Nutella, whipped cream, or cookies. Personally, I eat olives. I was glued to a jar of Saclà Italian ones, wearing shorts and a T-shirt, thinking about how useless my life was, when Luca made his appearance.

Mind you, he didn't just materialize out of thin air. He did knock and explain that he was there to talk about my ad. But *appearance* really is the right word—he transformed the place. For a moment, I swore I saw a hibiscus plant on the landing, a cascade of orchids raining down from the ceiling, and a tropical bird singing an exotic tune. He was as tan as I was pale, wearing a pair of jeans with ripped knees, a white T-shirt, and untied army-green canvas sneakers. A backpack was slung over one shoulder. He smiled. I stared at him like a moron, thunderstruck. I had just put an olive in my mouth, which was open in shock, and I could formulate only one thought: Did I shave my bikini line today?

"Is everything okay? Are you all right?" he asked me after about thirty seconds, speaking slowly, like I was old and deaf. I couldn't answer because the stupid olive decided to slip down my throat into the wrong pipe. I began to bray like a donkey. Luca threw his backpack on the ground, came up behind me, put his arms around me, and shook me like a rag doll. Basically, our first meeting will go down in history as the time when I almost choked to death on an olive and Luca made me spit it up on the carpet.

"Good thing I know the Heimlich maneuver," he said, regarding me the same way a lawyer would look at a farmer who made him milk a cow. I rubbed my sore abs, and a string of saliva rolled down my chin between coughs. "You'd better sit down. Where can I find glasses? Can I get you some water?"

As if I wasn't humiliated enough, he offered me a drink like I was *his* guest. He looked around a bit, made an amused comment about a moldy pear that had been sitting in the fruit bowl for weeks, and then asked me if the room was free.

"As free as can be," I replied, my voice still hoarse.

"I can take it?"

"Absolutely!"

"Great. And the lease?"

"Lease? What lease?"

"For the rent?"

"Oh, the rent, right."

"And don't you want to ask me for references? I could be a psycho-path or criminal, you know."

I wanted to tell him that his golden forearms were all the references I needed; with that smile, those eyes, those hands, those knees, he didn't need any other recommendations. But I didn't want to look man-crazy. It was better to act like I didn't give a shit how cool my new tenant was.

"Yes, I was going to get around to it," I said with an air of impor-tance that wasn't very credible, seeing as I was coughing and my ribs still hurt. I found out that he worked in a disco pub, that his cocktails were famous throughout Rome, and that he had held many jobs before that one. He had traveled a lot, and he wrote books in his spare time. He wanted to become a novelist. A famous one, if possible. We hammered out some kind of contract, he gave me three months' rent in advance, and we shook hands. We've been good friends ever since.

Just friends, unfortunately. He's a nice and fun guy. Sure, he makes a huge effort to seem macho and manly, but underneath is a sensitive soul. As far as I can tell, he has only one major flaw: he uses women like Kleenex. Apart from this nasty habit (and the post-apocalyptic state of his room), he's a great roommate.

Still, most nights I suffer while he's having fun in the other room. Once, I told him, "You're thirty-two years old! Don't you think it's time to act like an adult and try to settle down and fall in love? At least then I'd see the same thong around the apartment." He had smiled and shrugged. "Love doesn't exist, Carlotta," he said. "It's teenage bullshit, or at most, a treatable disease. I'm not a kid anymore, and I can assure you, I've met a lot of women, but my heart has never gone into overdrive. I've never wanted to see someone sleeping next to me on the other side of the bed. I just wanna get laid and then send them on home."

He's always crass like that. I've never once heard him use the term *make love*.

Suddenly I hear the signs of a discussion through the wall. I can tell it's a pissed-off monologue from the girl, who's just been told her services are no longer needed. I hear his footsteps on the floor, and her lisping about how men are thlimeballs. I hate to admit that she's right, and I can't blame her for feeling mortified. But I'm selfishly pleased at her expulsion. I'd love to slingshot her away with a rubber band, provided it disappeared into thin air immediately after, along with the piece of floss and anything else that's touched her. Luca turns the shower on; soon there will be a wading pool in the bathroom and wet footprints around the whole apartment. But I don't care. Now I can sleep, and so can the rest of the apartment complex.

As soon as I lie down and close my eyes, I hear a knock on my door. Luca comes in with a skimpy towel wrapped around his waist. Does he really think I'm as unfeeling as my nightstand? I'm blushing just thinking about his wrists and his elbows and his earlobes and—

"Are you asleep?" he asks. His voice is so beautiful that even if I had been asleep in the arms of the god of dreams, I would have kicked my way back down to earth. He doesn't wait for me to respond but comes in, dripping water like Hansel and Gretel dropped bread crumbs.

"I wanted to wish you good luck tomorrow, because I may not see you in the morning. I'm going to get some sleep and then write."

"Thanks," I say, as he drenches the bed.

"Sorry for the noise, but you know how it is . . ."

"No, I don't know how it is," I say. After more than a year of involuntary abstinence, I may as well be a virgin again.

"You're too uptight—you should go out with someone." He looks at me with a strange light in his eyes, his dripping hair threatening to short-circuit my nightstand lamp.

"So I can be thrown out of someone's house like Miss Perfect Ass? No thanks, I'd rather not."

"You could invite someone to come back here, so you'd be the one doing the throwing."

"Will anyone ever make you want to quit doing that?"

"No," he exclaims. "Never." The way that he talks about it, I think he'd rather swallow a live cockroach. "If you give a woman an inch, she'll take a mile. She'll start to want more than just sex—like attention."

"I'm a woman, too, remember?" I say, irritated not because of what he's saying about women, but because he's talking to me like I'm one of his friends at the bar. We're just about to start a pissing match or a burping contest.

"You're not a woman. Not in that sense."

"Thank you for that lovely compliment."

"You fool!"

He approaches me and the towel moves, highlighting his infamous manhood. He covers himself, laughing, and hugs me. He doesn't know how much it hurts and how much I want to show him that I am a woman, in every sense. My heart is beating a thousand times per minute, so I cough to hide the sound. I don't want him to find out that I belong to the ranks of those sentimental creatures who aren't satisfied with just sex and who would much rather clamor for his attention than get dressed in a hurry and run home cursing. I smell him from a distance like a dog sniffing for a buried bone. He smells damp, like seaweed, and soapy. God, I love him. Maybe I would be better off if I threw him out.

I hope that I get this job tomorrow and that they send me around the world or that I have to work the night shift so I won't be home for the next few conquests. Maybe I could soundproof the room. No, I'd die anyway. My imagination would take over. I reject him for the umpteenth time, pretending to be annoyed while I'm actually consumed with love and regret. Luca gets up, stretches, and claims to need sleep. He disappears, humming softly. I sigh, turn off the light, and fall asleep with the taste of chocolate on my tongue.

TWO

The Art Production headquarters is located on the Appian Way, in an ice-colored five-floor office building. The architect who designed it tried to give it a futuristic look, but it just looks like a jumble of cement and steel pipes, like a giant stove.

As I walk, I repeat to myself: "I can do this, I can do this, I can do this." I went to school at the Academy of Fine Arts, for God's sake! Besides this prestigious background, for years I've worked on the sets of school plays, television ads, and local fashion shows. I'm usually the one who locates the props or finds the best spots for photographing and filming. So far I haven't worked on anything major, but you really demonstrate your creativity and adaptability when you're forced to make do with a little money and a lot of hope. When it comes to good faith, imagination, and problem solving, nobody beats me. And I need this job. I can't afford to let it go. Although it's not in my nature, I'm ready to fight tooth and nail for it.

However, when I enter the lobby, I realize that the competition is far from grim. In fact, there is none. I'm the only one here besides a secretary with a platinum-blonde Marilyn Monroe hairstyle, typing on her cell phone behind the front desk. I walk over and realize that she's playing Candy Crush. I cough to get her attention. She looks up at me with blue eyes, clearly annoyed.

"I'm here for the set designer position."

She continues to scrutinize me up and down and finally shakes her head. "You seem too frail," she says.

"Is there heavy lifting involved?" I ask, remembering the time when, for an ecological antifur fashion show, I had to haul around a life-size papier-mâché walrus and the keel of a ship, practically by myself. Now that I think about it, I do still suffer from bouts of sciatica from that.

"No, nothing like that," she says. She leans toward me a little and whispers conspiratorially, "It's because of the director. He's heavy."

For a moment I imagine an obese boss in a wheelchair. "Look, I'm so sorry, but to be honest, I really don't want to be a caregiver."

"Oh, no, the bastard's doing just fine. Too fine, I'd say. He's heavy, meaning—how should I put it? He's sort of . . . unpleasant."

Coming from someone who doesn't strike me as particularly pleasant herself, this news is alarming. "How so?"

But the girl clearly does not intend to indulge my questions any further. As if she's already said too much, she pulls out a sheet of paper from a drawer. She fires off an array of questions, some of which are decidedly indiscreet. The company doesn't just want to know about my previous work experience, but also if I'm married, if I have children, where my family is from, and other probing and personal details. I want to tell her to mind her own business, but I hold my tongue. I got maybe two hours of sleep last night, I woke up late, and I had ten minutes to get ready. I just want this woman to hurry up.

"Cell phone number?" she asks.

"I actually don't have one."

"You don't have a cell phone?" She looks at me like I have six eyes and a donkey's tail for a nose.

"You know how it is," I say. "I went through three phones before I realized that enough is enough. I broke the first one by putting it in the oven instead of my frozen pizza, and I only realized it when I tried to call a friend with a slice of pepperoni. The second one got flushed, and the third one got lost or stolen—or maybe it ran away from me in fear. So now I do my part to stop the deaths of innocent cell phones."

"So what do you do if you're stuck on the side of the road?" she asks.

"Well, that doesn't normally happen. But I guess I'd try to find a pay phone. Or I'd send a telepathic message. Or just stick to taking the train."

"You're going to have to get one. You'll have to be available twenty-four hours a day for this job."

"It's not like he's a heart surgeon."

"Whatever, but without a cell phone, you won't be seen as competitive or professional."

"Why, because I can't play Candy Crush?"

My sarcasm is clearly lost on her, and she motions for me to sit down and wait my turn. I turn around and look at the empty room, at the faux wood chairs against the wall and the fly buzzing in a tireless, figure-eight search for an escape. I'd like to complain, but the fly was here before me.

I sit and wait. The fly suddenly finds the window and tries to fly through the glass. It rams the glass in the same spot with a stubbornness that evokes my sympathy. It reminds me of myself when I can't stop doing the wrong thing. Although I know I'll suffer, I shift into fourth gear and launch forward anyway. I feel sorry for it, so I crack the window. Under the secretary's puzzled gaze—she's stopped lining up her candy—I try to steer the fly into the fresh air. After another half dozen attempts, it finally finds its way out. At that very moment, the secretary tells me that I can go in.

"Take this and have him look it over," she tells me, handing me the questionnaire.

As I cross the threshold, I wonder, if the director really is an asshole, maybe the fly was smart to sneak out. But I need a job. Besides, I'm used to dealing with difficult people. My family is a disaster. I've withstood my Aunt Porzia's assaults for almost thirty years. I'm not afraid of anybody. So I enter the room.

I expect to find myself in front of some kind of armed force, but instead I come across two men, one sitting on the edge of a desk, and the other standing in front of a window, facing away from me. The man sitting down is so attractive that, for a moment, my nerves vanish like the fly through the window. His blond hair makes me think he must be from northern Europe. His eyebrows look like swan feathers. His eyes are Tiffany blue, his nose sharp and elegant, his skin almost translucent. He's wearing a gray suit over a T-shirt with a frog on it. He looks angelic, respectable, and efficient, all at the same time.

He invites me to come in with a smile and extends his hand. Friendly, but not too overzealous. He speaks with a faint accent— German, perhaps? His name is Franz Eisner, and he's the executive producer. He reads my questionnaire with interest while the other man continues to stare out the window, offering me the view of his back and a backside that resembles a dried plum. He's wearing black jeans, a sweater, and a white scarf that makes him look like Pavarotti.

The blond guy asks me some questions based on the questionnaire. I embellish my past work experience, turning white lies into big whoppers.

"What show is the job for?" I ask.

Franz hesitates a moment before replying. "It's a remake of Tennessee Williams's *The Glass Menagerie*. Are you familiar with the work?"

Of course I am. I've always loved it. I can already see myself hunting for props, especially timid Laura's collection of glass animals. Maybe even some records from the '40s and a record player. I definitely want this job. I want it with all my heart. But then Franz says something that alarms me.

"Obviously, it's a reworking. There's, uh, a few changes we're making in order to adapt it to the new style that the, uh, director and adapter of the text want."

All these uhs do not bode well. At that moment, as if summoned by God himself, the other man turns around. The results are unfortunate. He's as thin as his back end hinted, all edges, as if chiseled straight out of a concrete block. His eyes are deep-set, and he's painted on about three pounds of black eyeliner. Perhaps he wanted to achieve the coveted smoky-eye look, but to me, he just looks like a punk rocker or a panda bear. He walks toward me slowly. I don't think he's incapable of moving faster, but I suspect this lazy stride gives him an air of artistic exhaustion. I won't be fooled. His eyes confirm the secretary's comments—they're dark but icy.

"The original version of the work has been abused," he says coldly. "Mine is much more exciting and up to date. Art is about renewal, not slavish obedience to the past."

I want to tell him that I don't like remakes of famous works, but this is an interview, after all, and I can't alienate myself.

"Very interesting," I say. "Tell me more."

He stiffens and sucks in his cheeks. He holds a piece of his scarf between two fingers, studying it. "Franz, are you sure she isn't from the competition, trying to steal my idea?"

"I don't think so, Rocky," the blond man says, winking at me surreptitiously. "After all, we're going onstage in April, and it won't be easy to find the very . . . original . . . props that you're requiring. Assuming that Ms. Carlotta's references check out and that there aren't any other candidates, I'm inclined to trust her."

"I don't know," the director says, obviously disgusted. "I don't like her."

I've got half a mind to tell him that his aversion is reciprocated. He gives a last look at my questionnaire. An aristocratic frown darkens his face as he reads.

"Right, there we are," he says, as if he has just confirmed his theory. "I need someone brilliant. Her previous experience is just not up to par. What is this? She's clearly not up to the task. Plus, her family's from Calabria, and Calabrians are lazy by nature. She'd be great if we were looking for some Calabrian salami, but otherwise I find her to be incompetent."

As he speaks, I cannot quash the anger rising inside of me.

"Look here, Rocky Balboa," I say, fists on my hips. Now I'm pissed. "Your real name is probably Rocco, so I'd guess you come from the same place I do. As for the rest of your speech, I suspect that your remake is total bullshit, but I would have done my job well anyway. Once, for a music video, I had to carry a padlock that was ten feet tall. I did my best, even though that music video was a piece of shit. And you don't have to worry"—now I'm gesturing like an octopus—"I'm not Mata Hari, I don't work for the CIA, and I'm not part of some industrial espionage team. Now I'm leaving, because if I have to stay here another minute, I *will* want to find a pound of Calabrian salami and cram it down your throat."

I leave without saying good-bye. That's another opportunity that slipped out of my hands like an eel. I'm already dreading having to call my father and ask him for another loan. I've been unemployed for too long. I flee the building, chased by the secretary's dubious glance, and find myself in the street. It starts to rain, a thin but persistent drizzle that turns my coat into a sponge and seeps through my barbed-wire curls. I make my way back home while the city flows around me. Horns honk, the rain drizzles on the cobblestones, and a slight wind shushes. I pass hordes of Japanese tourists, boys whizzing by on mopeds, colorful train cars that resemble a gigantic accordion, and the muddy, lazy Tiber River flowing under the bridge.

I am chronically unable to get anywhere in life. I live my life the way the ancient people did: like the Italian proverb says, I take what's sweet, then throw away the rest.

Somehow, in the midst of this painful reflection, I am reminded of my mother. I wonder again how I, petite and wiry as I am, can really be her daughter, when she looks like a cross between Venus, Juno, and Monica Bellucci. My father is the artisan behind my insignificant appearance. He's a quiet, frail man, who, in a placid and submissive life, has only uttered one word of disappointment: a languid *wow* when he discovered four years ago that his wife was having an affair with a man named Gonzalo, who she met on a Mediterranean cruise. My mother had been hoping that her absence would go unnoticed, so she was quite surprised when my father filed for a divorce. It was almost as if she didn't understand how he could have come up with such an idea. My mother is incapable of realizing how she hurts other people, especially her ex-husband and her older daughter. With her younger daughter, though, she's very affectionate.

Oh, yeah. I forgot to mention Erika. Five years younger than me, she got everything from our mother. The beauty, the posture, the boobs, the long legs, the straight hair, and the tendency not to regard the opinions of others. Let's put it this way: I hadn't lost my virginity by the time I was twenty, so I reluctantly gave it up to a college friend. The only memory I have of the event is a flurry of grunts and excruciating pain. By this time, Erika had not only already given it up, but was quite skilled. She's basically the female version of Luca, except that she despises me deeply—to her, bearer of the highly coveted professional title of fashion model, I'm socially useless.

She doesn't parade around on haute couture catwalks or anything, and she's not the new Claudia Schiffer, but she's been in a lot of catalogs. She's the girl who poses, with her stomach sucked in and chest puffed out, in a lace bustier that costs as much as what I'd make in a month. She's the girl in the white dress no mortal woman could ever wear without looking like a layer cake, the girl with the latest shade of plumping lipstick, and the girl in the garden furniture catalogue who's pretending to pick daisies or lying in a hammock outside a quaint cottage.

So it goes without saying that Erika likes to show herself off. She lives in a fancy house in a fancy neighborhood, Parioli, and her walls are covered with sepia images of her own body: a glimpse of her breast, her navel, her back adorned with a pearl necklace, her bare feet on top of a glass cube. She parades a new guy around every Christmas and a different one by New Year's, causing confusion among our relatives. Although Erika swears she never went out with a Jess, Aunt Porzia remains fond of him to this day. I think my poor aunt (who is a bit deaf in her old age) is remembering a New Year's Eve three years ago, when at the stroke of midnight my dear sister was locked in the bathroom with a purple-haired guy, screaming, *Yes! Yes!*

In short, Erika's a real bitch. We go months without seeing each other, and when we talk on the phone, she only talks about herself. She ends each conversation with a perfunctory "Nothing new with you, right?"—her polite way of saying that she knows I'll never find a decent man, and even if I did, she'd snatch him up.

As I continue on my way, the rain stops, and the sun peeks out through the smog. I'm home, defeated and hungry, after an hour. I live in Trastevere, an old-world Roman neighborhood, on the top floor of a pink building with bright green window frames. Once I get inside my apartment, I fling my coat on the chair and push the button on my answering machine. There are a slew of messages, all within a few minutes of each other, from the girl from last night (whose name turns out to be Sandra, or rather, Thandra). The poor girl, clearly forgetting that she was thrown out, asks Luca to meet up again and repeats her number about a hundred times. Finally I get to the rest of the messages. When I hear my mother's voice, I shudder and wait for the blows to come. However, my dear mother only says that she'll call me later about something important. She closes by saying that she hopes I'm doing something constructive.

Hell, my head is spinning, my feet are on fire, and I feel like crying. I get up to go find something to eat. I'm not quite desperate enough for olives, but almost. I'm hoping there are some pretzels left. However, the pantry is empty. The only food is the cherries on the oil painting of a cherry tree I did a couple years ago that's hanging on the kitchen door—too bad it's not edible.

Just then, Luca comes in. The top of a golden baguette peeks out of the plastic bag he's holding. I am suddenly aware of tears pricking the corners of my eyes. Luca's actually a really sensitive guy when some naked chick isn't monopolizing his attention. He sets the bag on the table and comes over to me.

"What is it, little butterfly?" he asks. "Did it not go well? Don't tell me you made a bad joke."

"Kind of," I say, shrugging.

"You can't keep your mouth shut! That's why you lost that job for the French perfume ad a month ago."

"More like I can't keep my nose shut! Let's be honest, you can't sell a perfume that smells like sardines soaked in skunk sweat! That doesn't mean he should have been so offended and fired me. Oh well. Did you go shopping?"

"I bought some pasta, some tomatoes, a bottle of wine, and some oranges. And the bread, of course." He gestures at the old steel dinosaur covered in owl magnets. "I hope I didn't offend you, but I cleaned out your fridge."

"You're so great!" I say. It's true. If I were a cat, I'd spend all nine of my lives with him. "You're marriage material."

"Over my dead body," he says. "Marriage is not for me. The thought of being stuck with the same woman forever is nothing short of horrifying."

"But if you don't change your ways, you're going to need to review your precious philosophy."

Luca turns on the sink, rinses the tomatoes, and fills a pot with water. "What do you mean?" he asks casually, while turning on the gas stove.

"You sleep with a woman only once. Excluding those who are too young, too old, already in a relationship, and lesbians, you're eventually going to run out. You'll have to start over from the beginning."

"We don't need to exclude those who are already in relationships. Anyway, I don't even remember their faces the next day, so it wouldn't bother me to start over again. And in the meantime, the young ones will grow up."

"You're disgusting, do you know that? I hope you'll meet someone someday soon who treats you that way. I want to see you desperate for love."

"Never gonna happen."

"You never know. Oh, by the way, Miss Polka-Dot Thong called."

"Who?"

"The girl from last night? With the lisp, remember?"

"She had a lisp?" He laughs, puts the tomatoes in a pan, and uncorks the wine. "I didn't really pay much attention to how she spoke."

"Yeah, you probably wouldn't have noticed, given that she just moaned vowels all night. But her name is Sandra, and she wants to *thee you thoon*."

"That's her name? I couldn't remember last night when I said good-bye."

"You mean, when you threw her out."

"Yeah, I just couldn't remember. I wanted to be nice, but I think I called her Rebecca? Where did I come up with that?"

"The girl from three nights ago."

"How do you know that?"

"The answering machine, Luca! You never give them your cell phone number, so the poor seduced and abandoned things fill up the answering machine with their whining and insults!"

Luca sits down on the couch, laughing. He's so beautiful that I can't help but gaze at him, feeling enchanted. Just then, the phone rings, and my mother's voice bombards the machine. Even her *hello* is critical.

"Carlotta, honey, if you're at home, pick up the phone." It seems less like an invitation and more like a military order.

"Hi, Mom . . ." I grab the phone, pretending to sound distracted.

"I knew you were there! You're not the dining-out type."

"What do you want?"

"Make sure you're free in two weeks. Beatrice is getting married."

I roll my eyes. From what I remember, my mustached cousin Beatrice wants to be a Carmelite nun and firmly believes her virginity belongs to the Lord. Her protruding teeth and creepy smile terrified me. I must have heard wrong.

"Sorry, who?"

"Your cousin Beatrice! Are you starting to lose your memory?"

"But I thought she went to a convent?"

"Only for a while. You really are out of the loop. She had her teeth and nose done, spent a fortune on laser hair removal, met a Spanish guy, and now they're getting married."

How appalling. So Beatrice got plastic surgery. I wonder if there's anything original left on her body. "She must have really worked to keep it from me, since I'm finding out so late."

"But such controversy! Try to understand—that belly!"

"She had a tummy tuck, too?"

"I'm talking about the twins! Carlotta, have you been drinking?"

"What? Twins? Mom, I don't even know what you're talking about—"

"She's six months pregnant and she's huge. She wasn't sure about getting married before giving birth, but Aunt Palma really got after her."

"Ah . . ."

"Getting pregnant was a good thing for her. Time flies. You blink, and you've hit menopause! Don't you think it's time you got to it with some nice young man?"

"Mom!" I blush and my eyes dart involuntarily toward Luca, who's draining the spaghetti. Fortunately he can't hear a single word of my mother's delusional nonsense.

"You're not at all bad-looking, my dear!" she says in a burst of maternal generosity. "If you just committed yourself to it . . . But I've found you a perfect date for the wedding!"

I shudder and my stomach churns. This same thing happened when I was eighteen. I didn't have a date to the end-of-the-year dance at school—and I didn't care—but my mother set me up with the seventeen-year-old son of one of her bridge friends and forced me to go. He was seemingly innocuous, but once we were alone, he kept trying to root around under my dress. The thought of the adult version of a guy like that accompanying me to Beatrice's wedding makes my face burn. I fan myself with my hand.

Luca passes by, ruffling my hair. He points to the pasta and spreads his arms wide, whispering something about how much my mother loves to talk. Meanwhile, my mother, mistaking my silence for respectful attention, is waxing on about the importance of sowing your seeds while you're still young.

"I had you at twenty-six! That's only three years younger than you are now! Do you want your children to call you grandma?"

"Gotta go, Mom," I cut her off while Luca seasons the spaghetti and hang up the handset feeling sweaty, like I did the first time I saw *The Exorcist*. I'm on my way to the bathroom to rinse my face with cold water when the phone rings again. I'm tempted to ignore it, sure it's my mother again, but I don't want Luca to hear her ranting on the machine. I snatch up the phone. "If I get pregnant I'll let you know, but I'll decide who puts the bun in the oven!"

I realize too late that my mother is not on the other end of the line.

"Hello? Ms. Lieti? May I please speak to Ms. Carlotta Lieti?" It's a man.

"Yes, this is she. Who is this?"

"This is Franz Eisner."

The executive producer. The blond guy that winked at me.

"Oh, sure . . ."

Luca stares at me with curiosity.

"We met this morning, remember?"

"Of course." My mouth is wide open. I look like a fish gasping for breath. He's probably about to tell me that the director wants to sue me for emotional distress. I don't have the money to pay my lawyer. I don't even have a lawyer.

"We'd like to bring you on. If you're still interested, the job's yours."

"Wait, what?" I'm amazed that he hasn't asked if I'm drunk. Who would hire someone who picks up the phone sounding like she's sloshed at one in the afternoon?

"As I said, your resume is interesting, and I know how to convince Rocky. By the way, he's from Apulia, so you really are from the same area. Could you come sign your contract next week?"

With the phone wedged between my shoulder and my ear, I dance a ridiculous Zumba move. Then a memory nags me like a pebble in my shoe.

"Of course. But I have to ask you—what did you mean when you said I'll have to find some unusual items?"

I hear a laugh on the other end of the line.

"Even if his methods are questionable, Rocky is a genius in his own right," Franz says. "As I mentioned, he has reworked the entire text, setting the events in the modern day. So it only makes sense that some things have changed. For example, while Laura is still shy and romantic, she doesn't collect glass animals."

"She doesn't? Not even the unicorn?"

"Nope. She collects Barbies."

"Huh?"

"She has a collection of very rare, limited-edition Barbie dolls. That's her little menagerie."

For a few seconds, I'm appalled. Then a distant memory replaces the unicorn in my mind. I'm nine years old, and the mirror, like my mother, shows me no love. She'd spent the entire morning desperately trying to straighten my hair with brushes of all shapes and sizes, creams, sprays, and prayers to various patron saints. It was all in vain. My curls just wouldn't listen to reason. I almost felt bad for her. While all her nieces had hair as soft as silk sheets, her daughter was bushy-headed and freckled and had an unhealthy tendency to beat up the boys who teased her.

Little did she know then about Erika, who would become her shining star. For the time being, she had to be content with her first, mediocre daughter. She left me in front of the mirror in a fit of exasperation, as if it were all my fault, as if I had conspired with my hair to misbehave out of spite. My father came in at that point. "You're beautiful," he said and asked me to go for a drive with him because the sun was out—and the sun clears bad thoughts. He took me to the shopping center, and we walked around, my hand clinging to his thumb.

A window display of a small army of Barbie dolls at a toy store caught my attention. Nose and hands glued to the display window, I watched them rotate for the world to see. They were so beautiful, all so elegant in their soft-colored dresses, with hair that my mother would have loved. And then my heart stopped—for there was a Barbie doll with brown curly hair. I was convinced that she was smiling at me. She maybe even winked. She was wearing a strawberry-red dress with gold accents, and she was gorgeous. I turned to my father, but I didn't even need to speak. He already understood. That was *my* Barbie. That was *me* as a Barbie. Different and special. I kept her as a relic and never, ever tried to straighten her hair. She made me realize that everyone is special in their own way, and I'm grateful for it.

So I suppose the director's idea isn't completely terrible. It's definitely a crude interpretation of the text, but it intrigues me all the same.

Maybe I'm going a little crazy, but somehow I know that this job is for me.

"When you read the script, just do it calmly," Franz says. "We go onstage in a little over two months. Think you can do it?"

"Of course I can!" I say with conviction.

We make an appointment for the following Monday, and I'm beaming by the time we hang up. Luca looks at me questioningly. Taking advantage of my justified euphoria, I run to embrace him and let myself savor pressing against his sensational abs and feeling the heat radiate from my nether regions at his touch.

"I can't believe they picked me!" I say, leaping around the room. I run to wash my hands, then dash over to the table. Luca smiles, and I can tell that he's truly happy for me. I forget all about my mom and my cousin Beatrice's wedding. I don't care about having children who call me grandma. I have a job! I can buy those incredible boots I've been lusting after in the shop window! I eat with gusto and drain my wineglass.

"What makes you happier?" Luca asks me, watching me with curiosity. "The prospect of finding these props or just having a job?"

"Hey!" I say, a little drunk. I pretend to be offended, then burst out laughing. "Both, I suppose." Up until now, I really hadn't thought about how nice Franz's cheekbones are.

"How long has it been since you've had sex?" Luca asks me, peeling an orange. He stares at me, ruthless as only a man who works hard every night can be. He's suddenly serious, as if we were talking about a disease. He swallows an orange slice and then fiddles with a crumb on the table.

"That's my business," I say. "I'll clear the table. Did you write this morning?"

"You shouldn't be inactive for so long. It's not healthy. And then you run the risk of throwing yourself at the first guy who comes along. Excessive abstinence makes you a lot less selective, you know?"

"Says the most selective of us all!" I blurt. "Don't make me laugh."

"You don't see the difference?" He seems vaguely irritated, a rarity. I think he's even more beautiful when he's frowning. He continues to play with the crumb and doesn't look at me.

"There is no difference, unless you count chauvinism."

"Chauvinism has nothing to do with it." Anger tinges his voice. "The difference is that you're a foolish girl searching for the man of your dreams, and this makes you more inclined to do something drastic. You believe in eternal love, so you're stuck here like a jar of sun-dried tomatoes, hoping that a handsome prince will come along and put a ring on your finger. I don't expect anything from the women I entertain, except that they have fun with me. If someone doesn't meet my expectations, I'm not gonna go cry into my pillow."

"I don't cry into my pillow!"

"Carlotta . . ." He stops and shakes his head. "Don't you think I know you well enough to know that you're like a princess in search of rescue? For you, sex isn't just a way to get pleasure. You dream of falling asleep on Prince Charming's shoulder."

"Well, yeah, but—"

"The world is chock-full of guys like me, guys that are hoping to run down the stairs the second you're done having fun with them. These guys won't even listen to your voice messages, and they'll hardly remember your face, or your lisp."

His attitude is so defeatist. While I know he's trying to warn me, this level of harshness is unusual. I don't know what to say to him.

"You're wrong," I say, trying to sound confident, when in fact my legs are trembling under the table. "The world is also full of men willing to offer me their shoulder to sleep on. I don't know where they are, and they certainly don't look like you, but sooner or later, I'll find one. I'm sure of it—I'm not some totally helpless princess. But just because I haven't had sex in a year doesn't mean that I'm going to jump into bed with the first blond guy that walks by!"

And that's the truth.

I must be drunk. Or maybe I'm just hurt at the thought that he'll never be the prince whose shoulder I sleep on after a night of wild sex. Luca smiles, and he returns to his usual self. His comparison to a jar of sun-dried tomatoes was not at all flattering, but I'm too excited about my job to care. I tell him to get back to his writing. He gives me a playful slap on the cheek, then starts toward his room.

"I feel like your older brother, like it's my responsibility to open your eyes. Sometimes you can be too dreamy. The world sucks, my dear Carlotta."

"I know that all too well. Mostly thanks to you and your shining example."

"Well, at least my behavior has served some purpose. Now I'm going to go write. If anyone calls for me, just tell them I'm dead."

He keeps his writing shrouded in mystery. The pages he's already written are kept in a locked drawer, and he's explicitly forbidden me from using his computer. I suspect it's probably something violently passionate, maybe even erotic, because he occasionally emerges with a wild look in his eye to ask me bizarre questions. Elected special adviser on all things female, I help him out with the mysterious protagonist, whom he describes as a cross between an *L.A. Confidential* femme fatale and a Quentin Tarantino blood-covered bride. Most of the time I just stare, petrified, in response, offended that he lumps me together with the rest of my gender without thinking of me as an individual. But I can't help also imagining, at the same time, how a woman totally different from me would act in these situations, which are a cross between Grand Guignol and *Fifty Shades of Grey*.

"Will you read me a few pages?" I ask, just before he locks himself in his room.

"Not yet," he says as he has a million times before. "When I'm done. Actually, can I ask you a question?"

Here we go again. I prepare myself for another question about some woman with the sex drive of a rabbit, who relishes slicing her lovers with a Chinese sword.

"Which is more erogenous—the breasts or the stomach?"

"Huh?"

"Which is more pleasurable during foreplay?"

"Huh?"

"My experience tells me the breasts, but some women prefer their ears, or the back of their knees, or even their heels."

"Huh?"

"I want my main character to have a completely original thing. What would you suggest?"

"Huh?" I know, I sound like a broken record. But I can't formulate a more articulate answer. "Why the hell are you asking me these questions?" I say, when I manage to get my words back. "Can't you have the girls you sleep with take a survey? Have them fill it out before they leave?"

Luca laughs and then retreats with his questions unanswered. I hear him typing away as I submerge the dishes in the sink. I take a deep breath, trying to erase the image of Luca licking the back of a rapturous Sandra's knees.

My good mood lasts a little bit longer. I take another sip of wine straight from the bottle, toasting my long life as a sun-dried tomato.

THREE

I spend the whole morning feeling as happy as Gloria Swanson in *Sunset Boulevard* as she descends those famous steps. And I didn't even need to kill Luca and leave him in the swimming pool to achieve fame and fortune! Now I can tell people that I actually have a job. Although when my mother finds out, she'll probably tell me that searching for junk isn't a real job, that they're taking pity on me, and that at my age I'd better find myself a husband and pop out a little brat instead. When Erika finds out, she'll just smile like a cat plucking a sparrow.

Best to leave them both in the dark for now.

So I call Giovanna, one of my best friends. She's a few years younger than I am and is the most beautiful woman I know, even more so than Erika because her appearance isn't marred by resting bitch face. She's a makeup artist for some top fashion designers, and she always has antiwrinkle creams or mud, seaweed, and collagen masks for me. Unfortunately, she's working, so she cuts me off.

"I'm doing some model's makeup and I can't be distracted. This woman is so full of herself. She's hysterical about a pimple. She won't drink tap water. She says my perfume is too strong, and she's demanded absolute silence."

When I call Lara, my second and only other friend, I get the busy signal—not surprising, given her commitments as an excellent real estate agent, an anxious mother, and a perpetually pissed-off ex-wife. That exhausts my friends list—I can't exactly say I have a thriving social life. I've got important news, damn it, and there's no one to tell! I flip open an old phone book and close my eyes to pick a random person to call. When my index finger falls on a funeral home, I decide to give it up. You never know, I might end up signing onto a payment plan for a deluxe coffin.

Then I look at the clock and think of my father. He's been out of town for a few days at a flower festival, but he should be back by now. He undoubtedly belongs in the group of people that would delight in hearing about my happiness. But the phone rings in vain. It's not unusual for him to just not pick up the phone if he's lost in his plant paradise, which he created on his deck. From among his roses, cosmos, chervil, star anise clumps, potted palms, and Aspasia orchids, the telephone ring sounds just like a buzzing bee. Now I'm just talking to myself. So I decide to call a taxi and go see him.

He lives in upscale Prati, near the Vatican, on the top floor of an old, immaculately maintained building. The dark facade makes it look like a giant burnt cookie, but his terrace could give the Hanging Gardens of Babylon some serious competition. After he and my mother separated, my mother knocked down everything that he'd cared for so passionately. A fountain topped by a naked cherub supplanted the greenhouse. A white marble gazebo—reminiscent of a war monument—replaced the flowerbeds. The Japanese carp that filled the pond died almost immediately.

When I ring the doorbell, a woman opens the door, startling me. A woman? Who is she? She doesn't look very much at home; there's no towel in her hand or cobweb dangling from her ear. She's about fifty years old with blue eyes, cheeks as red as a Russian doll's, and a timid air. She's wearing a herringbone wool suit, and she's barefoot. Barefoot?

What is a barefoot nesting doll doing at my father's? Do I have the wrong apartment? I stammer and glance around to make sure I've got the right door. But this is indeed the top floor.

"Um . . . I . . .," I say uncertainly.

"You must be Carlotta," the woman murmurs.

My dad appears behind her, wearing gardening gloves and a child-like grin. She blushes, embarrassed, and whispers something to my father. Then she shakes my hand and walks away, still barefoot and still smiling.

"She's my neighbor," my dad hastens to clarify. "Every now and then, she comes and helps me with the plants."

I want to ask him more, especially when I head into the kitchen and see a juicy roast and a pan of shrimp on the counter, most definitely not his work. He's a magician with growing flora, but when it comes to cooking fauna, he's a disaster. For the moment, though, he doesn't seem inclined to say anything else. I can tell he's happy; there's a little light in his eyes that I know comes from the things he enjoys: good food, fresh flowers, mowed lawns, dewdrops, serenity, and gratitude. Plus he's plumper than usual, which, given the frailty we share, is equivalent to extravagance. I let him get away with not explaining—assuming there is any explaining to do.

His apartment is pretty bare on the inside; there are no paintings, no rugs, and just a few pieces of furniture. But out on the terrace, he abandons all modesty and becomes Baroque. The rooftop garden is bursting with vegetation. The plants seem to be laughing in the heat and humidity of the greenhouse that he built. Although it's late winter, the sun beats down like it's summer in here. I open a slightly dirty beach chair and sink into it. Just as I'm about to tell him about my professional success, he speaks.

"Erika will be glad to see you!" he exclaims.

I feel a slight jolt. It's not that I hate my sister—but the thought of seeing her makes me curse my decision to leave the Xanax at home. To be honest, it makes me curse my decision not to stay home myself. I'll never be nominated for the Older Sisters with a Heart of Gold championships, but Erika will never make the list of finalists in the Perfect Younger Sisters competition, either. I just have to fake it. My mouth contorts itself into a scary smile. Good thing Dad is too busy tending to a mandarin plant to notice.

"What a joy. My two girls together," he says, moving on to a Kentia palm.

Again, I'm about to tell him my sensational news when the doorbell rings. Okay, this is way too much suspense for my taste. As I go to open the door, I try out my Gloria Swanson walk again, but Erika looks at me like I'm an alien and stink of sulfur. She doesn't even say hello as she struts inside, merely nodding at me with her chin instead. Her perfume is stronger than the smell of Dad's entire nursery. She's wearing a cashmere sweater that's as soft as baby skin and leather gloves I doubt she takes off even at home.

Dad comes in, wearing his own muddy gloves, to give her a cheerful greeting. Careful lest she get dirty, too, she air-kisses him. It's weird that she's here; all she usually does is make her obligatory phone call every couple months.

The reason for her visit soon becomes clear. Among the few things that Dad kept after the divorce is a collection of ancient tapestries he inherited from his mother's mother. Frankly, I find them ugly. When I was little, I was careful not to touch them for fear that the fabric would turn into a chameleon's tongue and wrap me up. In one, the men and women, dressed in dark red, sit on the grass like they are enjoying a picnic, but stiffly, as if caught on the toilet. In another, glacial men stand with muskets drawn, as if ready to shoot me in the mouth. I wanted to get rid of them. Even now, as my dad is pulling them out, rolled up like papyrus, I hate to look at them. But Erika likes them. Or perhaps she likes the fact that she's discovered they're worth more than she originally thought. Either way, she's asked Dad if she can have one. Dad must hate them, too, or has only kept them out of respect for his grandmother, because he agrees enthusiastically.

After Erika examines them, she chooses the one I was most afraid of as a child. They chat while she puts the tapestry in a cardboard tube, all without ever taking off her gloves, like a thief who doesn't want to leave fingerprints. Suddenly, Dad turns to me.

"What was the wonderful news that you were about to tell me?"

Ugh, right now? I blush, and I catch Erika watching me out of the corner of her eye. She seems both curious and a little disappointed. *Is my prissy little sister challenging me?* What is it about me that bothers her so much? What did I ever do to her?

Just to spite her, I invent a mountain of bullshit, embellishing my tasks and quoting some ridiculous number for a salary. I talk about contracts I've already signed, promises of bonuses, Carlotta Lieti ready to conquer the world! My exaggerations make it sound like any day now I'll be whisked away to paint a fresco in the Oval Office. Dad believes me, and he's thrilled. Erika just smiles sardonically.

Suddenly, I'm ready to get out of here. I'm tired of doing my Gloria Swanson act, and I'm ready to munch on a chocolate bar in front of a *Grey's Anatomy* episode. But since Erika drove here and I walked, the beautiful sister offers to give the ugly one a ride. Before we leave, Dad gives me a small potted plant, handing it to me as if it were a jewel and asking me to take care of it.

Erika's car is a deep blue Mini Cooper with leather seats. There are no crumbs on the seats, not even an air freshener hanging from the rearview mirror, and the seat belts are covered in soft leather.

After a while, she says smugly, "So, soon you'll probably be running for president."

"I have just as much chance to become head of state as you do. Your work is so important that you'll get the Nobel Prize in peace, medicine, and literature all together."

"At least you can finally stop living off of Daddy."

"Look, I've had jobs. It's just that lately—"

"You might as well have not gotten your degree, really. What good did that do you?" She doesn't look at me as she speaks. She drives with a light touch, switching gears quietly. The only thing that moves is her hair every time she glances in the side mirror.

"Not everyone is lucky enough to land a job where it doesn't matter if you can draw a straight line," I say, rigid in my seat. Erika pulls away from me, her hands shaking as she grips the steering wheel. For a few minutes, silence prevails. I keep wondering why, why, *why* do we have to have these conversations? For us, blood has become water.

"How's your love life?" she asks after a while, as we're stopped at a traffic light. It's almost sunset. The streets are swarming with cars, and traffic roars like a metal leviathan.

"It's great," I say firmly.

"I'm going to venture a guess, given your business success, that you've managed to snag Johnny Depp."

"Even better."

"Tell me, tell me. I'm all ears!" She laughs this time, mocking me. We're almost to my place.

"I'm engaged to a wonderful guy. Johnny Depp pales in comparison. We'll be married soon. But your invitation might get lost and not arrive until after the wedding."

"What's his name?"

"Luca," I say without thinking. Damn it! I shouldn't have done that . . . Since we were teenagers, Erika has stolen everything from me. If I got a new dress or a new book, Erika had to have it, too. She didn't have to put up too much of a fuss either, because our mother was always willing to bestow beautiful things on her princess, more so than the pauper. So Erika would get two dresses and a subscription to *Top Girl* magazine. Later she began to steal boys, if she knew I really liked them. All I had to do was let one little comment escape about how I was vaguely interested in someone, and she'd jump on him, all claws and curves. He'd end up feeding her insatiable appetite. If she knew about Luca, she'd stop at nothing to get her hands on him. And Luca, who can't say no to any beautiful woman who offers herself to him, would jump at the chance to indulge. No, no, no! Luca is mine!

I hurry out of the car, clutching the seedling, to avoid further interrogation. Luckily Erika doesn't understand. She thinks I'm hurrying to avoid being forced to reveal my lie. But even though it's a lie, and Luca is just a seductive hallucination, a dream that will only come true when pigs fly, it's also true. It's true that he exists, it's true that I love him, and it's true that I have to protect him from Erika's clutches.

I leave without saying good-bye, and for the first time I'm glad I see sarcastic distrust in her eyes. *Don't believe me? Then get out of here!* But I still wonder, as I climb the stairs, why? Why are we so different? Why does a bridgeless abyss separate us? We were always together, practically attached at the hip, when we were little. She always followed me around, first crawling, then taking small, hesitant steps. She would draw stories about dragons and wizards, and I'd create puppet shows out of them—she'd laugh and clap her hands.

Then the spell broke. As we grew older, she became more and more beautiful, and I remained ordinary. That created a real gap between us. Our mother took her under her wing, while Dad and I hung back, as if she and Erika had gotten parts in a movie we'd been cut from because we weren't good enough. The only things I have left to remind myself of how we used to be are some pictures that I confess I still have in a nightstand drawer. I don't look at them often, but I need to know they're there, that those memories are real, and that it wasn't all a dream. Maybe one day we'll get back to the way we were.

I open the front door with a strange feeling of turmoil brewing in my chest. Feeling defeated, I'm almost tempted to call up Erika and ask her, "Remember how we used to be? Tell me what happened and whose fault it was." But then, when I get inside, I find Luca walking around with a towel around his waist, fresh out of the shower. As usual. When his hair is wet, it almost reaches his shoulders. That chest could have been carved by Michelangelo. He's half-naked, talking on the phone with God knows who. He smiles at me, and my insides turn to mush. There's no doubt about it. Erika, stay the hell away. I've had it with your little games. Don't even think about putting the *shadow* of the nail of your little finger on Luca. He may never be mine, but he'll never be yours.

Having made that satisfactory pact with myself, I move forward.

FOUR

It's Saturday night, and to celebrate my new job, Lara and Giovanna have arranged a blind triple date for me. Meeting a guy named Tony Boni is not exactly my idea of a perfect weekend. I'd rather watch a documentary on the mating rituals of hooved animals than worry about what to wear to please a stranger who doesn't even have the decency to change his name.

Luca left hours ago. He works late on the weekends and never gets back before dawn. I look in the mirror and grumble. Nothing new here. The same old Carlotta—the line "You've got a lot going for you" will never apply to me. I'm wearing a camel-colored wool skirt, black boots, an angora sweater that will certainly have me spitting out fluff all through dinner, and a coat. I've wrapped a striped scarf around my neck, Gryffindor-style. Anything but sexy. Not that I'm trying to be sexy, mind you, but I wonder if I could be. I search the corners of my mind for just one moment when someone has looked at me with approval. I remember the emerald-green dress with a sailor collar and a tulle skirt I wore to my third birthday party that was tolerable. Other than that, I come up short.

When Giovanna buzzes at the downstairs door, I quickly head out. She's in the seventh heaven phase of a new relationship. Not that she's new to such emotions, though. From a practical standpoint, her lifestyle isn't all that different from my sister's. The big difference is that Giovanna is always hoping to find Mr. Right. Her infatuations run like clockwork: on average, they last about twenty days and go from rags to riches at a dizzying speed. She suddenly and inevitably discovers that she has given herself to a total asshole, so she spends a week crying before she moves on to kiss the next frog. At the moment, she's head over heels for a young interior designer who's into minimalist homes and has forced her to replace her grandmother's furniture with more fashionable stuff. Her bed is currently a mattress thrown on the floor. Her clothes are hung up in the open, her windows have no curtains, and the only things on the walls are abstract prints with polka dots, like a connect-the-dots puzzle. He even tried to get her to upgrade her dog to a Chihuahua or a whippet, which he thought would be better than her fat, cumbersome sheepdog, Bear. Fortunately, Giovanna wouldn't budge on that. When this is over, I predict she'll miss her grandmother's things, including the huge lacquered armoire that hid her messiness and those nice, thick curtains that blocked the view of the Peeping Tom across the street.

Curtains or no curtains, Giovanna is happy right now, and she greets me with a hug. She's alone; we're meeting the others at the restaurant. She's wearing tight pants, a white blouse, a fuchsia leather coat without buttons, and heels that are so high she's practically walking on her tiptoes. She's very beautiful, so beautiful that she can't go anywhere without attracting looks. Her magnificent hair is long, black, and smooth as water. She's got blue eyes, she's tall even without heels, and she's never lacking in suitors or amazing clothes. As we walk, she tells me about Tony.

"He's an interesting guy. He's a painter, so you have a lot in common."

A shiver of panic runs up my spine. "That doesn't make me feel good. When you call someone interesting, that's because you're trying not to mention that they look like a Porta-Potty."

"I would never set you up with a Porta-Potty."

I look at her, perplexed, and half laugh. "You're forgetting about Eusebio. Remember him? The guy who wore flip-flops in December? He was pretty interesting, too . . ."

We look at each other and can't help but burst into laughter.

"He really was interesting!" she says "Remember how many jokes he knew?"

"Yeah, and they were all obscene. And he'd pound beers straight from the can, calling everyone who walked by a weirdo, without realizing he was the biggest weirdo of them all! And his laugh sounded like he was blowing raspberries."

"But you've gotta admit, you had fun that night."

"Yeah, right. Once I saw his checkered cardigan, I wanted to escape out the bathroom window. Too bad it was barred. If Tony is anything like that, I'm going to strangle you."

We reach Il Buco, a quiet, almost monastic restaurant. This place would be a good choice if I were going to have dinner with the man I love, but right now it just makes me feel uncomfortable. What if I don't know what to say or do in front of him? I'll embarrass myself with either silence or mindless babble. Whatever happens, the quiet atmosphere can't be good.

We go inside. The small room is full but silent. I get the feeling that everyone is staring at us. A cemetery in the wilds of Alaska would be livelier than this place. I see Lara at a table in the back with three men. One is her temporary flame, one is Giovanna's temporary flame, and I think the third one is my *very* temporary blind date.

As I get closer, I realize that Tony Boni, at least at first glance, is less disgusting than I pictured. I introduce myself, and we sit down. He's actually quite good-looking. He's tall and wearing glasses and a dark suit. He doesn't seem to have any weird tics, and he doesn't ask me if I've heard the one about the ice queen whose husband slept with a thermos. He's actually rather polite.

Lara won't take her eyes off of her phone, which she keeps on the table, lest she miss a call from Emma's babysitter. Now that her stormy marriage is over, Lara is disillusioned by men. She only goes out to make Giovanna happy and to give her vagina the occasional workout— although she worries the whole time that something could be happening to her little girl. While she's a lovely woman, with caramel-colored skin and a shiny bob right out of the roaring '20s, her negative experience with her ex-husband has left her in a permanent bad mood. To compensate, she eats like there's no tomorrow. Now she weighs almost 180 pounds and is more pissed off than ever, which makes her want to eat even more.

She met Filippo a few days ago. He's pretty buff, which makes her look slimmer, but he's got a really long face. The relationship won't last. Filippo will say, do, or think something wrong, and she'll say the same thing she always does: "I knew it. All men are assholes. I'm going to Google how to become a lesbian."

Armando scans the almost-bare walls and the few tables in the restaurant. "We were just noticing that this place is a bit too heavily decorated," he says. His words reverberate in the sepulchral silence.

"Oh . . . you're so right!" Giovanna says. "What would you do to make it more cutting-edge?"

"I'd get rid of some of the light, reduce the number of tables, and tone down all this shouting we're doing."

I have to wonder if he's just messing with us. I'd like to argue that a quartet of corpses would be more exuberant than we are, but Armando's kind of touchy, and I don't want to risk offending him. So I keep my mouth shut while he babbles on pompously. Lara fumbles with her phone, seeming to think she may have missed a call, but in here, the ringing would be as loud as a jet engine.

I get to talking to Tony Boni, and I discover that his real name is actually Antonio.

"I heard you paint," he says enthusiastically.

"Yeah, but I only do it for myself. I'm no Caravaggio."

"But who is? I'm not even sure I know how to paint seriously. I've never studied it, I've never had training," he explains. "My work isn't for everyone. I love still life and portraits, and I like to portray genuine, spontaneous, everyday things. How about you? Giovanna said you work in theater?"

I explain in detail what I do, and he listens with interest. Over dinner, I realize that Tony is actually much nicer than I expected. While Filippo and Lara silently stuff their faces and Armando harasses everyone with his theories, Tony pours me a drink and gives me an unexpected compliment about my hair.

"It's so lively and sinuous. I'd love to paint your face. You're very beautiful."

Beautiful? I laugh. "It'd end up looking like a caricature of a rabbit."

"I've never seen a face as extraordinary as yours," he says. "It amazes me that you aren't aware of that. As an artist, you should be able to recognize the details. Your upper lip is sublime. It's got a particular curve, like a small wave."

For a moment, I look at him as if he were wearing a straitjacket. And I feel stupidly excited.

I wonder why, when I do receive a compliment, I'm convinced it's a shameless lie told for the sole purpose of getting between my legs. Perhaps it's because no one has really admired me for, like, a century. Maybe it's because my mother called me this morning to remind me *again* of Beatrice's wedding. Or maybe it's because I'm thinking about Luca pouring alcohol into the glass of some woman who's willing to give it to him right there, right then, on the bar.

But sometimes it's nice to pretend I'm not the ugly version of my little sister. Also the red wine, which is full-bodied and fruity, is making me feel euphoric. I'm happy to be out, and the way Tony is staring at me certainly doesn't bother me.

When the waiters bring out our stuffed pigeon, he abandons his fork to separate it with his hands. He dismembers the bird's chest with four pairs of fingers, his pinkies politely arched downward. It seems strange to see him struggling with such a rugged task when he's dressed so nicely. Suddenly, he pulls out a chunk of shiny, juicy white meat covered in sauce; unexpectedly, he offers it to me. He holds out the piece of flesh with the thumb, index, and middle fingers of his left hand, his eyes inviting and suggestive. I do not accept. I say I'm a vegetarian. I'm probably blushing, but I feel like taking that bite would be an acceptance of an indecent proposal. It would be like admitting that, yes, I would very much like for his . . . paintbrush . . . to make some artistic sketch on my practically untouched canvas. I'm not that reckless. Sure, I'm flattered that he finds me desirable, but I suspect he'd treat any female the same way tonight.

When we leave the restaurant, rain has started to fall. Lara runs off to get a taxi with Filippo. Armando suggests after-dinner drinks at a local bar called Tabula Rasa. That name, combined with my knowledge of his bizarre tastes, makes me think it's a popular spot for small groups of chic radicals—aka pretentious assholes—to drink and languish. Luckily, Tony nixes Armando's idea.

"I know a great place on Cassia, it's called Chiodo," he counteroffers. "They just opened a few months ago. They make great drinks and there's good music."

A tremor rocks my chest. That's where Luca works. I've never been there because it's out of the way—and, to be honest, no one's ever invited me. Giovanna accepts with unseemly enthusiasm, which Armando doesn't approve of. But when Tony and I decide to go, he's forced to go with the flow.

When Tony and I are alone in his car, he seizes the opportunity to ask if he can draw me.

"I swear, you have a terrific face," he insists.

"The idea of staying still while someone stares at me, focusing on my flaws, embarrasses me a little bit."

"You're wrong, you know," he says. "In a face like yours, when it's scrutinized, the flaws disappear. You have the exact opposite problem. At first glance, your face seems imperfect, strange, inundated with freckles, but a keen eye will capture the treasure hidden behind the curtain. The big eyes that are the color of chestnut honey, the eyelashes that are so long they cast shadows on your cheeks, and your chin . . . I could try to copy the curve, but I'd never do it justice. And you know, Carlotta, you've got a neck that a swan would be jealous of."

I should probably ask him to stop, but I'm enjoying this. I confess, I'm a little bit excited. Not sexually, I mean. Emotionally. I feel like an awkward preteen who's been ensnared by a bunch of bullshit.

A beam of flashing lights crossing the sky leads us to Chiodo. Armando is so out of his element, he seems almost on the verge of hysterics. I won't let him get to me, though. We park the car near Luca's, and the ulcer in my stomach sears as we hit the red carpet. A bouncer who resembles a giant redwood checks us out, then we go inside. The place is huge. Stone arches separate it into several rooms, some with tables and some with sofas, and one dedicated to dancing. We check our coats and search for the bar. My nerves pound in my ears as loudly as the music. I must be losing it. I see Luca every day—I just saw him a few hours ago—but I'm acting as if I haven't seen him in a century.

As we approach the bar, Tony politely takes my elbow in his hand, and we walk over with Giovanna and a very distraught Armando. At the polished wooden counter, where drinkers crowd around like ants, we sit down on four leather stools. My eyes wander in search of Luca. All the bartenders are dressed like him, though: white shirt, dark pants, a hint of a beard, and an impish air. They pour out liquor with acrobatic skill, sliding the tumblers across the counter, smiling, winking, and waiting for the next customer who wants an extra dose of alcoholic pampering.

Finally, I see him. He's farther down the bar, laughing with a group of escort-free hens. All of a sudden, I feel hot. Tony asks everyone what we'd like to drink; I go for a cosmopolitan. The wine I drank with dinner should last me for seven lifetimes, but with a cosmo in hand, I'll look like Carrie in *Sex and the City*. Tony chooses a dry gin and gives the order to a bartender—not Luca. Then Luca switches spots with that bartender. Perhaps he's sick of pretending to flirt with those fifty-year-old cougars, who were clearly attempting to undress him with their eyes. He leans over to help a gorgeous blonde who's wearing something that resembles a towel. Perched on the stool, she strategically crosses her legs so that she offers him a quick glimpse of the equipment concealed between her thighs. He fills a glass for her, perhaps wondering what else of hers he can fill after his shift. Giovanna and Armando head off to the sofas. Tony whispers into my ear, asking me if I want to dance. I say yes at the exact moment that Luca sees us.

I can be satisfied. At least he recognizes me, and if only for a moment, I diverted his attention from the Scarlett Johansson look-alike. His expression is dazed, as if I were the last person he expected to see, but he nods and smiles at me, and the smile I give him back is happy. Then he frowns, suddenly serious, and his tiredness shows on his face.

The dance room is quieter—the music a slow sax solo—so we can talk. Tony hugs me with discreet energy, talking about himself and his art, while I sneak peeks over at the bar, only half listening and occasionally nodding. Suddenly, Giovanna appears through the crowd and drags me into the bathroom. She seems nervous.

"Nothing I ever do is good enough for him!" she blurts out when the door closes. "He says I'm too risqué and that some guy was just staring at my tits."

"It's weird that he doesn't like your shirt," I say. "I thought he was into minimalism."

"Oh, don't you start!" she says with a snort. She powders her nose and checks her neckline in the mirror. "I don't see anything!"

"Gio, you know that I love Armando like I love ex-lax in my lemonade, but you can't deny that you're practically naked. You're beautiful, but you're naked, and it's also raining."

"Oh stop it! You've been dancing dirty with Tony!" She's pretending to be angry, but it's all in good fun. "Do you think you're gonna sleep together?"

"Okay, you're about as delicate as a hippo."

"Then let me ask more politely. Do you think you'll allow him to end your prolonged chastity with his . . . bowling pin? And stop looking at me like that! He's obviously into you."

"I don't think—"

"Don't tell me you're still pining over your hunk of a roommate! He doesn't want you, sweetie. If he did, after six months of hanging out at home half-naked, you guys would have already done it. He'd find a way to make you understand. And then dive into some other pool."

"You're too . . . too . . ."

"I'm only being sincere, Carlotta. You have to get over him. It's a fact. *He doesn't want you.* So he's probably one of the hottest guys we've ever seen, but there are plenty of fish in the sea."

"And I end up getting a squid."

I look at my reflection while a lady in a leopard-print sheath dress puts a cigarette out in the sink. Giovanna has a point, I know, but she could at least be less dramatic about it. She continues as she powders her nose.

"That was blunt, but if I'm not, you'll never see inside another man's pants again. In any case, Luca is not the guy for you."

I sigh. My high from the night has been officially grounded. I'm almost tempted to inform her that Armando isn't the guy for her, either, but there's really no need, because she'll figure it out soon enough.

"We'd better get out of this bathroom," I say, my voice a little muffled. She's right; Luca doesn't want me that way. I feel like crying as

Giovanna tries to spruce me up and urges me to forget about that idiot who doesn't know what he's missing.

I leave and sneak over to the bar, feeling awful. Offended. Lonely. I climb onto a stool and order another cosmopolitan, then another, and down them in two gulps each. The burn travels from my throat to my stomach to my bowels. I stare at the empty glasses, thinking about what a poor fool I am. I'm neither young nor old, neither a virgin nor a whore, neither a teetotaler nor an alcoholic. I'm just a cluster of mediocre cells. My mother's right. I'm going to look like an idiot at Beatrice's wedding. I can just see the look on Erika's face, the way she'll silently insult me with her smile.

"Hey, don't overdo it. That stuff is heavy for someone who's already had a whole bottle of wine."

Luca's slightly sharp voice penetrates my thoughts. I look up and see him standing in front of me with his elbows on the counter. He's looking at my third cosmo—empty—and another glass of something else that slipped down my throat without protest and set my stomach on fire.

"Bring me another?" I say.

"I think you're done. You've had enough."

"I'm twenty-nine, almost thirty. I'm not driving. I can drink as much as I want."

"What's wrong? Did your knight dump you?" I don't reply. Right now, I hate him, because he wants every other girl except me. "I didn't know you were going out tonight," he continues.

"It's not like I tell you everything I do. I met a nice guy who's a painter. He said I'm beautiful."

"I think that's a good start." He walks away, and I watch him fill up the glasses of a few businessmen toasting some kind of success. When he turns, he smiles at me. I don't know whether it's the alcohol or the tears in my eyes, but my vision is skewed. My world twists as if I were looking through glasses with the wrong prescription, as if he were a total stranger. There's something abnormal about his smile that I can't figure out.

"Compliments are a quick, free pass to your underwear," he says to me and then moves away to the other side of the bar, where he works his magic with his bottles. The Scarlett Johansson doppelgänger hands him a note. I bet she'll be the lucky girl of the evening. He reads the note, and she speaks into his ear. I ask a different bartender for another drink. This guy has long hair that I'd just love to tear out and wear instead of my crazy curls.

He looks at me apologetically, then shrugs his muscular shoulders. "I can't. Your tab's closed."

I look at him askance. "What does that mean? Give me a drink!" My voice comes out distorted, as if I'm yelling underwater. The bartender glances at Luca, and then I understand. Luca must have told him not to serve me anything else. This infuriates me. I'm considering climbing on top of the bar to make a speech about my legitimate right to be hung over when I hear a voice behind me. I turn around. Tony Boni is smiling at me.

"There you are! Armando and Giovanna are gone," he tells me.

"They were fighting."

"What happened?"

"I don't know. I think it was about nipples? Giovanna's, I mean."

"Ah . . ."

"Apparently some guy was staring at them too much? But what was he supposed to do? They were out in plain sight, calling out hello. So the guy was just being polite by responding. Armando really shouldn't take offense."

"Shall we go?" Tony asks me, offering me his arm.

"Yes!" I reply immediately, jumping off the stool like a monkey.

I stumble and he grabs me with an "Upsy-daisy!" He steers me toward the coat check, and I don't look back.

It's cold outside, bitterly cold. The streets are brushed with a layer of shiny ice that crunches beneath my heels. Tony takes my hand, which is fine by me because I'm afraid I might fall over. We walk over to the parking lot. I wrap my scarf around my neck and take a deep breath, feeling the chill enter my nose and cleanse my brain.

"Do you want to do something else together?" he asks me. "Otherwise I can just take you straight home?"

"Of course! The night is young!" He doesn't seem to notice my sarcasm. The parking lot isn't very crowded, and the car windows are fogged with ice and the quiet. Tony continues to talk, but I'm not listening to a single syllable.

Suddenly, something unexpected happens. He stops right in the middle of the parking lot. Embraces me like an octopus and plants a kiss right on my mouth. It's not really a friendly kiss, either. His tongue pierces the barrier of my lips, manages to break through the stronghold of my teeth, and finally, moist and heavy, it meets my tongue, swirling it around. I don't participate much in this exhibition—things are getting hazy.

And then suddenly, I push Tony away and vomit onto the pavement, splattering his shoes. I suppose it's because of the kiss, but also the after-dinner vodka and the wine at dinner, and perhaps even the sparkling wine from last New Year's. It's not a pretty scene. All things considered, he's nice about it. He offers me his handkerchief and helps me climb into the car. Then things get fuzzy—there are lights, and some wind coming in through the open window, and an awkward, embarrassing silence. He drops me off at home; I doubt he'll ever so much as point a finger in my direction again.

I climb the stairs with the agility of a potted shrub and vomit again, crying now, into the toilet this time. I rinse my face under cold running water and emerge with my hair soaked, my mascara smeared everywhere. I feel my unhappiness all the way down to my toes.

I undress, dropping layers around the apartment, and to conclude this unforgettable evening, I fall asleep with my head on the kitchen table—in the exact spot where Sandra smashed her thighs a few nights ago. As I drift off to sleep, I vaguely wonder if I ever remembered to disinfect the table.

I wake up to the sound of footsteps on the stairs. My eyes fly to the clock on the wall. It's five thirty in the morning. Shit! Luca must be coming back from the bar with that girl. They're probably stripping outside the door. They can't find me here, also half-naked and looking like the creature from the Black Lagoon. My heart pounding, my hands pressed to my ribs to silence it, I run to my room. I collapse in bed, all ears. I think I can hear the gasps of the girl who passed him that note, and the rustle of footsteps in the hallway, but nothing that evokes the thrill of two passionate lovers. I curl up on my side and realize that I'm cold. After all, I'm only wearing underwear. As I slip out from the covers, Luca opens the door. It's not a pretty scene, either—my goose bumps and boobs are in plain sight. My mouth half opens to protest weakly, and then I collapse, my head dancing a rumba again. Luca stands there with my pantyhose in one hand, crumpled like used tissue. His expression is not pleasant. He comes closer, smelling of the outside world and the cold, then helps me get under the covers. He sits down on the bed with my pantyhose still in his hand.

"So tell me what happened."

That's weird. That girl is out there waiting for him, and he's in here hanging out with the girl who smells like vomit and can't even think straight.

"Where's the compliment guy?" he adds.

"How should I know? I threw up on him!"

"What?"

"He kissed me and I threw up on him. I don't think he's going to tell me I'm beautiful again."

"Right," he says coldly.

49

"You can go, it's all right, I'll allow it . . ." I wave my hand like a queen dismissing a subject. I don't want him to feel obligated to sit here and listen to my painful confessions while his blonde servant anxiously awaits him.

"Are you sure?"

"No, go ahead. Just don't make too much noise. My head is a mess."

"Do you want some chamomile tea?"

"No!" I'm starting to get nervous, and I don't know why. Maybe I want him to hurry up and get rid of that woman; tonight the thought of the impending wild sex is making me feel dirtier and more desperate than usual.

"Have you been drinking again?"

"No! I mean, yes. Water."

"Why is your bra in the blender?"

"I don't know! *I don't know.*"

"A little cranky, aren't you, butterfly?"

Then he leaves, his footsteps slow on the floor. His shadow disappears behind the door. How weird; the silence continues. Then I hear the roar of the shower and no cursing from the stairs. I don't understand. Somewhere outside, a clock chimes six times in a row. A blade of dawn filters in from the window. Luca goes into his room, closes the door, and then there's silence.

FIVE

The first thing I hear on Sunday is my mother's voice blabbering on the answering machine. I can't make out what she's saying, but the tone of her voice scares me. When I look at the bedside clock, it blinds me like a beacon. It's almost noon. I get up and my head feels like it's leaping around in a ballet.

Luca is standing in the kitchen, a cup of coffee in his hands. I'm sure he already went for a run, as he does most mornings, but he looks as fresh as a flower. He casts an amused glance at me.

"New fashion statement?" he asks. "Is today au naturel day?"

"What . . . ?" I look down and realize that I'm naked. Covering myself, I flee to the bathroom. I take a fifteen-minute shower under boiling water, with my curls stuffed inside a shower cap to make them easier to manage later. When I'm all dried off and wrapped in my bathrobe, I head back to the kitchen. I grab a goblet-sized coffee cup and take a sip that slightly burns my tongue. I immediately think of last night's nasty business—Tony's kiss and my vomit on his shoes. I shudder in horror.

"How are you feeling?" asks Luca.

"Like a piece of shit."

"Did you really puke on that guy, or did you just say that because you were drunk?"

"His tongue was a little . . . you know, wet, and with the vodka, it was just an indigestible combination. I couldn't help it."

"You know, tongues usually do tend to be wet."

"But not *this* wet!" I say. "I've kissed guys before, and I know that Tony's tongue was much wetter than average. And then there was the movement . . ."

"What movement?"

"Well, up and down, back and forth. It was like tongue choreography!"

"So what did you do?" Luca asks.

"I told you! I threw up."

"I meant before that. When he was playing tonsil hockey with you."

"I think I was paralyzed."

He laughs and almost spits out his coffee. I can't help but join in. Sure, if I think about that horrifying tongue or the fact that I let him explore my mouth with said tongue or how I gifted him with the slimy contents of my stomach in a show of gratitude, I want to smother myself with a pillow. But if I pretend that the mishap happened to some other moron who doesn't even know how to kiss, then I can see the humor of it.

"Anyway, it's not my fault," I say. "I'm a great kisser."

"I've got my doubts about that."

"You might be an expert when it comes to sex, but you've clearly got a lot to learn when it comes to kissing."

"How do you know that?"

"There's no way you can devote the proper amount of time to kissing when you're so busy howling."

"I kiss like I fuck—brilliantly."

"Are you offended?" I say.

"No, I'm just saying that someone as awkward as you doesn't really have any room to talk here."

"And I'm just saying that you're a conceited asshole."

"Come here, you distrustful little witch."

It all happens in the blink of an eye. He jumps up, grabs me by the collar of my robe, and kisses me. Oh. My. *God.* I let his tongue open my lips. It's slow, nothing choreographed, and tastes mildly like coffee. We break apart, and I bite my lip. He caresses me, then dives back in, this time embracing me. When he finally pulls away, there's an insolent smile on his lips.

"So? What'd you think?"

"Well . . ." I feign indifference, pretending that my legs have not turned to spaghetti under my robe. "I don't know, it wasn't anything mind-blowing . . ."

"You want a war?" he laughs. This time he picks me up and sets me on top of the table, cradling my head in his hands as he kisses me again. I tremble all over, inside and out.

Suddenly a voice brings me back down to earth. Behind us in the hall, a bunch of keys jangling in her hand, is my nuisance of a mother, dressed to the nines. She must have recently dyed her hair; I see new shades of cognac in an ombré pattern. She blinks like a porcelain doll, watching us with a mischievous look beneath two miles of eyelashes. Luca sees her and startles.

"No, my dear," she says shamelessly. "It's quite all right! I tried to call you all morning, Carlotta, so I just dropped by to see how you were doing. I have your keys, remember?"

I'm speechless. I open and close my mouth, and all I can hear is the amplified smack of my lips. I know exactly what she's thinking, and it's going to be impossible to explain to her that Luca and I were just kidding around, that there's nothing between us, that my perch on the table with my legs spread wide open has no sexual implication. I jump down and readjust my bathrobe, cursing the unfortunate moment when I gave her those keys.

Mom approaches Luca, shakes his hand, and sizes him up. She approves. Better, she's intrigued. They talk in the kitchen while I run to get dressed, and I hear her laughing at his jokes. I've forgotten my headache in the terror of trying to figure out how to get rid of her as soon as possible, before Luca decides to move out and leave me with just the memory of the taste of that amazing kiss. I throw on something haphazardly—jeans and a sweater, chainmail . . . I really have no idea. I'm so confused, I can't even see straight.

When I get back, my mother is informing Luca about my teenage years. In fact, she's so kind as to share that at eighteen, I was still desperately waiting for boobs—and envying thirteen-year-old Erika's enormous rack. Luca listens politely, obviously holding back laughter, with one eyebrow raised and his hands stuffed in his pants pockets.

"Um, Mom . . . I think you should give me back my keys."

"Oh, sure, sure, hold on. Here, my darling, now that I know you're all right, I won't have to worry anymore."

She insists that everything is fine, which I take to mean that as long as I'm with a guy that looks like Luca, she'll sleep soundly at night.

"Do you have anything going on this morning?" I ask, and it's my way of telling her to get out of here. Somehow I'm holding back my tears—maybe because Luca doesn't seem angry; instead, he seems to be enjoying all of this, as if it were a tennis match. His gaze bounces back and forth from me to my mother as he rests against the sink with his arms crossed over his chest.

I finally manage to convince my mother to leave. I guide her with a little push on the small of her back, open the door, and find something right in front of my nose. Or rather, someone. It's the girl with the polka-dot thong. The one with the lisp, who criticized my refrigerator. Or at least I think it is, because she's actually wearing clothes this time, and I only recognize her eyes and her horse mouth. My mother stops, sensing my tension at seeing the tearful, pissed-off young lady standing there. She doesn't budge; her sixth sense tells her that this girl isn't selling something door to door.

The girl looks behind us and zeroes in on Luca. He's probably pretty annoyed; he always is when his one-night stands dare to demand something else from him. Sandra, enraged by three days with no response to her messages, enters the apartment, brushing us aside as if we were made of papier-mâché. My mother looks at me, shocked that I'm allowing this tramp to make a beeline for my man. I don't even have time to grope for an explanation when Sandra bursts.

"You thtupid bathtard! You fucked me for an hour thtraight the other night, and now you're pretending not to know me? You owe me a little more conthideration! What do you think, that I'm thome kind of thtupid bitch?"

Luca's answer isn't exactly cryptic. "Yes," he says, not bothered in the least. "That about sums it up."

I'm worried that any minute now she's going to pull a revolver out of her purse and hold it to his head. My mom, however, is ready to kick back, relax, order a bucket of popcorn, and enjoy the show. I drag her outside, lock the door behind us, and accompany her resolutely outside to the sidewalk. It's frigid out here.

"You shouldn't leave him alone with that girl," she says. "She had an incredible ass and her perfume smelled expensive."

"Don't worry, Luca will handle her."

"That's the problem."

"What?"

"That young lady seemed intent on nabbing your suitor, and if you're not careful, she'll steal him right out from under your nose. I bet she's good in bed, but I'm not as optimistic about you."

"Mom! You're always thinking about the same thing."

"Sex is important. If you had more of it, you wouldn't have all this acne under your chin, see?" She tips my head back as if I were a horse getting its teeth examined. "Erika has skin as soft as apricots," she says loudly.

"Oh, I'm sure she does!" I say, humiliated.

"Let's go back in and see what happens."

"I'm going back inside, Mom. *You* need to go!" Now I'm practically screaming, and a few passersby stare at me in horror.

"I could help you."

"I don't even want to know what kind of help you could give me, and I'm begging you to please just go home. I can take care of myself."

"You must bring Luca to the wedding—to show him to all of the aunts!" she says, as if he's some kind of trophy.

"I don't even know if I'm going, and if I do, I'm not bringing Luca."

"Why not?"

"He can't go. He's busy."

If I attempted to tell her the truth, and if I said I didn't want to be like Sandra or any of his other ephemeral flings because I couldn't stand the embarrassment and discomfort that would follow—and that I don't just want sex from him, but his mind, his soul, his breath, his memories, his future, too—all I'd do is convince her that I'm both crazy and conceited.

A cab pulls up to the curb, and I'm about to flag it for my mother when Giovanna jumps out of it. She races over and grabs me like a piranha.

"I told that useless piece of shit Armando to go to hell!" she shrieks before I can say anything. "He kept bringing up all these awful things from last night, saying that my boobs were on display, and that that guy from the bar was staring at me . . . He even told me again I had to get rid of Bear, this time because he wags his tail too loud! And then our make-up sex lasted four—yes, *four*—minutes total, including foreplay! That's it! I can't take it anymore. So I told him that we were through, that he should go buy some Viagra and find someone else to wipe his ass for him! Then he accused me of going out last night basically naked! How dare he!"

She opens her coat, and I realize that she's still wearing her outfit from last night. "Do I look naked?" she yells, shaking her boobs for everyone on the sidewalk. A bearded jogger stops dead at the sight. Giovanna closes her coat, disappointing the wide-eyed athlete, and promptly bursts into tears. My mother, on the other hand, looks very satisfied. She's clearly enjoying this extraordinary morning, so much that I don't think she's noticed her breath looks like speech bubbles in the freezing air. She must be storing up gossip to report to the aunts.

Eventually, I just give Giovanna a hug to get her moving, because I'm freezing and Sandra hasn't come down yet, which can only mean something bad. Giovanna hails a taxi with her arm outstretched and her coat wide open. A taxi driver slams on his brakes and asks her see-through shirt where he can take it. My mother, wrapped in her fur coat, does not intend to let go of our argument.

"Anyway, back to Luca," she says as soon as Giovanna is gone. "I can see he's got a wild side. I don't know if you can keep up with him. You should spice things up more! How about a nice outfit like Giovanna's? Or a padded push-up bra? I have a friend who swears by push-up pantyhose."

"Thank you, Mother. I'm sure you're right, as always. But all of my body parts would thud to the ground when I undressed. And there are noise restrictions in our apartment complex."

"You should wear more makeup. You have such a mouth, and your hair—why don't you ever use a flatiron?"

"I'll just make an appointment with the dry cleaner to steam clean my head." I'm tired and sullen. The cold has permeated every inch of my body, and I'm pretty sure that an icicle will form on the end of my nose any second now. When another taxi finally pulls up to the curb, I pray that it's not Tony seeking damages for the vomit on his nice shoes. The taxi is empty, but my mother's still not ready to leave.

"Oh, I forgot. I also came here to tell you something from your cousin Beatrice. She wants you to be her maid of honor."

"Ah . . ." is all I can get out. My reaction obviously horrifies her—she thinks I should be jumping for joy and delighting the passersby with some sidewalk acrobatics. "Thank Beatrice for me, but tell her that I cannot accept."

"But you've already accepted!"

"What? When? You heard me actually say yes? I don't think so."

"I accepted for you—I told her you'd love to."

"And when were you planning on telling me?"

"You can't back out," my mother says. "She already had the seamstress work on your dress, and your name has been printed on the programs."

I wish I could nudge the nearby manhole cover open with my heel and disappear inside. I stifle a scream, and a pinprick of unhappiness begins to pierce my heart.

"Is she getting in or not?" the taxi driver demands before continuing on his way, leaving me to be her prisoner.

"When were you planning on telling me?" I repeat. "I suppose you were going to wait until the wedding day, if I even showed up, to let me know that my dear cousin wants me to walk down the aisle dressed like a cupcake, while all the aunts murmur, 'Poor insignificant Carlotta, she'll never get married and she makes barely any money—'"

"You're being unfair, as usual," she says, not letting me have the last word. "You're going to be the maid of honor and make me proud for once in your life. The dress is almost ready. I'll send it to you in a week. I'm sure it'll be fine. We took measurements from Lisa."

"Beatrice's sister? But she's twelve years old!"

"And she has a bigger bosom than you. But it'll work."

I'm about to say something when someone grabs me by the shoulders.

"Pervert!" Sandra yells into my ear.

I turn around as my mother's delight meter shoots up to the stars.

"What?"

"You dirty bitch!"

I have no idea why she's calling me this, and I tell her so.

Sandra puffs out her cheeks. "Looking the way you do, how dare you act like that!"

"Dirty bitch?" I say again, while a family walking by stares at me like I'm dealing drugs to children.

"Whore!" Sandra yells. She hops into a cab, and my mother, burning with a desire to learn more about her daughter's sleazy side, jumps into the cab with her without a good-bye. I stand paralyzed on the sidewalk, a halo of icy breath framing my face.

Finally, I go back to the apartment, unable to make sense of this. Luca is still in the kitchen, putting a frozen chicken in the oven. He looks pensive as he scrubs a potato under running water.

"Hey," I say, entering.

"Hey," he says. "Do you want fries with the chicken? Here, peel this potato."

I take a knife and start to peel it, hands shaking with confusion and anxiety. "I hope my mother didn't freak you out," I say. "I'm sure she told you quite a few tall tales."

"She thought we were together?"

"Well, you've gotta admit—"

"Right."

"I get the feeling that Sandra hates me," I say, watching him out of the corner of my eye.

He turns, looking both amused and guilty. "You're not wrong."

"What did you say?" Sandra's choice words rattle around in my mind like marbles.

"If there's one thing I can't deal with, it's crying women. Especially when it's a crying woman I don't even know coming into my apartment and accusing me of—"

"But you do know Sandra," I say. "You slept with her three nights ago."

"—God knows what kind of treachery," he continues as if I hadn't interrupted him. "I can't stand it when women come home with me once and then act like we're engaged! My intentions are clear. So I just explained to her that—"

"What did you explain to her?" I demand, the potato in my left hand and the knife in the other.

"That I'm a slave to your deprivation, that we're actually together but you forced me to bring Sandra back here because you get off listening to me having sex with other women," he says. "That I'm in love with you, but you're kinky and treat me like a doormat. That I'm seeing a psychiatrist to help me figure out how to leave you. And that if I do leave you, she'll be the first person I call."

I can't even believe this.

"You're a fucking . . . asshole!" The potato tumbles to the ground with a thud, and my face turns fuchsia. "There are other ways you could have resolved that! Do you know what she called me in front of my mother?" The knife falls to the ground, too. He just might be next. "Luca! Do you realize what she's going to say to my mother? They left in a taxi together!"

"I wouldn't worry about your mother. She might even be relieved to hear it. She asked me if you still kiss like you did when you were sixteen. Apparently your boyfriend at the time publicly complained about your lack of tongue."

"Holy crap." I collapse onto a chair, for fear of melting into the floor, and repeat that about eight times.

"I told her that your tongue has since risen to the challenge."

If I still had the knife in my hand, I swear I'd use his back for target practice.

"By the way, no more messing around like that." He pretends to zip up his lips. "No more kissing, I mean."

"Am I that disgusting?"

"You're not disgusting at all, butterfly. The truth is, we shouldn't play around with things that might lead to misunderstandings. I know, I started it, and I'll bang my head against the fridge as punishment. But I don't want that to ever happen again. Sex or anything remotely resembling it should be off the table for us. We're friends, damn it, and if we let something like that get in the way, even if it's just a joke, it might mess things up."

"You're right," I whisper. I feel like a raw fish that's been chopped up by a hysterical sushi chef.

We change the subject and set the table while the chicken cooks and the potatoes turn golden. Luca turns on some music on the radio, and then holes up in his room for half an hour to call a friend. Then we eat, but my stomach is sealed shut. I don't let myself show any emotion until I can hear him typing on his keyboard.

At least I don't repulse him, but I read him loud and clear. There will be no sex between us, no love. Just me and him, one here and one there—never us. But this is the first time I've ever truly been in love with someone. In a way, I'm still a virgin! Virginity is in your heart, not your hymen. It's an emotion. I love him, and that scares me.

While I load the dishwasher, Luca pops out wearing his reading glasses. He gestures to the answering machine.

"I forgot to tell you that while you were down there with your mom, Michelangelo called."

"Who?"

"What's-his-name. The tongue guy that you puked on last night. The message is on the machine."

He disappears, closing the door behind him, but the typing doesn't start back up again. I wipe my hands, stunned, and press the flashing button. Tony's voice is cheerful, much to my dismay. He swears he's not offended; Giovanna told him I rarely drink and that I threw up because of all the alcohol. He clearly does not understand that his saliva was the catalyst for my regurgitation. He's still determined to paint my portrait and repeats that I have a very interesting face. He leaves me his number, asking me to call him back, and I scribble it down on a piece of scrap paper. I sit on the couch and giggle. I don't know if I'll call him back. If he tries to kiss me again when I haven't had any alcohol and I puke, he may realize something's up.

I lie down with my head on the armrest. Light snowfall shimmers beyond the window, and I drift off to sleep. At some point I feel a wave of air on my warm cheek and am barely conscious of Luca draping a plaid blanket over my curled-up body.

SIX

The Knights Theater isn't much more than a closet, and it's sat unused for thirty years. The dust pinches my nose and throat. The curtain looks as scraggly as a mop, and the forty seats in the auditorium are covered in cobwebs. One thing's for sure: this ain't Broadway. And yet, I like this cubbyhole. I imagine what it will look like after a vigorous cleaning: the pistachio-green granite floor, the red chairs, the mahogany fixtures ready to shine in the dark like flames. I can already hear the footsteps of the audience flooding in, their voices hushed like in church, the whoosh of the curtain sliding open, and a shower of applause.

I've always loved this world. During the show, I'll be backstage preparing the props for upcoming scenes, and my heart never fails to skip a beat from the emotion.

I have no hope, however, for improving the director. On Monday, I signed my contract and learned that my salary will allow me to feast on dry bread and spring water. Luckily, Rocky wasn't there. It was just Franz, who shook my hand with the usual vigor and smiled at me with that good-guy smile. He gave me the script, which I devoured in one night. I was shocked at how, despite the substantial changes to the setting, the story had been left unchanged. Laura's loneliness, Amanda's intrusiveness, and Tom's intolerance are all the same. The Barbie doll collection is different, though. I guess the dolls are much more suited to modern times than glass animals. I'm enough of a Barbie expert to know that the ones Rocky has requested are like the Gronchi Rosa stamp for stamp collectors. I hope he's aware that he'll need a much bigger budget to obtain them.

As I walk down a side aisle, I see him sitting in the front row, dressed all in white. He's wearing a Korean-style gown that comes down to his calves, a scarf wrapped around his neck, and a headband. I swear. His hair shouldn't be pushed back like that; it brutally highlights his cheekbones, his shark-fin nose, and his eyes, which are devoid of kindness but well equipped with kohl eyeliner. He's shouting instructions to both the technicians and the actors, waving his arms around like a conductor, but not bothering to get up from his chair. He frowns and rolls his eyes when he sees me.

"Here she is," he murmurs. "Late. Zero professionalism."

I hold back a retort. I had prepared a little speech about the impossibility of finding the entire Barbie collection with a budget of only five hundred euro, but I'm afraid that once I start, I won't be able to hold back. Better to postpone it. This is only the second time we've met, and Franz isn't around this time to protect me.

Rocky condemns me with a look, not even thinking to introduce me to the rest of the crew. He moves on to the man sitting next to him, who nods emphatically as Rocky waves his script.

I sit down, feeling uncomfortable. I don't know anyone here apart from the bird man in the scarf. I'd feel weird getting up onstage and introducing myself, like a new student in an elementary school class. While I'm sitting there wondering what to do, a set builder in overalls emerges from one of the wings. He waves an arm and calls my name. It takes me a few seconds to realize that it's Franz! In those clothes, with his hair all mussed up, he looks completely different—but definitely not in a bad way. Next to him is a young girl who's shorter than I am but very full-bodied. Her red hair is plaited in two French braids, and her nose is sprinkled with freckles. She's very pretty, but why is there a teenager in this theater?

"Carlotta, welcome!" says Franz, leaning down from the stage to shake my hand. His fingers are a little dirty, and there's a splash of black paint on his nose. "Forgive me for my outfit, but with such a small production, you have to get down and dirty and do whatever needs to be done. This is Iriza, the set design architect. Iriza, this is Carlotta, who will be a big help."

"I know what you're gonna say," says the girl with a smile. "Everyone reacts the same way. I'm a baby face! But I'm thirty-two."

I stare at her in amazement. This girl with pigtail braids is thirty-two years old? But she looks sixteen! And where are her wrinkles, the ones that begin to creep up around your eyes just as you near thirty? She laughs, but her skin stays as smooth as porcelain. She doesn't look like she gets Botox, either. Maybe I got her wrinkles instead.

One thing, however, is immediately clear. Iriza has a crush on Franz. She looks at him the way I looked at Luke Perry when I was thirteen years old. He doesn't seem to notice, though. He's friendly and basically indifferent. Since I have some experience in unrequited feelings, I immediately recognize the signal she's broadcasting: *We're just friends, but I'm not letting you touch him with a ten-foot pole.* I immediately like Iriza a whole lot more. We share a disease—we both want someone who won't even give us a second glance.

Rocky interrupts our pleasantries. "This isn't a holiday party," he shouts. "You're here to work."

Franz gets back to work, and Iriza invites me to follow her onstage. She enthusiastically explains her stage design ideas to me. The few pieces of furniture will be made of plexiglass, and the details of the house will be a painted on the background. The actors will wear pale, almost phosphorescent, makeup to suggest an air of fragility. At the end of the show, when the curtain closes, the set will break from an earthquake special effect to express the rift that is created in the characters' lives before and after the events in the play. After all, no matter how well maintained or protected it may be, a world of glass is destined to shatter.

While we're talking—quietly, so that Rocky doesn't come yell at us again—a new voice sneaks up behind me and makes me jump in fright.

"Hey there." A mammoth stands an inch away from my left ear. "Our Franz has a nice ass, huh?" She says this so loud that audiences as far away as the La Scala in Milan probably heard her. But no one seems bothered: not the arrogant director, and not even Franz with the aforementioned nice ass.

Urged by her comment, my gaze shifts lightning fast over to Franz. Mind you, the woman's not wrong. Iriza whispers to me that her name is Rose, but she's nowhere near as graceful as her floral name might suggest.

"You know what they say about a guy with a big nose? He's also big down south," she declares openly, without a hint of embarrassment and (amazingly) without Rocky telling her to go to hell. "The sound engineer must be small—his nose is the size of a tiny potato."

I want to sink into the ground, but instead I turn so I can see her better—and almost scream. All she's missing is an eye on her forehead, and she'd be the spitting image of two-hundred-year-old Polyphemus (although I don't believe Polyphemus ever made foul comments about the length of Ulysses's nose). Rose, meanwhile, continues to giggle as she spouts more coarse jokes—with no response from Rocky.

Iriza seems to read my mind. "She's the director's grandmother," she says. "She's the only human being on this planet that Rocky shows even the slightest bit of affection to. She doesn't bother any of us anymore. Be careful, though. She's going to ask you your favorite sexual position, and you'd better have an answer—she won't leave you alone until you do."

I fear that Rose will be disappointed in me. Not only has it been centuries since I've engaged in the art of lovemaking, but in my few experiences, I never strayed from your basic choreography. The classic guy-on-top, girl-on-bottom, a few minutes of frenetic bustle, thank you, I'll call you, you'll call me, and life goes on.

Suddenly, Rocky seems to remember that we're actually in the theater, and he calls the actors up on the stage. Iriza and I move aside toward Franz, who is caulking a damaged floorboard, and continue to whisper. The actors are perfectly cast according to Rocky's vision. They all look like they've been fasting for a month, and they're pale as eggshells, too. The woman who's playing Amanda looks like a thinner Sigourney Weaver. Laura is a tall blond girl with Slavic cheekbones, who sort of looks like Cate Blanchett. The guy who plays Jim, the family's guest whom Laura is secretly in love with, fits the part. But the guy who plays Tom seems out of place. According to the new script, Laura's brother is an aspiring heavy metal musician forced to work in a bank and is oppressed by an omnipresent mother. But he's got eyes as innocent as Bashful from *Snow White and the Seven Dwarves*. I can't see him dreaming about smashing guitars and humping microphone stands.

While the actors run their lines, pausing every so often to move left or right according to Rocky's instructions, I wander backstage. The world back here is my secret garden—everything still has yet to be placed, everything is still possible, radiating with the charm of undiscovered treasures and unsolved mysteries. Walking around back here, I feel like I'm rummaging through an attic. For a moment, I imagine the Phantom of the Opera emerging from a tunnel and kidnapping me. I'm so focused on my fantasies of hidden passages behind the walls that I don't notice the irregularity in the flooring. At one wrong step, a wooden board gives way underneath my weight. It cracks like a breaking walnut. I find myself facedown on the ground with my legs trapped in a hole, my rear in the air, and my skirt raised completely up over my waist.

For a moment, my mind goes blank. Then I start to process the situation, and panic strikes. There's no one back here. No one saw me fall, and it's no use trying to pull my skirt down because the back is completely torn and hooked on a ledge like a flag. I take a deep breath, and two dust balls fly up my nose. Ann Darrow must have felt more or less like this when King Kong captured her. So what now? Will everyone else come looking for me? What if they don't? What if they think I left? Why do I keep finding myself in these ridiculous situations? Why doesn't anything normal ever happen to me?

I hear actors' voices in the distance and the occasional hammer. I just have to ask for help. Mortified, I begin to call out. At first, my voice is so quiet that I think only the cockroaches could hear me, so I call out louder. Sitting here waiting to be ridiculed by the public, I feel like I'm caught in a slapstick comedy show. A sharp pain pierces my legs; by some miracle my nose doesn't seem to be broken. But the thought that haunts me most as I hear people respond to my cries is that today I decided to wear a pair of panties with bleach stains.

Everyone trickles in, both curious and alarmed. As soon as they realize what happened, the giggles intensify. Franz and Iriza rush to help me, not laughing at all. Rocky doesn't laugh either, but not out of compassion. His stare is murderous. I've interrupted his rehearsal, and he wants to reduce me to sawdust for it. I get up with great effort, suppressing a string of curse words that would make a sailor blush. My tights are snagged, my skirt shredded, my knee skinned. Flushed with embarrassment and trembling like a leaf, I sneeze half a dozen times before I can breathe regularly again.

"How are you doing? You all right?" Franz asks with touching solidarity.

Grandmother Rose approaches. "Congratulations. You've got a nice ass, too."

Hooray, now everyone will remember me as a great bumbling fool. It won't even matter if I do my job well. I'm permanently marked. It'll go like this:

Carlotta? Who is that? I don't think I know her.

Oh, she's done incredible work for some of the best directors in Europe. She graduated with honors from the Academy of Fine Arts and wrote her thesis on twentieth-century theater scenes. I think Woody Allen wanted her for his film that was set in Rome. You don't remember her?

No, I swear I don't.

She's the one who fell into the hole and got stuck with her rear hanging out on her first day of work.

Oh, yeah, her! I know her!

While I limp away, Franz, who has since donned a coat, takes me by the arm. He insists on taking me to the emergency room, but I refuse.

"There's no need, really. It's only my dignity that's hurt, and I don't think there's any medicine for that."

"Let me at least take you home. Your skirt is completely torn, and you shouldn't be walking around like that."

"You have no idea. My mood is completely shot," I say, accepting his offer of mercy.

In the car, I'm silent for a long time, wallowing. Not because I feel victimized, but because I'm criticizing myself. After a while, Franz turns to me and smiles indulgently.

"Nothing serious happened, come on. Don't make that face."

"Nothing serious, sure. I could have been seriously injured, and instead I'm well enough to be able to think about how stupid I am."

"How is it your fault if that theater is littered with traps?"

"Has anyone else ever fallen through the floor?"

"Well, no, actually."

"Because that trap was waiting for me. I shouldn't have gone back there," I say. "I knew I'd end up like this. My life could have been written by Zucker, Abrahams, and Zucker. I've seen it all. Once I was even attacked by pigeons in Piazza San Marco—like in that Hitchcock movie! When I was younger, I was the one who always fell down the stairs at school, slipped love letters into the wrong guy's pocket, or got stung by bees if I picked a flower and put it in my hair. And don't even get me started on my adult life. Would you believe me if I told you that I even mixed up the recipients of two note cards? I sent one expressing condolences to a friend that was getting married and my warmest congratulations to another one who just became a widow! Of course something like this would happen to me. Perhaps in a past life I tortured angels, and now karma is retaliating. I should add these wonderful experiences to my resume. Maybe some director who's even nicer than Rocky would appreciate them."

"At least with you, we'll never be bored," Franz offers.

"A little monotony is good for your health and your reputation."

"Is that what your boyfriend says?"

I shrug, my way of admitting that I don't have a boyfriend.

"I thought I heard that you lived with a guy, but maybe I was wrong."

I stare at him. He thought he heard *what*? Do people just go around spreading gossip about me all over Rome? I'm vaguely irritated. Franz, seeming to sense my bitterness, quickly explains.

"It was written in your paperwork. They must have taken it from your initial questionnaire."

"The initial questionnaire. Right! What extremely pertinent questions. I didn't lie, though. I do live with a man . . . And if that offends the decency of our dear director or his holy grandmother . . . tell them that the man I live with helps pay the rent, since my wages are miserable wages."

"No! It intrigued me. It was as good a way as any to find out if you're engaged." He's silent, shifting gears. He has a nice profile. His lips are slightly protruding now, like he's sulking. I stammer something. I point out where he needs to turn, feeling dumb. I'm not so arrogant as to believe that he likes me, but if he does, I'll have to tell him that my love life is a total mess, I dream of having sex with my tenant, a young painter named Tony Boni called me back *again* this morning, and my mother will probably set me up with some creep at my cousin's wedding if I don't bring Luca. Of course, I don't say any of this. I'm crazy, but not entirely stupid.

We arrive at my place. I thank him and leap out of the car unathletically. We say good-bye awkwardly, the way people do when one person saw the other with her ass in the air for a solid minute.

I hear Luca's voice from the landing before I've even opened the apartment door. Wouldn't it be just glorious if he were chatting with my mother? I'm tempted to take refuge on the terrace until the nuisance has left. But I can make out only his voice. It's strangely high-pitched, and I wonder if he's discovered some drug-induced paradise for frustrated writers. He's talking nonsense about bees and rabbits—an obscure addict language? Finally, I hear another voice. I swear, if I find him whispering obscenities in some woman's ear, I will evict him on the spot.

I open the door abruptly, and there he is, sitting on the couch next to little Emma, who is listening intently as he reads her a story from a picture book that's bigger than she is. They both startle, and Emma looks bewildered. She was absorbed in a world of bees and bunnies, and I practically kicked in the door like a member of a vice squad. Luca gives me a dirty look.

"Aunt Carlotta! Come in but be quiet!" Emma exclaims.

"Yeah, come in but be quiet!" Luca echoes. "There's a chubby bumblebee that's afraid to fly, so he always ends up falling to the ground, and a mischievous bunny that keeps the whole forest awake by tapping his foot . . ."

How absurd! They explain the story so that I know what's going on. But maybe he really is drugged, under the strange influence of children that even a thirty-two-year-old writer of erotica can't escape. I listen, sitting on a chair, until it's clear to me that the bee has learned to fly and the bunny has learned a little discipline. When the story ends, Emma jumps off the couch and rushes to hug me. I don't have the faintest idea what she's doing here with her big colorful book, but her vanilla scent intoxicates me.

"What happened to you, Aunt Carlotta?" she asks me, looking at my tights and skirt and a cobweb dangling from my shoulder. Even Luca finally notices my sorry state. He asks me the same question more colorfully.

"What happened to you, little butterfly? Do I have to go smash someone's face in?"

"Nothing serious. I just fell on the job," I say, continuing to hug Emma. "But what are you doing here, cutie?"

"Lara brought her over an hour ago," Luca informs me. "She had an appointment with someone. I don't know what or where, but she needed someone to look after Emma. Apparently the babysitter from the other night was incompetent."

Seeing him so paternal, so patient, so strangely comfortable with a little girl he's seen maybe three times is having a crazy effect on me. He's too good. Dangerously good. It's so much easier to hate him (or at least try to) when he's playing the virile male in the next room. But this complicates things. It wouldn't be enough for me to make love to him and wake up in the same bed the next morning. I want him to be the father of my children. I need to grow old with him. I want us to be buried next to each other. Completely unaware of my burial plans, Luca nudges me.

"After Emma leaves, tell me what happened," he whispers. "Can you take care of her for now? I read her two stories, I told her about a fairy that lives in the fridge, and I made her a glass of warm milk, but now I want to write."

"I'm on it," I say. Emma steals my attention. I give her a cookie, we draw together, I comb her hair. It's fun to be a mom for a while. I think I could learn to be good with kids. I'm not much taller than they are, I know how to make animal noises, and I can still see things that many other women my age haven't been able to see for years: monsters under the bed when the storm rages outside and ghosts behind the billowing curtains. I think I'd be a good mother. But it'll never happen. I just know it. I want to have children to give and receive love—not just to satisfy my biological clock or feel included in a society where motherhood is trendy again. I'm easily satisfied when it comes to many things, but not this. With this, it's all or nothing. And it seems that nothing is the most likely option for me.

Enough! I hate self-pity. I'm actually not doing too bad. I'm working in the entertainment world, I live with a ridiculously hot guy, I have a suitor who calls, and next Saturday, I'm going to be somebody's maid of honor. Sure, I just made a complete spectacle of myself, and Facebook and Twitter will probably have pictures soon, but I'm used to that kind of thing by now. Like Franz says, at least the people in my life will never be bored. I brush Emma's hair while I console myself with these painful lies.

"Is Luca your boyfriend?" she suddenly asks me as I'm braiding her hair.

"No, he's a friend of mine, just like your mom," I say. Although her mother has never sucked on my bottom lip like a popsicle.

"Then can he be my boyfriend?"

Four years is pretty young to start trusting these bastards. Luckily, her mother will set her straight soon. We go to my room, and she takes the liberty of poking around my things while I change.

We're rolling around on the carpet pretending we're underwater when the phone rings. It's my mother. She's been calling me nonstop lately. Maybe I should change my number. Meanwhile, I'll let the machine get it.

"Erika is just dying to meet Luca! You should bring him to the wedding; otherwise, you'll be going with Catello."

I wonder if she intends to keep him fresh in a freezer bag so she can pull him out if necessary. But I have another reason to go alone: to prevent Erika from hooking up with Luca. Mom must have described him well, because my loving sister is clearly already scheming to snatch him from under my nose. This will mean that I'll have to put up with Catello. It would help if I could remember anything about him. Mom says I've met him before, but I don't remember ever meeting anyone with such a ridiculous name.

Lara comes to get Emma that evening. Luca showers and dresses. He's got a date somewhere with someone I don't know. While he ties his shoes, he asks me about my workday. I tell him about my latest adventure, and he looks at me for a moment, eyes wide with shock. Then he bursts into laughter, first laughing at me, then laughing with me, throwing himself down on the bed with all his weight.

"You are a wonderful catastrophe," he exclaims, running a hand through his hair and offering me a view of his magnificent neck and five o'clock shadow. "I don't know what I'd do without you. I had a hellish morning, but you always make me smile."

"Why, what happened to you?"

He shrugs and smiles again, but I can tell that he doesn't seem his happy self. I don't understand why, and I suddenly feel worried about him. I love him—I can't stand to see him sad.

"If something's going on, you know you can talk to me, right?" I say.

"I know, butterfly. I'm sure you would give me advice worthy of a Dear Abby column."

"I would, I learned from the best."

He stares at me for a moment. "Do you think a person who has closed off his heart and doesn't want to let people in would be able to handle sudden, strong emotion?"

My mouth gapes for a minute. My heart somersaults like a trapeze artist at the circus. I preferred his questions about breasts and high heels.

"You mean . . . Is this a personal thing? Or . . . is it for your book?"

"For my book, of course," he says. "The sex and revenge scenes are fine, but now that's she's fallen in love in spite of herself, I'm in trouble. I have to make this woman's love realistic, without it sounding ridiculous."

Despite my boasts about my worth as a counselor, my tongue is tied up in knots. For some reason, I can't shake the feeling that he's not talking about his book at all. He's turned my heart into pulp. He doesn't notice my silence, though, because his own overshadows it. Tense, distracted, and impatient, he seems lost in a thousand thoughts.

When he leaves, he's wearing a simple blazer with a white shirt, jeans, and a padded trench coat. This is different from his usual detached air; he's acting like this is a tryst. The pain this causes me makes the torment I suffer over his moans in the other room seem inconsequential. A monster thrashes in my stomach. My hands shake. It's like the earth has opened up and sucked me down into its darkest depths.

I can't resist peeking out the window. Luca is standing on the sidewalk, whipped by the cold wind. A car stops. I see a woman's slender hand on the steering wheel. He gets in, they drive off, and the sleet swallows them.

I spend the evening drawing and eating Mini Ritz crackers. I have an album full of images like the one I'm drawing tonight: always the same subject, drawn in pencil, charcoal, chalk, pastels . . . The images are my stolen glimpses. Luca looking thoughtful as he stares at the computer screen, rereading the last lines he's written, chin propped on his hand. Luca sleeping alone, with the sheets clinging to him like a woman's legs. Luca in the shower, the frosted glass revealing only the shadow of his muscles and the wave of his hair. I know I'm halfway to stalker status, because he doesn't know about these drawings. But I need them, not just so I can marvel at the beauty of his features, but so I can see the beauty that his emotions reveal. Tonight, I draw him with the same sad eyes I saw before he left.

Around midnight, I hear the sound of a car on the road, and I cautiously look outside again. It's the same car from earlier, and Luca and the woman get out. The snow has stopped, and the light of a streetlamp illuminates them. She's young, and from what I can see from up here, she's beautiful. Elegant and graceful, she doesn't look like the women that usually traipse through here. A green silk scarf is wrapped around her short hair, which I think is the same color as honey. They talk, and even from above I sense excitement between them. He takes her hand and squeezes it as if to warm her. Then they embrace. For a moment, my heart stops. I'm seriously ready to throw myself out the window and splatter on the sidewalk like a spilled scoop of ice cream. But first, I'd like to have some bionic ears so I can hear what they're saying. There's something sweet in the way they're standing, something infinitely worse than the wild encounters I'm used to seeing.

I scramble away from the window just as Luca opens the front door of the apartment complex. The woman doesn't follow him up; instead, she gets in her car and drives away. I hide my drawings and rush to the couch, then stretch out as if I've been asleep. When he opens the door, I pretend that the noise wakes me up. He looks dreamy, as if his mind is somewhere else, perhaps still with the beautiful girl with the scarf and the slender hands.

"How'd it go?" I ask him with hypocritical nonchalance.

"It was nothing special."

"Did you make a new friend?"

He doesn't answer me or even say good night—he just tells me that he's going to bed. I'm left alone with the sound of the TV. Suddenly I realize this is what it's going to be like when he leaves. There's no doubt in my mind that he will. He'll fall in love, and he'll leave me, forgetting all his theories about the illusion of love. The weight of this thought is heavy, and I arch my back under it. Who is this mysterious woman who is bringing out his tender side? Yesterday Luca was his usual self, a ruthless womanizer. What happened, and when? This morning, while I was gone? Was it love at first sight? While I gave an audience of complete strangers a show, did Luca feel butterflies in his stomach and fall in love?

I seem to have lost him.

Except he was never mine in the first place.

I listen for the sound of his feet on the floor before I get up. As I walk barefoot down the hall, I'm tempted to barge into his room and tell him that I love him.

But wisdom sends me to my room.

SEVEN

Luca has been acting increasingly strange lately. He doesn't talk much, he writes for hours without a break, and he disappears every night, even when he's not bartending. One night he didn't even come back home until eight in the morning, as I was drinking a five-shot espresso with trembling hands. He looked tired and pale. He smiled, gave me a peck on the cheek, and went to shower.

Fortunately, work has kept me busy. After the first week on the job, Iriza invited me to go to a cafe that serves the most delicious hot chocolate in the world. While sipping our heavenly drinks, she handed me a booklet with the stage design marked out, down to the smallest details, even those only hinted at in the script. Getting the few pieces of furniture won't be difficult, as they are fairly ordinary and so minimalist that I think the staged house will look like the family is in the process of moving out. But I'm worried that Laura's Barbie doll collection is going to drive me crazy—the sadistic Rocky has demanded the original versions. Finding the first Barbie—from the 1960s, with a black-and-white striped dress, jaunty ponytail, and seductive gaze—will be like finding an endangered monk seal.

Iriza is so nice. All of a sudden, we find ourselves talking about our private lives. I discover that she was married and that her husband passed away from cancer. It doesn't seem possible that her fresh face and friendly personality hide a painful past. Now my worries about trivial things like a broken heart and a few over-the-top relatives seem juvenile and whiny.

"Don't make that face," she says kindly. "It's been so long, and time has been good to me. My work is exciting, and I have room for more things in my life. By the way, I'm sorry to tell you that your job isn't going to be as easy as it might have sounded."

"It hasn't seemed easy at all. I want to talk to Rocky, but he makes me want to pull that scarf tighter around his neck and I forget what I was going to say. Oops—are you friends with him?"

She smiles, shrugging. "Rocky doesn't have friends. He lives in his own delusional world and dislikes everyone for random reasons. In your case, he hates you because a long time ago a girlfriend from Calabria dumped him out of the blue. Ever since then, he's had a visceral hatred for everyone who reminds him of that area. It's nothing personal."

"So he doesn't like me because I'm from Calabria, just like his ex-girlfriend?"

"Yeah, but it would have been the same thing if you were from Umbria—like the plumber who screwed up the irrigation system in his garden—or if you were from the Philippines—like the maid that left him to return to her home without even giving him notice. He's moody and neurotic, and he's convinced he's a misunderstood genius. But his ideas do work. I've worked with him before, and his shows aren't bad. One time he reworked *The Story of an Abandoned Doll*, but instead of two little girls fighting over a doll in a chalk circle, he made them two women vying for a man. The one that let him go was the winner. Men are like that. They don't want to feel trapped. It's better to be seen as a friend or companion rather than possessive. Then there's hope they'll notice you."

My sixth sense picks up that she's talking about Franz. But she's also talking about me, even though she doesn't know it. I smile. "Then there are the men who need to feel the heel on their necks to be happy. But really, men are on the same level as earthworms to me."

"Are you with anyone?"

"I'm currently out of the chalk circle, waiting for the man I love to realize that I'm the right woman for him."

Iriza explodes in crystalline laughter. "Then you're like the winner in Rocky's adaptation. Or Penelope from *The Odyssey*, the woman who waits confidently. Hopefully that will pay off."

"I've always wondered if Penelope really does win in the end," I say. "Ulysses basically just leaves her again after a while. It's typical—men hardly stop for long. They make us believe they're here for good, but then the sea calls to them. Who knows, maybe Ulysses went back to have another go with Circe."

Iriza winces playfully. "I hope not."

"Don't worry," I say in a guru-like tone. "Perhaps there is a solution—Penelope is seriously detrimental to his mental health by herself. Even Circe, after she's used up all her seduction techniques, will become boring. I think it's all about balance. A little bit domestic and a little bit slutty, you know?"

"Does that work for you?"

"Oh, I haven't tested my theory yet. I guess I'll try it out and let you know!"

Iriza nods to the waiter to bring us our bill, and she insists on paying.

My social life has blossomed. Tony called me again. Given the terrible way I acted, I'm beginning to think that he either really likes me, or that vomit turns him on. I haven't called him back, just like I haven't called back Giovanna or my mother, who have both left me a handful of delusional messages. Giovanna called to tell me that she's met a great guy, and my mother to say that my bridesmaid's dress is on its way—and that she's sending a message from Catello with it.

Strangely, Erika calls one evening. Unfortunately, Luca picks up as I'm locked in the bathroom with a wax-strip Groucho Marx mustache under my nose. Through the door, I hear his voice turning overly polite, and then he says her name and alarm bells blare in my mind. I burst out of the bathroom screaming "Noooo!" in a manner worthy of Renata Tebaldi. I dive onto the couch and snatch the phone from his hands like a soccer goalie blocking a penalty kick with a textbook dive.

Luca looks at me, stunned, his last words—"Yes, we live together"—hanging in the air. The look I give him is a cross between Freddy Krueger and a fawn: ruthless and pleading. As I talk to Erika, however, I lose the fawn part.

"What do you want," I say, not even bothering to phrase it like a question.

"For how educated you are, you have the manners of a truck driver. Were you singing just now, or do you not want me to meet Luca?"

A growl rises up inside of me—either my stomach rumbling, or my soul churning with anger. "Why are you calling me? It's not my birthday. It's not even my funeral."

"I hear you've been chosen as maid of honor," she says, making no effort to disguise the mockery in her voice. "Congratulations!"

"Do you want to take my place?"

"I would never deprive you of such a glorious moment."

"Then what do you want?"

"Carlotta, you're so tense. Relax, okay?"

"I'm relaxed! I am very relaxed!" I say, sounding as relaxed as someone about to be subjected to lethal injection.

"Luca's such a nice guy, and he has a beautiful voice. Mom said he was very interesting."

"Mom thinks a lot of things are interesting—Aunt Porzia's broccoli cake, for example."

"I'll just see him at the wedding, then. You're bringing him, right?"

"I have to go," I say, without answering her question.

"You don't always have to be so uptight, little sister. Irritability gives you wrinkles."

"And hypocrisy gives you hemorrhoids."

With that, I end the conversation by throwing the phone on the couch. I'm breathing hard when Luca comes to check on me before he goes out.

"What's wrong?" he asks, giving me a pat on the cheek. I'd like to bare my soul to him about my senseless struggle with my sister and our stupid competition to see who can crush the other (which I've never won, of course). I'd like to wrest the promise from him that if she calls again, he will treat her like a butler would, completely detached, and not give her a second glance if he meets her. But such promises—if he would be so magnanimous as to make them—would be meaningless. We're not together. He's not my boyfriend, and I have no right to extort such oaths from him.

Moreover, he's not the problem. I am. As long as things are so fragile that just the idea of Erika makes me seriously fear losing him, I will never be happy, and our relationship will never be more than this exhausting game of war. I don't know much, but I do know this: the battle will turn once I get my hands on something she can't touch. A job that I'm proud of, true love, and above all else, deep self-love. Until then, my feelings will never change. So I just tell Luca that sometimes my family makes me hysterical. Then I run to the bathroom, as the wax has turned into wallpaper glue.

On Friday morning, the package containing my bridesmaid dress arrives. Entirely taffeta, the color dung-brown, it's worse than even my most horrifying speculations. Along with the dress is the nice message from Catello that my mother promised she would pass along. It's written in kindergartenesque handwriting on the back of the invitation.

"I can't weit to see you again."

Weit?

After a lot of thinking, I've decided he must be one of two guys that my mother tried to set me up with a few years ago, during an end-of-the-year party at her aunt Ermellina's house. One of the two was pretty cool; he was tall and dark, had great hair and a tiny nose ring, and smoked enough for four Turks. He wasn't that bad, except that he kept trying to reach out and touch me. The other guy, however, had a spittle problem, a receding hairline, and glasses that made his pupils look like watermelon seeds. I spent the whole evening trying to escape the nightmare that was both of these guys. I hope I don't have to do the same thing this time around.

The whole wedding is making me nervous. The thought of seeing all my relatives (especially Erika) increases my despair as well as my desire to invent an excuse and stay home. But I want to see my dad—who will surely be there, as he has kept a civil relationship with my mother's side of the family—and that's stronger than everything else.

Saturday afternoon, I do my makeup under the watchful eyes of three Barbie dolls that I just bought on the Internet. They're the only ones I've managed to find quickly online. While I almost pinch my eyelids with my eyelash curler, the three plastic women peek out from the dressing table, still in their pink boxes. Peach Blossom Barbie probably feels sorry for me, but the other two are laughing at me behind my back. Killer Barbie, with her knife and little black dress, looks at me with contempt. Tattoo Barbie, with her beautiful bob, an anthology of tattoos on her arms, and leopard-print leggings, would probably tell me to throw out the bridesmaid dress—to hell with Beatrice and all seven generations of my family! If only I had the courage . . .

Suddenly, Luca interrupts my silent conversation with the dolls. Stopping out in the hall, he leans against the doorjamb and stares at me.

"You're prettier without makeup," he says with a smile, and it's not even sarcastic. As always, he's half-naked. Damn him. He's wearing blue cutoffs that used to be suit pants. They're already sitting low on his waist, but he thrusts his hands in his pockets with so much energy that it's a miracle the pants don't fall to the floor. He'd probably laugh and show off his goods with pride.

"Am I?" I fake disinterest while flames lick the inside of my stomach.

"Yeah. It hides your freckles," he says, coming in and sitting down on my bed. Peeking at him in the mirror, I feel like an ice cube on a sunny windowsill.

"The idea was to make me look less like a strawberry."

"I like your strawberry face. Your freckles and your hair are fun."

"Fun like a roller coaster ride." But I'm happy he's talking to me. He seems more peaceful. I wonder what it would be like to lick his face, like licking the frosting of a donut . . .

"You're beautiful, Carlotta, and that's coming from an expert."

I gasp and accidentally smear mascara all over my cheek. A wave of heat ripples through me, and I unconsciously clench my crossed legs.

I try to joke. "Yeah, beautiful for a freak of nature." He watches me with attention that I don't understand. My heart pounds against my poor ribs. If he doesn't stop, I might faint.

"Don't make jokes, butterfly. I'm just being brotherly. No ulterior motives."

He gets up, comes over to the dressing table, and starts to play with one of my curls while I dab at the mascara stain on my cheek. As I watch his abdomen in the mirror, I wish we were on the cover of a romance novel, me half-naked as well, with his powerful arms wrapped around me, his nostrils flaring with desire. Instead, I point to the dress that's laid out on the chair.

"Will I be able to look elegant in my diarrhea-colored bridesmaid dress?"

"Mmm," he mumbles. He's probably not saying anything so he won't offend me.

He keeps fiddling with my hair, and my stomach quivers as if I've swallowed a full-size python. He bends down, pecks me on the cheek, smiles, shakes his head, and goes into the kitchen. In a little while, he'll probably go out for one of his usual nights at the bar. I put on the dress and immediately cover it with my coat, which is long enough to conceal every reproachful inch. Then I go to the kitchen, too.

"I just hope Catello has stopped his inappropriate touching or spitting habits," I sigh, slipping on my shoes.

Luca gulps black coffee. "Who's Catello?"

"The guy that my mother wants me to sleep with," I say with a shrug. Luca winces. If I were a bit more confident, I'd think that the idea of me and Catello has upset him.

I laugh. "Just know that I'm undergoing this torture all to save you." He doesn't laugh at all. He swallows the last sip of coffee and leans on the table with his arms crossed. "Catello is the toll that I must pay for your freedom from Aunt Porzia, Aunt Palma, and Aunt Ermelline." And Erika, whose attacks I fear the most. Still silent, he gives me a strange look. I move to the doorway. "Okay, I'm going. I probably won't come back tonight. I'm afraid I'll be sleeping at my mom's place." I have an overnight bag with me that contains everything I'll need to spend the night in the loony bin with my dear mother for a warden.

"With Catello?" he asks. He smiles a bit, then waves good-bye.

The very thought of the night ending with Catello makes me break out into a cold sweat. If Catello even thinks about coming near me, I'll crush him. I should have let Lara give me pepper spray. For lack of a better option, I take the armed Barbie doll out of her box. Perhaps I'll defend myself with her, or maybe having her in my purse will give me what I need not to succumb to such destruction. I swear, I'm the only bridesmaid on earth with such an item in my bag.

My family lives in the suburb of Camilluccia, in a cluster of villas surrounded by plants and trees. Thirty-two years ago, when my mother met my father, she moved from Calabria to the sunny suburbs with delusions of grandeur about what it would be like to have a wealthy husband. Her delusions were quickly stifled. But all the aunts followed her lead, migrating like a flock of hawks to turn the neighborhood into their own microvillage. Their stretch of houses—with their large gardens, kidney-shaped swimming pools, tiny dogs, and garish fountains—look like they belong in Los Angeles.

I open the gate and walk very slowly up my Aunt Palma's driveway, enjoying the silence that pulses through the trees. Furious chaos awaits me a few hundred feet away—a swarm of people and lights, and a circus tent erected in the garden. I've never seen so many tulips. They must have wiped the Netherlands clean to fill the lawn, the balconies, the Aphrodite-shaped fountain, the steps, and the gazebo.

When I see my mother with Aunt Porzia, I try to hide behind a giant cactus plant. But she notices me immediately and drags my aunt over.

"Are you alone?" she says without even saying hello. "Well then, I'm going to call Catello."

She disappears, while Aunt Porzia eyes me from behind her Swarovski-studded glasses. She's shorter than I am, but her hug crushes me. She is wearing a ridiculous headscarf, and she's so tan she must have spent the last month in a tanning bed. I ask how she's doing after we exchange pleasantries.

She pinches my cheek, frowns, and says loudly, "You're too skinny. Are you too poor to buy food?"

"I either go to the soup kitchen or feed on roots and berries. It depends on the day."

"Didn't you bring your boyfriend? You can't keep a man! You should learn from your sister, with that pretty boy, Jess. They've been together for a lifetime."

"No doubt," I say under my breath. "Erika knows how to do things for a lifetime."

"If you don't find a husband," Aunt Porzia goes on, "you'll never have children, and you'll die without heirs."

"That just means no one will be killed over the division of my assets."

"Always witty, aren't you, big sister?" Erika's charming and treacherous voice catches me off guard. To say that she is beautiful would be like saying the sun is warm. She's wearing gloves and a long, backless sapphire dress with a slit that goes all the way to her pubic region. She looks like she's not wearing makeup (which means she spent several hours in front of the mirror to achieve this look), and her hair slides down her bare back like a silk cloth, swaying with every movement. A bald, muscular guy is standing next to her. Aunt Porzia practically forces him to kneel to receive her affection and kisses. She calls him Jess, which would make him the thousandth Jess in my little sister's sex life.

"This dress is so pretty," Erika says in a tone that a stranger might perceive as caring. But I know her too well. I shift the coat to make sure the dress is completely shielded, and she lifts a corner of her mouth. "It looks great on you. It makes you look tan."

"At least I don't have to worry about getting sick," I say, pointing to her outfit, which is really more of an optical illusion than a dress. "Won't your colon freeze?"

"Oh, I'm still so young, I won't get cold. So why are you here alone?" She smiles, and I can tell she's swinging between the displeasure of having her sex appeal taken down a notch and the triumph of knowing I'm as alone as an unmatched sock.

At that moment, my mother returns, Catello in tow. It's the touchy guy with the nose ring, only it's gone, and so is the hair. He's not quite completely bald, but his forehead—topped with a horrid comb-over—glistens under the lights. He's a little pudgy, and he hasn't kicked his smoking habit. He's wearing a red jacket and a pair of black jeans. He shakes my hand and licks the tip of his cigarette in a way that warns me I'll be in danger the whole evening.

Luckily, just then the bridesmaids are called to duty. Inside the house, I get rid of the coat and overnight bag and emerge in all my poop-colored glory. Beatrice is in her room just finishing getting dressed. The room is full of women all over the age of forty, and for a moment I think I'm in the wrong place. It's only the abundance of brown garments that lets me know I'm not. Beatrice has chosen only spinsters as her bridesmaids, and I'm the only one not on the verge of menopause. What an honor to be first in a line of losers. I don't see Beatrice at first, and then I remember that I shouldn't be looking for a nun with a mustache, but a pregnant bride dressed in white. And then I see her. She's dressed in dazzling white. Her injected lips are boatlike, her new nose too small, and her eyebrows dyed to match her newly blonde hair. As we wave hello, my eyes burn from the glow of her dress. Aunt Palma squeezes me, and so do all my mother's sisters.

Once the procession of spinsters begins, I'm embarrassed to find myself part of a wedding that seems to be straight out of a rom-com. We descend the stairs holding bouquets of thorny thistles, then head over to the gazebo, where the tulle-covered wooden benches for the guests resemble clouds. The ashen sky threatens snow, but only a few guests are hiding underneath puffy fur coats.

Photographers hop around like grasshoppers. A few babies start to cry. The organist plays the wedding march. I must admit the groom, Pablo, is rather handsome; his long hair is tied back in a ponytail, and he has strong Spanish features and a sensual expression. I wonder where they met—he doesn't seem like the type of guy to frequent a monastery. The bridesmaids take their places as the celebrant speaks of eternal love. A tenor sings Schubert's "Ave Maria" in the background. Finally, deafening cheers ring out.

After about eight hundred more or less identical photographs, we reach the refreshments tent. I grab a glass of champagne and hover close to the walls to try to hide from Catello. I must look like a spy on the run. Just when I think I'm safe, half hidden behind a decorative urn at the back of the tent, my persecutor hunts me down.

"There's my beautiful partner!"

"Um . . .," I say, folding my arms tightly across my breasts like a freshly embalmed corpse to prevent Catello from grabbing onto them.

"Can I get you a sandwich? Would you like to dance? Tell me what you want to do; I'm here for you!"

"Thanks, but—"

"Would you like to take a walk, just the two of us?" Both his eyes and his forehead glisten. I shudder. If we were alone, I'm sure he'd make some kind of obscene proposal, and I'd have to crush his balls.

"I wouldn't mind a sandwich," I say, hoping that will send him away. But I underestimated him. He yells out to a waiter, and soon a tray appears for us. It's full of adorable brown bites that closely resemble my dress. While Catello talks, I circle the tent slowly, hoping to find my father in the crowd. He's the only one who can save me from this brute.

"You're even more beautiful," Catello says.

"Now, now," I say tactfully.

"I've lost some hair, haven't I?"

"No! What are you talking about?"

My mother is obviously thrilled—she's walking around talking to people like she's the pope and introducing everyone to her beautiful, practically naked daughter. Then, in the midst of all the chaos, I finally see my dad. I raise a hand to get his attention, and Catello seizes the opportunity. In two seconds his arm is snaked around my waist and his fingers clutched around my left breast. What a disgusting date! I'm getting ready to castrate him when someone swoops in and saves me.

I must have fainted and woken up in a dream. This can't be true— my life is a disaster show, not a feel-good romantic movie. But it is totally, incredibly, and absurdly true: the pinch I'm giving my arm hurts—and bad!

Luca leans toward Catello and removes his hand. It must be forceful, because Catello cries out.

"If you touch her again, I'll shatter your teeth," Luca says with a smile, as if he were giving out friendly advice. I stare at Luca in a daze, almost expecting him to dissolve into thin air. But Luca takes my hand and asks me to dance. What is going on?

"Hey," he says. "If you don't shut your mouth, you'll catch flies."

"What are you doing here? Aren't you supposed to be working?"

"I asked for the night off."

"But how did you get here? How did you get the address?"

"There was an invitation on your bed. Geez, Carlotta, do you want me to leave? Do you want to go back to that guy?"

"No!" I yelp, grabbing him by the lapel. "I'm just amazed that someone who escaped the clutches of my family decided to show up here on purpose."

"Were you a good bridesmaid?" he asks, holding me as we start to dance—not too tight, but just tight enough that I can feel his body enveloping mine. He looks very elegant. I don't know where he got the tuxedo, but it fits him perfectly, emphasizing his shoulders.

"I was great! But . . . um . . . why did you come?"

"To keep you company," Luca says. "Families can be cruel. You need to be able to make fun of them with someone. We'll tell them that we're madly in love, we're going to have a big wedding just like this, we want to get pregnant within a year, and a whole lot of details to satisfy your aunts. All right?"

Confused and a little excited, I can barely whisper, "Sure!" We dance until my mother's scream breaks the spell.

"Luca!" she cries. It's so loud that the only people on earth who don't hear are a couple of Eskimo tribes. Suddenly proud of her eldest daughter, she parades me around just like Erika. I can't really blame her. Luca is quite appetizing, and she's trembling with the desire to inform everyone that Carlotta has finally managed to do something right. The aunts crowd around us like goats around a single clump of tender grass. Luca smiles, feigns admiration for everything, and above all, listens to their bullshit patiently. I love him even more for it.

I escape the crowd after a minute and glance around. Catello has fortunately disappeared—perhaps my mother has stuffed him back in his freezer bag. I grab another glass of champagne and a sandwich, then head over to my father. The Russian nesting doll I met at his house is with him. I learn that her name is Coretta. She's shy and gentle and smiles with her mouth closed.

"Your mother is so loud," my father says, as my mother hoots like an owl a few feet away. "She's so strung out that she introduced me to your sister. And then she almost crushed my wrist trying to show me that fine young man you were dancing with."

"Mom's always like this, even at funerals. Remember when great-aunt Prisca died?"

"They had to slap her when she laughed."

"You look great, Dad."

"So do you."

As we talk, I discover that Coretta is an excellent listener. And it's weird—this is only the second time I've met her, but I feel completely at ease around her. As people dance around us, I hear that my cousin Lisa has a boyfriend (whom Aunt Porzia also calls Jess). My dad invites me to dance with him as his quiet date grabs some dessert and holes up behind a plant like a hedgehog. He's shorter than I am, and he dances like a child. He asks me about my life and wants to know if I have a boyfriend—with none of my mother's motives, just the hope that I find completeness in my life.

He tells me a little bit about Coretta. A widow, she's his same age. They share passions for gardening and cooking. She seems to be reserved, simple, and thoughtful. His eyes sparkle as he speaks of her. At the end of the song, he goes back to her, and they hold hands like teenagers. I smile as I watch them, but it immediately disappears when I realize I've lost sight of Luca.

I scan the crowd, sifting through the people dancing, the people stealing slices of cake, the people drinking too much, and the whole lot of people yawning in boredom before I find him. My mother has just introduced him to Erika, then left them alone to save the ice swans that have become the ball in a kids' game of catch. Damn it! Erika's date, who's scarfing down food like he's ending a hunger strike, is about to be replaced. I want to run over there and stop them, but instead I hover here near the Aphrodite fountain. I already know how this hackneyed plot will turn out. Lost in thought about how to dodge my family's sympathy, I realize too late that the groom is crouched beside me. He's taken his hair out of the ponytail and removed his jacket.

"*Tengo permiso de mi amada esposa para bailar un tango con usted.*"

I look at him aghast.

"What? Dance a tango? No way. Go ask someone who—"

Ignoring my resistance, Pablo drags me to the dance floor. The guests all move back into a wide circle, ready to watch (or, more likely, murder me for my lack of tango skills). Pablo leads me along to the dramatic music, his cheek pressed to mine, his face fixed in an erotic expression reserved for the tango. Pablo bites his lip, leaves me, takes me, dips me, and I'm sure I look like a rubber doll being tossed around. When it's over, the audience applauds, and Beatrice looks ecstatic.

I run away with what little strength I have left before anyone has the chance to suggest an encore. Champagne churns in my belly, threatening to climb up to my mouth. At least if I throw up, no one will notice, as my dress will camouflage it nicely. As I stand by myself, hands pressed to my cheeks, Luca comes out from behind the gazebo.

"Always the center of attention, huh?" he says sarcastically.

"You defend yourself well," I say. "You've finally met my sister."

"She's pretty great."

I don't reply; it's a mean joke. My mother interrupts our short silence, pouncing on us like a lurking lioness.

"You'll be staying at my house tonight, of course?" she asks.

"Actually, we don't—"

"Of course!" Luca interrupts me with a grin. He winks and nudges me. I stare at him like a gaping fish.

"Have you met your father's new girlfriend?" my mom continues, her voice venomous. "Beatrice insisted that we invite him, and he brought her along. What a dull woman! Always so quiet and brooding. She never laughs. I can't stand people like that. Am I right, Luca?"

"A lady is never fully dressed without a smile," he says innocently. Game, set, match.

As we eat cake, Erika suddenly seems to remember that she has a sister. She pretends to buzz around me—buzzing around Luca, actually—her body quivering with excitement. Luca brushes her off and holds my hand, but he still pays attention to her, which is all she needs to feel victorious.

I hate them. I hate this little game. I hate thinking about the pity I'll get from my aunts. Suddenly I'm too tired, too fed up, and too mortified. I'm getting out of here. I grab my coat and purse and ditch the party.

My mom's house, the house I grew up in, isn't far from here. I walk the road as the snow dances around me. It's late, it's cold, and I feel sad. The formula of Luca plus Erika is almost chemical in nature, and inevitable: they will end up sleeping together. I don't know if I should feel relieved—at least he's not thinking about the unknown woman he was so sweet with—or angry—because he's with someone who isn't me and who happens to be my sister. Now that I don't have to worry about running into a compassionate aunt, I let my mascara run freely.

Teresa, my mother's distant cousin who tends the house in exchange for room and board, opens the door. She hugs me, surprised that I'm already here. I learn that some other distant cousins are sleeping here tonight, and the rooms are ready.

My mother has changed everything about my childhood home. Now my room is a guest room with a gigantic fireplace—Mom wanted fireplaces in every room—that illuminates the bed and ceiling. The room seems very chic, like a cabin in Aspen. I put my coat and purse on the bed and crouch down in front of the fire that Teresa started. Meanwhile, she gives me some pajamas, since I cleverly left my overnight bag at Beatrice's. Outside the window, the snow dances, its choreography driven by the wind. Tomorrow morning it will probably have melted, but tonight, it seems endless.

Suddenly, I hear a racket downstairs—the clan has arrived. I hear my mother asking about me. I go out onto the landing and peek out, like a little girl. I start in surprise—Luca's there. Erika's there, too. She must have managed to get a last-minute room from our dear mother. Knowing their vocal abilities, I'm not getting any sleep tonight. Or maybe I still have time to call a taxi? The phone's in my mother's room. I head in that direction, but then the guests start to climb the stairs. I shut myself in my room, foolishly intimidated. When Luca enters, I stare at him like he's a stranger.

"What's the matter? Have you seen a ghost?" he asks. His smile fades to a tender look. "Carlotta, you're so pale . . . Are you feeling okay?"

"I'm fine. What do you want?"

"What do I want?" He shakes his head and sits down on the bed. "We're engaged, aren't we? Strip down, my love!" He says this last part loud enough to be heard outside. He smiles at me, pecks me on the cheek, lies down on his back, and chuckles softly, his hands on his abdomen.

"Quit the bullshit!" I say softly. "Anyone can see that you're into my sister. No one will buy our story."

He gets up, still cheerful, takes off his jacket, and throws it at me. "Your sister's a knockout, but that's not why I'm here. I had much more fun duping your family."

He grabs me and throws me on the bed. A fire ignites within me as Luca climbs over me, laughing, and starts jumping on the bed. The springs groan faintly and the headboard knocks against the wall. I stare at him, as shocked as if he'd just called forth lightning from the ceiling. Suddenly, something presses into my neck. I reach underneath me and Killer Barbie rolls out of my purse. Luca stops jumping.

"You're nuts!" he exclaims. "Most girls keep makeup or condoms in their purses, but you carry a psychopathic doll?"

"I thought she would be the most suitable escort."

"She's perfect for the situation. But since I'm your escort now"—he puts the Barbie doll on the floor—"and since everyone's in the hallway eavesdropping, how about if we give the people what they want?"

"They're probably making bets. They've set the odds at slim to none that we'll—"

"So let them all lose. Let's do it." He hits me with that smile. "Just pretending, of course."

"Of course, of course," I say resignedly.

"We'll start off small," he says softly, brushing his lips against me. I'm already flushed and breathless. "Soft kisses on your mouth, your throat, on every inch of your skin. I taste your tongue. I kiss you until you're completely breathless, and—" Suddenly he stops, shattering the entire scene. "Come on, Carlotta, you have to make some noise every now and then. Otherwise they'll think I'm having sex with a corpse."

I gasp, still paralyzed by his words, but obey him. My heart pounds as he whispers his smut, softly telling me all about an act that I haven't partaken of in so long, that I've maybe never taken seriously. Now and then he raises his voice, moaning and breathing heavily, for the benefit of the audience in the hall. It seems so real that I'm afraid I'll lose it just listening to him.

"Carlotta, doll, if you want it to be credible, you're going to have to breathe."

"But how—"

He laughs—a howl to the spies outside—winks, and tickles my hips, knowing that I'm quite ticklish there. I cry out, half a laugh, half a scream, to defend myself. Suddenly we're in an all-out tickle fight, rolling around and grabbing pillows as the bed rocks in place. I decide to play the game, too, even though it's passionless and I'm embarrassed to fake a sexual encounter that still seems all too real to me, given my past. But I'm happy with the racket we're making. Pleasure is pain. When it's over, Luca lies down next to me.

"You were fantastic, baby," he says, still loudly. "That was better than that one time in the bathroom of the plane during that turbulence."

He's so handsome and messy; he looks like we really did just make love. He reaches out and strokes my wrist with his thumb. I can't even bear it. I shake him off.

"Carlotta, what's wrong?" he asks, playing with my curls.

I stick my tongue out at him. He smiles and kisses the tip of my nose. But there's something strange and lost in his eyes. He stares at me as if something is bothering him. I hope he can't see the desire behind my discomfort. I hate to imagine what he'd think of me. We're just friends. Our only sex is pretend sex.

He closes his eyes, his hand still tight around my wrist. The fire crackles and spits in the fireplace. It's the only light in the room as the snow whirls around outside. Luca falls asleep quickly, and soon I can watch him without getting caught. I wish I had my sketchbook and a pencil so I could capture the true beauty of his soul that shows through his relaxed face.

Maybe it would be better if he were out of my life completely. It may be all fun and games to him, but to me, this is no joke.

EIGHT

Tony has called me again, for the umpteenth time. I listen to his message and I wonder if I'm willing to tolerate his tongue again.

"What does the house painter want now?" Luca asks, looking contemptuous. I'm curious—recently, his bad mood only seems to be worsening. He's often nervous and sullen, and whenever I bring up Tony, his response is always cutting.

"He's not a house painter. He's an artist. He's showing at an exhibition, and he doesn't have enough work to put up. He wants to draw my portrait."

Luca laughs sardonically. "He wants to immortalize your vagina," he says.

My mouth hangs open. "What the . . . ?"

"He obviously wants to fuck you."

"There's no need to be so explicit!" I exclaim. "And besides, why do you care? Maybe I'd like that. Tony's an interesting guy."

"You're being a little bitchy."

"Excuse me? What do you mean by that?"

"Just what I said. All you talk about lately is the painter guy and the other guy, the blond German one you work with. Just sleep with them and be done with it."

"Maybe I will. I don't need your advice," I say, furious.

So, nearly a month after the vomiting episode, I decide to call Tony back. We agree to meet for coffee in a cafe near the theater.

I arrive late, sweaty and out of breath from the battle I just won with a vintage toy salesman who wanted an exorbitant sum for a 1965 Astronaut Barbie. Tony is already waiting for me at the cafe. We chat over our espressos, and he tells me about his upcoming exhibition, then asks me about my work.

"At the moment, I'm hunting down these." I show him the pretty space traveler with almost maternal pride.

He casts a rude look at the Barbie. "I suppose little girls like them. But if I were a father, I wouldn't buy that for my daughter."

"Oh . . . Why not?"

"Why give her a false image of womanhood? It would humiliate her. Barbie dolls are tall and beautiful, too goddess-like. Women just aren't like that. Real women look like you."

"So that makes me . . . what? Chopped liver?" I ask, swallowing the last sip of my coffee and feeling like a cat whose tail was just rudely trampled.

He raises his hands in surrender and shakes his head. "I didn't mean that. I think you're very beautiful, you know."

I suppose I deserve it after the whole vomit incident, so I accept his apology. But although I don't mind the veiled insult, I do mind the way he spoke of the Barbie doll. It reminds me of Lara's intransigent attitude toward men. "There's nothing different between these dolls and the princesses in the fairy tales that we've read for generations. They were the most beautiful women in the land, right?"

"Yeah, maybe you're right," Tony says, "but I just don't like the emphasis on their plastic appearance. My paintings are interior portraits.

Although your beauty is not only interior, mind you. You're beautiful all the way to the tips of your hair."

My hair has always been my soft spot. Compliment these crazy locks, and I'll melt like a Popsicle in the sun. What harm could there be in granting him the privilege of portraying these features? So I agree to pose for him. After all, it's not like I have to ask anyone else's permission.

A few nights later, as I'm getting ready to go to Tony's studio, Luca passes by me. He takes a drag from his cigar, then blows the smoke at me, making me cough. His eyes are very green and cold as diamonds.

"Are you on the pill?" he asks suddenly.

"Huh?"

"Are you going to use some method of birth control?"

"That's none of your business."

"Here," he says, slipping something into my purse.

A condom.

I look at it as if it were a bloody severed hand.

"Do you know how to use it? Or do I have to explain? That fool might not know how."

"Luca!" I shout, flushed with anger and discomfort. "I know how to use it, and anyway, just stop! You know, once you get going, you can really get nasty as hell."

"I don't know anything about this guy. I just want to save your ass and keep you from getting pregnant."

I have no intention of sleeping with Tony, but I don't need him to know that. "I don't need your advice."

I leave the house without looking back, reining in my wild desire to kick him where it hurts.

The studio is in Testaccio, a hipster neighborhood by the river. Tony lets me in. In his paint-spattered sweater, he actually looks like a painter. In fact, he looks like a painting himself. He's not wearing his glasses, and his hair is unkempt.

Inside, I take in the surroundings. The studio is a loft on the top floor of an old building. Its walls are exposed brick, its windows curtainless. Dozens of canvases are stacked everywhere, covered with red-stained sheets. And oh boy . . . There's a giant bed in the center of the room. I must not jump to conclusions. I'm sure he only intends to be hospitable. If he wants to keep his bed in the middle of his work space, then by all means, he should. And if, by chance, the bed is where he makes me sit while he paints my portrait, then I must not mistake this for lustful intent.

While he sketches me, though, he barely peeks out from behind his canvas except to adjust my posture and shower me with compliments. And he doesn't ask for anything more than my beautiful face for his sketches. It's two hours before he lets me move again. My neck feels rusty, like a piston without oil.

"Hey," he realizes. "Did I make you stand still for too long?"

"Art involves some sacrifice, right?"

"Come here, forgive me . . ." He looks like a wolf as he comes closer. He kneels on the bed behind me and starts to massage my neck, even though his hands are slightly dirty from painting. It's a relief—he's also an artist at giving neck rubs. His hands move masterfully from my shoulders to my neck to my hair. And he talks and he talks and he talks . . . He talks way too much. Tony might have some great qualities, but knowing when to shut up is not one of them.

After his fingertips work their magic, he asks me if I'm hungry. Fortunately there's no innuendo in the question—he orders Chinese food over the phone, and half an hour later it arrives. We eat sitting on the bed, and Tony continues to talk as he uses his chopsticks expertly. He sucks noodles between his lips like a snake, and devours steamed dumplings with a pleasure that is almost carnal. When he asks me if I want the cookie, it startles me. Am I so depraved that I distort even the most innocent allusion to a fortune cookie?

I break it open and read the message: it tells me to be careful because when it rains, it pours. Tony's fortune urges him to eat when he's hungry. The way I've been interpreting everything since I got here, the two fortunes are clearly double entendres. But I prefer to believe that rain is rain and hunger is hunger.

After dinner, he throws away the containers and clears the bed. I sit near him, and he continues to blather on about his exhibition and how great my portrait will look in it. Then, suddenly, there's the first warning sign: silence. An unusual development.

He smiles. "You're so beautiful," he says again (he's actually said this so many times that I feel like Venus incarnate). Then he puts a hand on my cheek and kisses me. What a brave man to try once more to dive into a sea that I once banned him from entering so ungracefully. Again, his tongue dances inside my mouth, tasting like fortune cookie and steamed rice. It's so hectic and sloppy that I think I'm going to be sick all over again. But this time, I repress the gag reflex. I think about ice cream, hot chocolate, and toffee, but above all . . . Luca. It doesn't do anything to help me relax, but at least I can pretend to respond to his advances with enthusiasm, as if all the pleasures of the universe were concentrated in his bustling tongue.

At the same time, Tony attempts to insert two fingers under my sweater. My hand is quicker, and I cut him off. He grumbles something and tries again. After three unsuccessful attempts, he embarks on a more ambitious mission. He grabs my wrist and slaps my hand on the flap of his pants. He seems to have a .22 semiautomatic hidden in his jeans. Oh my God—now it's not in his jeans anymore. When did he pull it out? Is there a sliding door in his pants that reads his mind?

Tony mumbles something I can't understand. I haven't touched a man in this region in months, and now I'm discovering that I'd actually rather keep it that way. I feel dirty and lonely, and I really want to leave. I keep firmly rejecting Tony, but he's either pretending not to understand, or interpreting my reluctance as some kind of provocative game. Finally, he looks me in the eye, a mixture of anger and disgust written on his face.

"Are you not enjoying this?" he asks, his voice hoarse.

"What do you think?" I want to say. "I've been wiggling like an eel for ten minutes. I'm playing hide and seek with your hand. You're chasing me all over the bed. Don't even get me started on your kissing, which I initially tolerated for educational purposes and decided to give a second chance after I made a fool of myself last time . . . Have you not noticed that you're paralyzing me? Back off, okay?"

But of course, I just say, "Tony, it's a bit too soon. I don't really know you that well . . ."

Even if I'd known him for three generations and our grandparents had made polenta together, I still wouldn't want him. But I need him to believe I'm merely a woman of archaic principles—and that maybe in a century and a half, he'll be able to get to second base.

"Okay . . .," he whispers, clearly disappointed. He lets out a whistle. "Carlotta, I'm as turned on as a bison."

I don't know much about bison, so I don't say anything, but I'd say he's more like an anteater, at least his tongue. He rearranges his soldier, still at attention, and zips up his pants. We get up from the bed. I get the impression that he's eager to get rid of me, but I don't think it's because he doesn't want to see me again—he keeps telling me that he'll call me, that we have to go out again, that we have to get to know each other better. I think he just wants to be alone.

On the bus ride home, I commit an act of incivility. I chuck the condom out the window. I just want to get home, take a shower, and, above all, brush my teeth. So happy to be back, away from Tony and his wandering hands, I climb the stairs at last and go inside. But providence is not forgiving. Although the time is a bit unusual—it's just past midnight—the moans I can hear are anything but. Luca's already got a girl in his room. His door is ajar, so the sounds are amplified. I can hear vowels, syllables, even words.

I know that voice.

Suddenly I'm cold, as if a flurry of snow just burst in through the window. I know I'll suffer, I know I should just go to my room and turn a blind eye, but I can't help it. I approach the door. A halo of light filters through the crack. The lampshade on the bedside table dims the light in the room, but the scene is all too clear. There's Luca, naked on his back. And on top of him is Erika, her hair swishing as usual, her spine twisting like a snake. I stand motionless in the middle of the hallway, my fists clenched and my jaw so tight that I'd need a crowbar to pry it open. Pain courses through me in a shock wave extending from my feet to my ears. By chance, Luca opens his eyes. It's a coincidence, as I haven't made any noise. He sees me. At first, he looks surprised. But then his gaze immediately turns wicked. He moves faster as he stares at me, lowering his eyelids.

I run away.

It's raining outside, a dirty, black rain that seems to ooze. The streets are empty except for a few passersby. I walk quickly. I don't know where I'm headed. I just want to get lost under the beating rain. I walk for a long time, without feeling the weight of passing time. I ache. No, scratch that. I'm dying. With each step, I age a century. The only word I can think of, the only word in the midst of the tumult, is *why*.

Why, Luca?

Why, Erika?

Just for a few minutes of pelvic thrusting, after which you'll both feel like strangers? Does it not matter that the same blood runs through our veins? Despite the way things are now, I have never been able to forget the two girls who played together and dreamed of futures as princesses, astronauts, ballerinas. Something—but what?—has left us on opposite banks of an impassable river. But was it not enough to despise each other from afar? I never thought she'd really go so far as to try to drown me.

And Luca . . . I thought he was my friend, but he's no more than a dirty bastard. My mind wanders to my mother's triumph and my aunts' hypocritical commiseration. I must look like a psychopath, chasing ghosts through a stormy night. I'm ready to die now. I'm going to die now. I'm dying now.

But I don't die. Instead, I walk for miles.

A few hours before dawn, I finally summon the strength to go back home. I'm tired and soaking wet. I get inside, and Luca is in the kitchen, smoking a cigar and drinking coffee. He looks like he spent a sleepless night. I just hope that Erika had the decency to leave. I don't even look at him. I don't even say hi. I go right to my room and sit down on the bed, dripping on the blanket. I don't have time to unzip my boots before Luca comes in.

"What's wrong with you?" he asks. I know he's trying to provoke me. He's well aware of what sparked my reaction.

"Nothing. I just want you to get out of my room." All my anger disappeared while I was walking. Now I'm only left with disappointment and pain.

"Well, too bad. I'm not leaving. Damn it, Carlotta, you're acting ridiculous! Why did you come into my room? Were you spying on me? And don't pull that 'I demand an explanation' bullshit with me. You know I hate to feel controlled."

"I'm not trying to control you!" I shout, exasperated. "When have I ever said anything like that? I have to listen to your noises every night. There are always random women pissing in my toilet, rummaging through my fridge, stealing my things, and I've never said a thing! But please, I'm dying to know . . . Of all the women in the world, why did you feel the need to sleep with my sister? Did you really have to go on the Ride of the Valkyries with Erika?"

"For your information, she came here and ripped my pants off!"

"Oh, you poor thing! Don't pretend like she violated you. Are you some kind of animal in heat, one that absolutely has to satisfy its carnal instincts?"

My words, in my jumble of emotions, are vulgar and harsh. Luca runs around the room like a hurricane, still shirtless and smoking with ferocity.

"And you think you're so much better than me? What good does your hypocritical holier-than-thou attitude do for you? 'Oh, I don't sleep with anyone unless it means something. Oh, other women are sluts, but I'm so chaste. I'm just waiting for my prince.' And then some guy comes along and gives you some shitty compliment. You don't know anything about anything, so you go along with it, and he makes you puke when he kisses you!"

His nastiness and words all baffle me. But I won't let him win.

"It's not the same thing! I'm talking about my sister. I'm not telling you what to do with your dick; just don't put it in Erika! Even with all your theories about doing it with people to avoid complications, you thought you could just do my sister and it wouldn't matter? Don't you see how complicated it is? My whole family thinks we're together. Did you forget that? And now they think that my boyfriend has to cheat on me because I can't satisfy him. Poor Carlotta, the loser, who finally had sex for the first time when she was twenty just to get rid of her virginity. Poor Carlotta who can't keep a man, who will die without ever having kids because only a complete Neanderthal would want to procreate with her. Who's only ever been with grabby Catello and drooling Tony Boni! Do you understand what I'm saying?"

Wrinkles knot between his eyebrows as he stares at me. He bites his lower lip and asks me a stupid question that exasperates me.

"Did you sleep with Tony?"

"You know, Luca, I think you're right," I say. "It's useless for me to pose as a prude, because the truth is, I like sex. I like sex a lot. If I want to sleep with a man, I will. Isn't that your go-to advice? Haven't you told me millions of times to just go out with somebody? I think the time has come to act on that advice."

"So is that a yes?"

"What?"

"You didn't answer my question," he says. "Is that a yes?"

"Are you jealous or something?" I say, trying to provoke him.

"Carlotta!" He spreads his arms, apparently discouraged and sick of me. "Is that what you think? That is so fucking ridiculous. Jealous? Me? Over you? If I wasn't so pissed off, that would make me laugh. I even gave you a condom before you left, remember? Excuse me for caring about you. From now on, I'm just going to mind my own business. You should do the same."

He leaves the room, whisking his cigar and his anger away with him. It's as if, suddenly, a mountain collapses on our home. I hear him slam his bedroom door and collapse on his bed. I wouldn't be surprised if he decides to move out, and I wouldn't be surprised if he asks me if I want him to. Right now, I just lay my head down on the pillow and try to fall asleep.

I'm still cold even with my pajamas on, so I seek refuge under the covers. Submerged and alone, I let myself cry. No one can spy on me here. A part of my soul, perhaps the best part, disappears along with my tears.

NINE

"Soft kitty, warm kitty, little ball of fur! Happy kitty, sleepy kitty, purr, purr, purr . . ."

Neither Sheldon Cooper nor his mother is singing this song to me. It's Emma. I don't know how she learned it, but she sings it with conviction, as if it were a spell that will heal my invisible wounds. The morning after that awful night, I took a taxi straight to Lara's. I need Emma's innocence. I need this hushed peace. She caresses me and sings to me even though she doesn't know what's bothering me. But it only lasts until she goes off to kindergarten for the day. Then Lara and Giovanna decide to hold a war council. They plot revenge sitting around the sofa where I'm curled up.

"What Luca's done is unforgivable, but your sister is a grade-A bitch," Giovanna growls. With her high-heeled boots, she's almost as tall as the ceiling—and formidable.

"Yes, but Luca is a pig. As usual, he just thinks with his little head, not his big head," Lara mutters. She's not very tall, but the anger she's accumulated against all the men on the planet makes her seem like a giant.

"But how do you explain all this shit?" Giovanna asks me. "I mean, you and Erika are sisters! This behavior is just so exaggerated. Are you sure you didn't do anything to provoke them?"

"He must have forced her into it," Lara says. "If men are even remotely decent-looking, they think they can do whatever they want."

"It didn't seem forced," I murmur, remembering how Erika's back danced. "Luca doesn't have to force women. I don't know, guys. I often wonder what I did, but I've never figured it out. We were like two peas in a pod when we were kids. Then she grew up and became beautiful. Our mother taught her what she had wanted to teach me and couldn't—to use my looks to get what I want. It was like Erika was brainwashed, and it was only a matter of time before funny, weird Carlotta wasn't worthy of her presence anymore. Then she enrolled in private school and started hanging out with catty girls. We just drifted apart."

"You know what I think of your mother," Lara says. "She's horribly sexist. She only values women if they're the eighth wonder of the world. Who knows what she put in Erika's mind? Of course, her classmates probably didn't help, either. That's why my daughter is going to public school and why she'll never have anything expensive until she can buy it with her own money. But you have to kick Luca out immediately. You can't keep turning a blind eye. If you weren't in love with him, you'd never excuse his behavior. He transforms your apartment into a brothel every night. Let me look over the lease, and I'll dismantle it in two seconds so you can kick him out on his ass."

Giovanna immediately sides with Lara. "This has been going on for such a long time. It makes no sense, Carlotta. Are you hoping that one day he'll fall in love with you? That only happens in the movies. In real life, he's going to keep this up until he's fifty."

"Luca's not like that," I declare, surprising myself.

"Not like what?" Lara looks like a lioness whose cubs were just threatened.

"He's not bad," I insist, knowing that's a contemptible opinion. And how could it not be? I came here with mascara running down my cheeks, my hair in tangles, and a cry for help streaming from my lips. I can't expect my best friends, who have both taken the day off work to be with me, to show any kindness toward the person who ruined me. Especially when the air is foggy with "I told you so." But I just can't think badly of Luca. I can't hate him. A part of me knows he is a better man than his actions show.

"Please," I whisper, my eyes burning with tears again. "Can you stop giving me advice? I know it's for my own good, but can you just treat me like Emma did for a little bit? I swear I'll really think it all over. I'll figure out what to do about Luca. But right now I just want to sleep and cry—and sleep some more."

Giovanna comes to sit next to me and strokes my hair. "You're in a sorry state, little one," she whispers. Lara heads into the kitchen to make me one of her infamous cups of tea that she claims are good for your health but really taste like toilet paper. I sip it slowly. I don't like it, but it was made with love—that's good enough for me.

I close my eyes after I finish my tea. Lara starts to hum the song Emma was singing, and then Giovanna chimes in. After a few minutes, both of my friends are tenderly singing together, cradling me with the repetitive melody.

"Soft kitty, warm kitty, little ball of fur. Happy kitty, sleepy kitty, purr, purr, purr."

And I fall asleep.

I know. I have to do something. I need to get Luca out of my heart. I should ask him to move out. But I don't have the courage, cunning, or stupidity to do it. I prefer cold war to bloodshed.

We haven't spoken since that night. I don't see him very much, but I'm okay with that. When I get up in the morning, he's already out for a run. When I come home in the evening, he's always just about to go out. We greet each other coolly and exchange a few awkward words. We are two distant planets sharing the apartment, two parallel lines observing each other from afar and hoping not to run into each other. The thing that hurts the most is that I know I'm right, but he couldn't care less.

I'm too upset to call Erika. She would see right through me, and her feelings of triumph would triple. It's better to leave her alone. But I do imagine the kind of medieval torture I'd subject her to if I could . . . Which scares even me.

Meanwhile, my work at the theater has become even more complicated than Franz said it would. Internet research has confirmed my suspicions. Most of the dolls that Rocky wants are either unavailable or outrageously expensive. How am I supposed to snag Scarlett O'Hara Barbie in her green dress, or Happy Family Barbie with her third-trimester belly, or Talking Barbie with her fundamentally important phrase, "Who do you have a crush on?"

One afternoon, Giovanna calls me as I'm leaving the theater to check out some toy stores.

"Can you please watch Bear tonight? Something came up at work and I have to run back to the set, but if he stays locked up inside much longer he'll start howling like a werewolf and tearing the couch apart!"

I readily say yes. Bear and I are very similar. We're both a little crazy and have a lot of hair. We don't like to be on a leash, so we jerk around whoever's walking us—him to chase other dogs and invisible smells, me to check out cute clothes in shop windows. Neither of us ever gets what we want—whether that's buying everything or quarreling with a particularly unpleasant pug—but it's the chase itself that we enjoy.

My hairy escort in tow, I head into an old, windowless toy shop full of shelves packed with colorful boxes. Flirty plastic girls peek out from them. It seems more like a junk shop, with boxes stacked everywhere and secondhand toys strewn about on dark wooden shelves. The shopkeeper sells and repairs vintage and antique toys. A young girl who looks to be about five or six is here with her mother. She solemnly hands the shopkeeper a doll.

"Make her better," she tells him. He nods and sizes up the doll. She's small and plump, with big eyes, a floral-print dress, and black flats with bows. One of her arms is detached, and there's a cut on her cheek. I'm almost tempted to ask what happened, as if we were in a doctor's office waiting room.

"She'll be ready to go home in three days," the shopkeeper says. He's small and stout, with white hair, like an elf. Feeling reassured that her little baby will be all better soon, the little girl leaves. Unfortunately, as I list all the dolls I'm looking for, he shakes his head sadly.

"I'm sorry. At the moment, I don't have any of those. They're rare and very expensive. The first Barbie you mentioned goes for about seven thousand euro. They're collectibles, not children's toys."

"I know. I scoured the Internet, but they're either impossible to get or crazily expensive. I don't know what else to do."

"You won't be able to find them in stores. You should try talking to collectors."

"Do you know any?" I say, as solemn and pleading as the girl who left him the broken doll.

"You're in luck. I sold some of these dolls to some amateurs a while ago. I think they wanted to complete their collection. They ended up asking me to buy them back, but they're too expensive. And what if I couldn't find a buyer? With the state of the economy, sometimes this business is tough. I can't afford it. Maybe you can contact them and see if they'll offer you a better price."

"Probably not, but it can't hurt to try."

He writes down the names and addresses on a sheet of paper, and I thank him. As I'm about to leave, I turn and ask him, "Will you make her better? That little girl's doll, I mean."

"I'll make her better," he says. He smiles at me the way my father did when I brought him a hurt caterpillar I'd found while playing outside.

I take Bear to the park. He goes crazy, straining against the leash and wagging his tail, once he catches a whiff of the earth, so different from the smells of asphalt and smog. He sniffs the butts of Labradors, Great Danes, and Pomeranians, and they all courteously reciprocate. I feel bad about keeping him on the leash when he so desperately wants to run free, so I make him swear—paw to his heart—that he'll behave, and then I let him go.

It's hot today, and the sky looks like an upside-down ocean. Bear seems as happy as only a dog chasing other dogs in the emerald-green grass can be. I get emotional watching him. I'd love to be him, a simple, trusting creature who just needs a good run and a sniff under the tail to feel at peace with the universe. I sit down on the grass and watch him chase the joy of living. Run, my furry friend, run!

Oh, God. Don't run too far!

I lose sight of him as he disappears into the trees ringing the park. I told Giovanna to get him neutered to spare him the suffering of chasing after female dogs. People think it's nice when male dogs go after a female in heat. Nice, my ass! At the very least, you risk them fighting with other dogs; at the worst, he'll father dozens of puppies. What if they're not purebred and no one wants them?

I head into the trees to look for Bear, calling him with increasing desperation. After what seems like hours, the culprit appears, all fresh and combed. By which I mean, he's covered in mud and weeds, and a lizard's tail is sticking out of his mouth. If I scold him, he'll think I'm saying, "Bad dog! You shouldn't have come back." So I pet him in spite of myself.

I put him back on the leash and take him to a fountain to try to clean him up. He paddles around, very pleased with himself. The scenery is beautiful. In the distance, a pond glitters like silver paper, and nearby a park cafe's tables and umbrellas are clustered under a clump of trees. I decide to sit down and order a drink. Finally exhausted, Bear falls asleep under the table.

As the waiter passes by, he ignores me completely—perhaps he has no work ethic, or perhaps he was just not captured by my radiant beauty. Tall and lanky, he looks like he just came from his grandmother's funeral. So, looking like the nerdy student who knows all the answers, I raise my hand to get his attention. But this giraffe-man hybrid walks right by me again, tray in hand, toward tables hidden among the trees as if I'm not even here. More and more people sit down around me, and the lanky guy continues to ignore me—and insolently, too.

Now I'm just pissed off. I don't want anything to drink anymore, but he can't just treat me like some insignificant shrub. As he passes by with two iced coffees on his fake silver tray, I sneakily extend my leg and trip him. He sways for a few seconds, and the glasses slide—an impossible balancing act. He curses as they tumble to the ground. The iced coffee splatters everywhere; whipped cream lands in his ear. Bear raises an eyelid as if to say, *Please be quiet; can't you see that I'm resting?* I hold back laughter while the waiter glares at me.

"You did that on purpose!" he says.

"What do you mean?" I say. "I'm not even here, am I? You're talking to a shrub!"

He gets up, mumbling. If he did get it, he pretends not to. He goes over to someone sitting a few tables over and explains that he needs to resubmit their order because a crazy lady tripped him. I get up, ready to do it again, but then I sit right back down. The voice I hear responding to the waiter belongs to Luca, and he's not alone. I get up and, protected by the trees, follow his voice. I could recognize it in the middle of a U2 concert, no matter what sound he was making—a laugh, a moan, a yell, and lately, the silence that feels like a slap in the face.

I peek out from behind a hedge and see them sitting at a table under an umbrella. He's with *her*. There's no doubt in my mind that this is the elegant young woman that I saw him with outside of the apartment. Close up, even with the hedge obstructing my view, she's even lovelier than I thought, and she's not wearing sophisticated makeup or expensive clothes. Her hair is pixie short.

From here, as I listen to snippets of their conversation, I feel unsettled and slimy, like a snake. He's slightly tense, sighing like a teenage boy in love. In a nasty tone, he says something about not letting her father get in the way. I feel like crap, and not just because I'm playing secret agent over here with a twig in my right nostril and bird poop on my shoulder. It's because I can tell that Luca loves this woman. She seems to belong to the traditionally wealthy class. The watch on her wrist could pay for my apartment. I'm willing to bet that dear old dad learned that his daughter has the hots for a guy like him (read: a statuesque guy with a modest savings account) and has decided to exile the guy and lock up the girl. If only.

Luca alternates between nervousness and moments of strange sweetness. All of a sudden, he starts to talk about their love. "It's a crazy thing!" he says, his elbows propped on his knees and his chin in his hands. "Damn, Paola, I feel like I'm high."

"My darling," she says. "I'm happy. It amuses me, too, to see you so flustered."

"Are you mocking me?" His eyes glisten. He looks lost.

"No, my dear. I'm just relieved. You know, bad boy Luca, the guy who devours women and spits them out. . . To see you so uncertain . . . and then to find out . . ."

"Hey, I didn't say I'm in love. There's something unusual and strong between us, but I don't know if I can go that far. I just feel weird, like there's a hole in my stomach. It could just be indigestion, or maybe an allergy. Let's not get too carried away here."

Her expression turns sulky. If I were her, I'd kick him. A young, unhappy billionaire trying to get her tyrannical father to accept Luca as a son, when he's not even sure he really loves her? It makes me feel terribly cynical.

They're still talking, but I hear someone coming. I don't want to be seen lurking around like a creep so I get down and try to blend in with the bush like a chameleon for what seems like a century. Meanwhile, Luca and the woman leave. I'm just about to get up and leave myself when I hear a voice from above. It's not God admonishing me for my sin of curiosity, but the telephone-pole waiter staring at me as if I were insane.

"I knew you were crazy!" he says. "What a freak!"

I grab Bear's leash; he gets up feebly, and we race off along the path that leads out of the park. Once we hit the street, I finally let myself relax and burst out laughing.

"We're quite a sight, aren't we, Bear?"

He demonstrates his agreement by peeing on a tree trunk and then licking it.

It all comes rushing back to me soon after. Luca's face. His voice, troubled from feelings he can't understand. Paola. I can't compete with a woman like her. She didn't seem like another one of his conquests. She seems like someone nice, someone who picks daisies (probably gold-plated ones) in her spare time.

She seems like someone who's bound to win.

TEN

Should I talk to him or keep ignoring him?

Through his bedroom door, I hear Luca typing on his laptop. Keeping up the silent treatment would probably be best. He doesn't deserve my trust or even a shadow of forgiveness.

Yet here I am. I reach out to touch the door handle, then pull my hand back. I do the same thing several times. I'm just about to retreat when the door suddenly opens. Luca winces and frowns when he sees me. Damn it. It would be so much easier if he could just look gross once in a while. But he never does. He's wearing the same ripped jeans he wore when we first met, a cotton V-neck sweater, and no shoes or socks. He runs one hand through his hair, holding a cigar stub in the other. After a moment of surprise, he steps back into his room.

"I thought you were out," he murmurs. Everything and anything could be written in those eyes, but I can't decipher a single word.

"Can I use your computer for a second?" I say bluntly. "My laptop's been dead for a while, as you know . . . I was going to go to an Internet cafe, but it's raining."

He nods and invites me to come in. Our bodies brush momentarily as I pass by, and for a split second I feel like he touched me with his shoulder on purpose. Obviously I'm imagining things.

Luca's room smells like cigars and grapefruit-scented aftershave and looks like a typical guy's room. There are no added frills, just a bed, a dresser, and a desk. Nothing is on the floor except a stack of papers, an empty beer bottle, and a dune of cigar ashes in a glass. Now that I think about it, there haven't even been any women in here the past few days. After his erotic encounter with Erika, he stopped having houseguests. He comes home late every night like always, but he's alone. Once upon a time, I would have been thrilled. But now, with what I know about Paola and the conversation I overheard in the park, his metamorphosis isn't comforting. He isn't bringing home girls anymore because he's falling in love with her. Other girls have become invisible.

I swallow a spasm of pain as I approach the computer. Just then, Luca squawks and rushes over to close an open file that he obviously does not want me to read.

"Don't worry. I won't look at your masterpiece," I say curtly. But I did see that it was a letter. Perhaps to Paola. I hope it wasn't to Erika. I clench my fists. Luca's still hovering. Does he not trust me? I'm the one who doesn't trust *him*, until he's proven me wrong!

"You can relax," I say. "I'm not going to go through your stuff."

"I know that," he says, but less rudely than before. He puts out the cigar in the glass of ashes and waves away the smoke as if to keep it away from me. I try to ignore his kind gesture and pull up Google Maps. I have to figure out how to get to the collectors that the toy store owner gave me. It's not easy to do with Luca hovering over me like an angel. Or like a devil.

Silence reigns for several minutes. I write down the collectors' phone numbers, copy and paste some images, and pretend to surf the Web a little longer even though I'm very much done. Then Luca's voice rings out. It's so unexpected that his voice is momentarily unrecognizable.

"I shouldn't have done it."

I gasp, my mouth falling open as the computer screen blurs before me. I don't say anything. I don't turn around. I don't ask him to explain. I know exactly what he's talking about.

"With your sister. I shouldn't have done it," he continues softly, as if he doesn't want anyone else to hear. Sighing deeply, I get up. I'm grateful for this admission—knowing him, it's equivalent to kneeling on a carpet of broken glass. But it's not enough of an antidote to eradicate the poison. It doesn't erase the memory of their two bodies intertwined, his cruel eyes when he saw me in the doorway, or the words he said afterward. I head for the door, still silent. I can feel his eyes following me, step by step. Just before I leave, he comes out with it.

"Have you been sleeping with Tony?"

I stifle a wince. "That is still none of your business," I say coldly.

As I expected, taking the Metro would have required about a million changes, so I take a taxi. I'm very nervous by the time I arrive at my destination. I blame Rocky and his damn adaptation. I blame Luca and his chutzpah. Did he really think it would be enough to just admit he made a mistake and that everything would go back to the way it was before? The former didn't work, and the latter remains to be seen, but the outcome does not look good.

Damn it, I have to focus on my job today. I can't afford to be distracted. As the taxi drives away, I feel a chill. The collector's cottage is cute and sweet—almost too sweet, just like all the houses in this neighborhood. Judging by the immaculate streets and the homes' pastel facades, you'd think Disney princesses lived here. The cottage is pink, with lace curtains in the windows and a disturbing number of gnomes in the garden. Some are hanging from tree branches, some are attached to tree trunks, and several seem to be emerging from the ground through fake manholes. While they're supposed to cheer the place up, to me they just look scary, like they'll turn nasty once the clock strikes midnight or the sprinklers come on.

For a moment, I'm transported back to a childhood memory. It was the morning of my sixth birthday. My mother thought it would be a good idea to put Chucky's twin sister on the pillow next to me before I woke up. I opened my eyes and there she was, staring at me with turquoise glass eyes and an evil grin. I screamed and threw her into my closet—a throw deserving of an Olympic bronze in shot put at the very least. I distinctly remember the thud she made as she fell to the floor. I swear that as she landed, her hair momentarily transformed into a tangle of snakes.

As I walk up to the house, I stifle a scream just like that one. I'm almost tempted to leave. After all, my phone call yesterday with the collector was not reassuring at all. A shrill, yet seemingly friendly woman picked up the phone. As soon as I explained who I was and who had given me her name, she fell silent. I thought the line had gone dead. Then I heard a string of quiet mutterings, of which I only caught the phrases *find a girlfriend* and *get your ass out of the chair*. She started to yell. "It's just the census lady! She might drop by tomorrow! I'll be home!" So the owner of the props I need might be a dangerous schizophrenic, but I can't run away or Rocky will fire me for sure.

I ring the bell and a bird chirps for about thirty seconds. I plug my ears and grit my teeth. The door, which has a terrifying knocker in the shape of a child, opens to reveal a woman who fits right in with the house and the gnomes. She's tiny, dark, and dressed in cream and fuchsia. She flashes me a smile out of a '60s ad.

"Please, please, come in! You're here for those dolls, right?"

I nod and follow her inside. She makes me sit in a living room overflowing with crocheted doilies and antique porcelain. She insists on serving me a cup of tea that looks like sewer water. Then she starts to talk about censuses—very loudly—and doesn't let me get a word in edgewise. Occasionally she leaves the room to peer warily up a staircase with a railing that's bedecked in fringed trimmings. A glimmer of uneasiness starts to bother me. Maybe I should slip out. I don't want her to suddenly turn into Norman Bates. I glance at the door, contemplating my escape. This woman clearly does not collect Barbie dolls: just gnomes, porcelain plates, and lace doilies. And probably also human heads, which she must keep in the freezer. Suddenly, she comes back over to me and lowers her voice.

"It's so Massimo doesn't find out, you know?"

"No, I don't know. Who is Massimo?"

"My son. If he knew that I was attempting to give away his little women, he would make quite a fuss."

Finally, a light of understanding pierces the darkness. This woman isn't crazy, at least not clinically. She's just a busybody mother. A slightly nuts busybody mother, I must admit.

"When he started the collection, I didn't see anything wrong with it," she continues. "I love collections, too."

"I noticed."

"But then it got out of hand. It's one thing to collect teacups, stamps, coins, garden gnomes . . . Did you see them outside?"

"Yes. They're lovely."

"Aren't they? Anyway, it's quite another thing to keep buying these half-naked dolls. So I decided to get rid of them."

"And your son's okay with that?"

"He doesn't know. He must not suspect anything because, like I said, he'd never agree to it! He's always in his room on the computer or sleeping or reading magazines with naked ladies in them," she confesses, looking shocked. "He's seventeen. He's a real sweetheart. I'd love for him to start dating. I've even got someone lined up for him. She's a good girl. Her name's Rossana. She's my cousin's daughter. But Massimo doesn't even want to meet her."

I'd like to remind her that relations between relatives usually result in children with seven fingers on each hand, but I'm here on a mission. I show her the pictures I printed out.

"Yes, I think we have three or four of these. Just look at their short skirts! Why do you want these dolls, by the way?" she asks, suddenly attentive.

"I need them for an exhibit that will showcase the failures of contemporary society."

"Ah, well, if that's the case, then you might as well take them. I was worried you were a collector, too. Come with me."

"Can you first tell me how much they cost?"

"Cost? Oh, I'm not looking to sell them to you! I'll give them to you for free."

"You'll give them to me?" But my happiness is short-lived. I can't take any of these dolls without her knowing how expensive they are. I'd feel like a thief, or at least like I was preying on elderly, anxious mothers. And if she sold them, she could buy tons of crocheted doilies. But I underestimated her.

"I know what you're thinking," she says. "Who do you think paid for the dolls? After his father's death, I tried to do everything I could to make Massimo happy. But I never thought it would come to this. It's just not normal for a young man to collect Barbie dolls! At first, I wanted to sell them, but I've since made a vow. If I give them away and receive nothing in return, then perhaps Massimo will end up engaged to Rossana, and in a few years I'll have a beautiful grandson with golden curls."

What can I say? It's a flawless plan.

The woman rises and invites me to follow her into another room. As soon as I enter, I feel like I've contracted claustrophobia and gotten trapped in an elevator. This room is the apotheosis of pathological collecting. There are flamingos everywhere—flamingo porcelain dishes, flamingo paintings, flamingo pillows, and flamingo-patterned curtains. Some gnomes have infiltrated from outside.

Massimo's collection stands out from all of this. I spot Malibu Barbie among the clutter, as well as Playboy Bunny Barbie with rabbit ears and Drag Queen Barbie with a glittery, sparkling miniskirt. I'm ready to thank this woman and get out of this little shop of horrors— resisting the temptation to suggest that she sign up to be on the TV show *Hoarders*. Suddenly, a male voice makes me tremble.

"Mom, what are you doing?"

Massimo appears in the doorway. He's a disheveled, pimply boy, and he looks like he spends an awful lot of time alone. He does not seem at all pleased to see us here.

"Those are mine!" he says, practically growling.

His mother stands her ground like a saint preparing for martyrdom. "You're wrong. They're actually mine, seeing as I paid for them." She turns to me. "Get out of here. I'll handle him."

The next few moments pass in a blur. I dash off in my heels. Massimo chases after me, yelling out words that must be insults in some alien language, and his mother attempts to stop him. With the dolls in a bag and my heart in my throat, I stride down the street with Massimo after me and the mother after him. I keep running even when the chase ends, thanks to the mother's ankle grab that fells Massimo. Completely out of breath and drenched in sweat, I can't help but laugh. I laugh myself silly all the way to the taxi stand. I keep laughing even once I'm in the taxi, gasping for air as something stabs near my spleen.

What a strange feeling. I feel alive. It's as if the escape, the race, and the convulsions of laughter have washed everything else away. All the pain from the last few weeks transforms into a pink flamingo and flies away, light and lithe, over the taxi and into the sky.

ELEVEN

My mother has started to torment me with phone calls asking me what I want for my birthday. On June first, I'll be thirty years old. The more I try to forget about it, the harder she works to remind me.

"I know it's still far off, but organizing a good party takes time. Tell me what you want! Jewelry? Shoes? Face creams? Maybe a spa gift certificate?"

"Please don't try to fool me into thinking you're going to buy me a Tiffany necklace, and then surprise me with a loofah. And no parties, I beg you. I'm sick of pretending to be surprised every time."

"I'll make the coconut cake, okay?"

"No, please don't. Coconut is gross."

"Since when?"

"Since I was born. Erika's the one who loves coconut cake."

"That's so weird. I'm sure you're wrong."

"I think I know what I like," I say. "Anyway, I don't want a cake."

"Would you rather have cupcakes?"

"I don't want any damn sweets!"

"Try to be more refined, dear."

"Refined? Aren't you the one who wants me to sleep around more because sex helps keep the neck wrinkle-free?"

As always, when I say something she doesn't understand, she pretends like she doesn't hear it. "Wait until you see the treat that Oreste got you."

"Oreste? Who's that? Don't tell me it's another Catello!"

"Oreste is my new friend." She says the word *friend* with clear satisfaction, as if she means something else entirely. I'm appalled. Does my mom have a new boyfriend? "He's such a sweet boy," she continues, cackling like a hen.

"Boy?"

"He's twenty years younger than I am," she says, sounding victorious. "He sells women's lingerie."

"He sells underwear?"

"He sells intimates. He has a chain of stores. He gave me some lace corsets that—"

"I don't want to know!" I shout, instinctively moving the phone away from my ear. "And I don't want any gifts from Oreste! I don't want any gifts at all. I don't want a party, and I don't want any relatives giving me the third degree about how much money I make or what I'm doing with my life. Please just forget that I was ever born."

"How could I, darling? I have stretch marks on my stomach because of you. Every time I look at them, I think of you."

I hang up. What wonderful news. My mother has a new boyfriend who is young enough to be her son. She only remembers me because I marred her skin. And I'll have to deal with a damn coconut cake on my birthday.

When I accepted Tony's invitation to come to his art show, I had no intention of taking our relationship any further. I actually declined his invitation three separate times, accompanied by imaginative excuses, before I accepted, in case he expected sentimental developments. Then I took advantage of his good mood to unequivocally inform him that he mustn't break my heart. But I'm not planning on giving it to him in this life. Or the next.

The invitation-only gallery event is full. Everyone seems very snooty, as is customary at these kinds of events. Spotlights cleverly focused on the large canvases illuminate the gallery. Waitresses mill about carrying trays overflowing with flutes of champagne and tiny canapés.

Giovanna and her new beau come over to greet me. His name is Tommaso. He's not the jealous type at all. In fact, he encourages her to sleep around. I don't know how Giovanna feels about this. She may find it exciting now, but that can't last long.

As I'm about to move on, Luca greets me vaguely and gives me another one of those looks that I don't understand. Since the day of his confession, things between us have improved. We can talk without forcing it or sounding hateful. My anger has subdued. But things still aren't perfect, even on his end. He doesn't ask me for advice on his female characters anymore. He's still seeing Paola. They must meet at her place, because he doesn't bring any women over to our place. Not a single one—neither naked nor clothed, dyed nor natural, hairy nor bald. I doubt that Luca has taken a vow of chastity, so he must be getting busy elsewhere. Sometimes, I get the feeling he's just about to tell me that he's fallen for someone. He'll stare at me, then close his open mouth as if one syllable away from divulging a deep secret. I certainly don't help him along, because I don't want to know anything yet. He can tell me later, when I'm stronger.

However, tonight, I'm out with Tony. I'm pretending to enjoy myself. I think I look nice enough. I'm wearing a new blue silk dress, an old pink cardigan knotted at my waist, and caramel-colored heels. I tried to tame my hair with a bevy of glittery bobby pins, but it just made me look even more ridiculous than usual.

I stand in front of Tony's portrait of me, completely puzzled. I've never liked abstract art—maybe it's just beyond me. I don't get the portrait, with its neurotic, sparse brushstrokes in four intersecting rows flanked by a cut in the canvas. When I think of how many hours I was forced to stand still and listen to him blather! He might as well have painted a Barbie doll instead. But here I am, a confused lump of colors, with a circular gash where my mouth should be. I don't see anything that resembles me in this painting, assuming that really is supposed to be me. It's called *Carlotta on the Bed*. Well, now everyone will think we slept together. Although, to be honest, everyone who knows me already thinks we did. Luca thinks so, Giovanna thinks so, Tommaso probably even thinks so. While I'm admiring the piece, Tony comes up to me and hugs me from behind.

"You wonderful woman!" he whispers. "You are magnificent. I'm glad you came. So, what do you think?" I string together a few words about the brushstrokes and the deeply tormented emotions reflected in the piece. He's pleased that I've captured the essence of his creation. He looks elegant. I think he's even dyed his hair, as it reflects shades of plum that I've never noticed. He kisses me on the cheek and goes off to cajole his guests into buying his strange paintings. I walk the halls with a glass of champagne, then stop at a huge canvas. It boasts a set of sketches that, with a little imagination, form an erect male organ. The work's enigmatic title is *Anchored Fisherman*. And then I run into Erika.

She looks perfect, smooth, and insolent as usual, but strangely, she's alone. Erika? Alone at a social event? This is not only strange; it's downright catastrophic. She looks down at me from atop her six-inch heels.

"Carlotta, you're here, too," she murmurs. "I've been running into you so much lately. What a pleasure."

"The pleasure's all mine," I say. "Did you buy this piece? It's right up your alley."

"You're funny," she says dryly. "I heard that you're a friend of the painter. His painting of you looks just like you. Of course, I'm sure the allusion to the bed is only allegorical."

"You're wrong," I say in a high-pitched voice. "There's nothing allegorical about it."

"Okay, don't get mad. I'm glad you're having fun. There's actually something I need to talk to you about. It's been bothering me for weeks."

"It must really be haunting you," I say. "If we hadn't run into each other, you'd never have thought to tell me . . ."

"No, I wanted to call you. I just . . . I was really busy. But I'm hoping with all my heart that you and Luca aren't together anymore."

"And why are you hoping that?" I ask, trying not to boil over at the thought of her buttocks on Luca's hips.

"He made a pass at me. One night, I came to see you. And he . . . he sat me down and almost pounced on me. Believe me, it was atrocious."

"How awful! You must have slapped him."

"What do you want from me?" Erika says. "I'm no saint. I tried to resist, but Luca knows just what to do, you know. And ever since we met, he'd been badgering me wherever I went! Of course I turned him down. How could I do that to you? I thought that confessing was the right thing to do, so that you know you can't trust him."

"That's very kind of you," I whisper with a gentleness that throws her off a little. "Thank you for the nice words, but you don't need to worry. Luca is not the one for me. I never really cared about him. As you said yourself, he knows just what to do, but . . . he's not my type."

"Ah, well . . ." She has nothing else to say.

I walk away with a smile. She must be disappointed. I don't know what sisters are supposed to be like, but mine's a real piece of work.

I feel her eyes following me as I take Tony's arm, flaunting him about as if to show that he's only for my use and consumption. One thing is certain: Erika came on to Luca. The fact that it would upset me was just the cherry on top. As I come to this conclusion, Giovanna approaches me, and Tony wanders away. It seems that Tommaso has taken a liking to a painting entitled *Orgy in the Parlor*. It's a canvas covered in yellow brushstrokes, all converging on a central hole that represents many possible symbolic meanings. He'll probably buy it. It would make a nice addition to his bedroom.

"Is that your sister?" she suddenly exclaims.

"Yeah," I say wearily, without following Giovanna's stare. "We've talked."

"I'd be careful if I were you. I know you keep telling me that there's nothing going on between you and Tony, but I still think you should know that she's all over him right now."

I spin around, and she's right. Erika is rubbing herself all over him. She needs to win again. She thinks that there's something between us, she's irritated that a painting with my name on it is featured in an exhibition, and she's pissed that I reacted calmly to her hypocritical admission of guilt. I don't give a shit about Tony. He could do the entire national women's soccer team and it wouldn't bother me. But seeing Erika trying to deliver yet another low blow infuriates me. If she knew how I felt about Franz, she'd march right over to the theater and offer herself to him wrapped up naked in the stage curtain. She'd probably even try to nail my postman if she thought I had a crush on him. I quiver with anger at this person who somehow shares my genes.

I head over toward them, and soon Erika and I find ourselves battling for a guy we don't even like, just to spite each other. We shower him with compliments and touch his hands and arms and back, like two hungry animals. This isn't me; this is me pretending to be my sister. I hate her. I shouldn't say it, but it's true.

As the evening progresses, Tony is very intrigued by what's happening. He doesn't understand it, but I'm sure it excites him. And I know that Erika will eventually win because she's willing to play dirty. The humiliation stings, and I'm sure the anger she sees in me makes all her efforts worth it.

Toward the end of the night, after Giovanna and Tommaso have left, I get ready to leave—Tony has offered to give me a ride. But Erika has secured a spot in Tony's car, as well. That's it; she's won. He's moved on to her.

Erika pretends to greet me warmly when I get in. I'll go home alone, and she will add Tony to her list of late-night snacks. As we drive through the city, Tony and the fourth passenger, his agent, talk about how successful the evening was, completely unaware of the war-like atmosphere in the car. Something dangerous worms its way into my mind. All the hatred that I've managed to suppress in the past few weeks since I saw Luca and Erika together takes possession of my soul. If I were stronger, I wouldn't do this. But I'm weak. My heart is broken. I want a man who I will never have. When Tony gets out at my place to say good night to me, I allow my suffering to speak in my place. It's not my voice, but the voice of a secret pain hidden in the depths of my soul: I ask him to come upstairs. Tony grins and accepts my offer. Looking like he's preparing to devour me, he tells his agent to take Erika home.

This is the only enjoyable moment of the whole evening. Erika looks stunned, ready to burst into flame. Her eyes shoot sparks. But we head upstairs, and Tony, with great distinction, firmly grasps my butt, whispering about what awaits. We go inside, and I hope Luca is home so that he'll finally have to hear me have sex. Or rescue me. But he's not here.

Tony starts to kiss me. I can't afford to be squeamish, so I let it happen. As I fiddle with the buttons on my cardigan, I think to myself how shitty my life is. I'm almost thirty years old. I should have realized before now that romance is just a fantasy. Isn't that what Luca says? He sleeps with women for exercise, for the thrill of pleasure, and that's it. Tony asks me where my room is, and I point to it with my eyes. As we

Amabile Giusti

move, Tony slowly drops his jacket, his shirt, and his shoes, like a toy falling to pieces, as his tongue swirls in my mouth.

We enter my room, and he climbs on the bed. In spite of myself, I close the door. I stand motionless at the threshold. My dress is slightly crumpled, and I'm only wearing one shoe, so I'm tilted to one side like a leaning tower. He snaps his fingers and jerks his neck, a signal to approach that should appear erotic to me . . . but he really just looks like an old sea turtle. Nevertheless, I sit down on the edge of the bed. He gets naked in three seconds. Seriously, there must be some kind of automated mechanism in his pants. Or perhaps they're Velcro, like the kind that strippers use. *Voilà, madames et messieurs*, here are my crown jewels, ready for use!

He tries to tear my clothes off, but I don't want to ruin my new dress, so I do it myself. I let him fight with the hooks of my bra and tear my silk panties to the ground. Now his soldier is staring at me with one attentive eye. He fiddles with the condom, which I'm glad for—I would not have had the courage to try my hand at that. He says something I can't hear as I fight back tears.

Suddenly, Tony begins to chant. It sounds like he's praying in Turkish. He prepares himself in record time, continuing to make this repetitive whining noise. Then, with the delicacy of a crowbar, he opens my legs with his knee. Sleeping with a guy who doesn't love you is awful. It is painful. I feel like a whore, worse than Erika, because this gives me no pleasure. The whine drones in my ears, the bed creaks, Tony makes orgasmic faces, and I just want to get it over with. I stay still, occasionally crying out in the spirit of hospitality. In between noises, he announces that he's about to finish. As he explodes, I hear a noise outside my room. Luca must have just gotten home. What a welcome. He slams the door and traipses through the apartment as if his shoes were made of stone. Tony collapses into the mattress. The sheets swallow me up. He smiles and asks me how I'm feeling.

"I'm great," I whisper. Great because it's over and now he can leave.

130

"Me, too," he says, nestling down beside me.

His little friend touches my leg. Tony reaches out, takes it, and pinches my side, showing no signs of leaving. I should be grateful, right, that he's lingering? He gives my cheek one of his slobbery kisses and seems ready to doze off. Please, no. I did not sign up for this. Should I tell him? *Hey, Tony, could you please peel yourself off my mattress?* Is there a correct way to banish him from my sight forever without offending him? Considering that he's already snoring—how is he asleep already?—I don't know what to do. Do I just push him off the bed? Right now, I'd better just get dressed.

I free myself from his sweaty weight and slip on a shirt. He continues to snore. The condom falls to the floor, looking like a crushed worm. The apartment is silent; Luca must have gone back out again. I go to the bathroom to wash up. I still feel awful. Is this really what young women do? They just let themselves be used, without passion or pleasure, for reasons that are probably more valid than mine? I curl up on the couch. I want to cry.

At that moment, Luca's door opens, and his face appears in the shadows. He stares at me for a long time without blinking. He must be alone, because he still has his jacket on. I watch him, then make a daring foray into conversation.

"You're back early." I try to be strong, but it doesn't work. Bland statements just don't hold up to post-sex tears that have nothing to do with happiness.

"What's wrong?" he asks me seriously.

"Nothing . . .," I say as a sob overtakes my voice.

Luca sits down on the couch and looks toward my room. Tony's snoring is still going strong. "Why are you crying? Did that asshole force you to do something? Because if he did . . ." He jumps to his feet, his fists hard as rocks.

"Absolutely not."

"How long is he gonna stay here?"

"I don't know."

"What do you mean, you don't know? Is he going to stay all night?"

"Shh . . . Luca, he'll hear you."

"Hey, at least I had the decency to come check on you."

"I don't know how to act," I whisper very quietly.

"What do you mean?"

"I don't know how to make him leave without offending him."

"What the fuck do you care if he gets offended? Tell him to get the hell out, and that's it! It doesn't take much, just a few words."

"I can't. Not like that," I say.

"Okay, then write him a poem and sing it to him, but get him out of here. Unless you really do want him to stay."

"I don't want him to stay. I want to kick him out without offending him."

"You're too sensitive, Carlotta," he says, his voice sharp. "You worry too much about hurting other people's feelings. I can tell him for you if you want."

"No way! I told you, I don't want to offend him. You'd be mean."

"You bet I'd be mean. So, what are you going to do?"

"I don't know. Let me think."

"Think fast, or I'll do it myself."

"Shut up! Listen," I say, frightened by a sudden noise from the bedroom.

"Wait here," he orders. He gets up, leaves the apartment, and closes the door. I don't have time to wonder where he's gone, as Tony emerges from my room, still naked. He grabs me by the shoulders and sneaks a hand under my shirt.

"Tony . . . Maybe you should . . ."

At that moment, Luca swings open the door as if just returning home from work. He stops and stares at me and then at Tony with wide eyes.

"Whore!" he screams. Tony, startled, quickly covers his junk with one hand. I'm paralyzed with surprise, my mouth stuck in a giant O. "You dirty whore!" Luca yells. "You swore to me you wouldn't do this again. And you! You filthy, disgusting creep. How dare you touch my woman? You won't get away with it this time. I'm gonna kill both of you."

"Hey!" Tony exclaims, genuinely frightened. "Carlotta, I thought you said—"

"Women lie, didn't you know that?" Luca says. He comes closer, and I realize that Tony actually believes he's my husband! I have to hold back a laugh even though Luca is so angry that his lips tremble. A vein pulses in his temple like a blue snake. He's doing such a great job that even I can barely remember it's just pretend. "If you touch her again, if you even dare to come anywhere near her, I swear I'll break your legs." He punctuates this by jabbing a finger in Tony's chest, and then promptly punches him right in the nose. This is reaching the peak of realism. Luca grabs Tony again and punches him in the jaw. Tony tries to reciprocate but, fearing an attack on Little Tony and the boys, bends over to protect them.

Now the foyer of my apartment is a boxing ring, and I suddenly feel the need to intervene. But in my heroic attempt to dive between them before the clothed man beats the naked one to a pulp, I catch one of Luca's punches. This error ends the match. Tony quickly gets dressed and runs out without another word.

I feel awful. If this was Luca's idea of getting him to leave without making me feel guilty, his plan didn't work. I feel worse than before. In addition to my total lack of self-esteem and the pain between my legs, my head feels like a gong, and I can't even keep my eye open. At least Luca is upset. He puts ice in a towel and makes me sit down, mumbling something about how stupid he was. I'm tempted to tell him he's right. But I like that he's taking care of me, that he cares about how I feel. I'm so close that I can feel his breath. Somehow, I find myself lying on the couch, my cheek resting in his lap and his hands running through my hair.

"Luca," I say suddenly. "I'm going to become a nun."

"What did you say?" he snorts.

"I've decided. I'm going to lock myself in a convent."

"It might just be the punch talking, but you're making less sense than usual."

"No, the punch enlightened me. I don't want anything to do with sex. I will dedicate myself to gardening and embroidery, and I will pray for my unfortunate sisters who still allow men to hurt them."

"I told you I'm sorry. I meant to punch *his* face, not yours."

"No, I was thinking about everything that happened tonight with Tony. Sex is shit. I don't need it. I am fine just by myself! What does sex even get you?"

"You're crazy." He raises one eyebrow. "What the hell happened to make you arrive at such a drastic conclusion?"

"I let a stranger get inside me. Now I feel like a disgusting, slimy booger, and I'll be walking funny for the next two months."

"Carlotta . . ."

Don't look at me with those eyes, Luca. Don't let that faint smile play over your lips. Don't make me weak with your tenderness. Just shut up and let my name hang suspended in the air, like a puff of breeze.

He gets up, and I fear the worst. I stay on the couch, the ice dripping on my face now. He returns a moment later carrying a blanket. He understands that I can't go back into my room tonight, that I don't want to offend my nose with the smell of the sex that barely even involved me. It's not really Tony's fault. He was simply an instrument of my despair.

As my eyelids grow heavy, Luca goes back to his room, but he leaves the door open. The sound of his breathing close by makes me feel at home.

TWELVE

I clean my room as if I'd hosted an Ebola patient last night. I cleaned myself the same way, with a forty-five-minute shower and an entire bottle of body wash. I know that this is not a normal reaction. After all, Tony did not force himself on me. He's not a contemptible man; actually, he's quite pleasant. But I'm still toying with the idea of joining a convent. It would mean I could eliminate the men from my life without being considered a loser. Plus, I wouldn't have to shave as often.

Above all, I could get away from Luca and the frightening certainty that he's going to tell me all the sordid details about his new love, Paola. I feel his eyes on me around the apartment. He's as neurotic as a toy soldier who has been wound too tightly. I think he can tell I'm avoiding him.

He's going to the bar tonight, and while I'm scrubbing the floor of my room, he suddenly appears in my doorway. He leans against the frame and looks at me.

"I have to tell you something," he begins after thirty seconds of silence.

Nerves beat in me like a dragonfly's wings. I don't answer right away. I stay kneeling on the floor, thinking about a million things in the span of one second. I decide to play tough.

"Do we have to do this right now? As you can see, I'm busy," I say gruffly.

"Let me know when you're available, then. You're harder to get ahold of than Madonna these days." He sounds annoyed. He drums two fingers on the edge of the door. "I know you're still pissed at me because of Erika. I can see a thousand-page tome on the flaws of men in your eyes whenever you look at me. And I understand, you have every right to be angry."

I'm tempted to tell him that a thousand pages is a pretty low estimate, but I decide against it.

"Anyway, I wanted your opinion on whether I should . . . leave . . ."

"What's up? Are you about to embark on an adventure?" I ask with feigned nonchalance.

"No, you don't understand. I meant, like, leave the apartment. For good."

"Wha—" I can't even finish the word.

"It's clear that we're not getting along very well. Something changed. I know that you're upset. You've changed, or at least your attitude toward me has changed. I get it, and I don't want to force my presence on you."

As he speaks, I'm thinking that it's not just me who's changed. He has, too. He's different, and that is what bothers me about our strange routine. But his little performance with Erika undoubtedly helped me to close myself off from him, and since I discovered his interest in Paola, my heart has been filled with cracks.

"No," I say. "It's not that I don't want you here. And I'm over what happened with Erika, really. After all, you're free to be with whoever you want to be with. It's just that . . . This new version of you scares me a little."

"What do you mean?"

"This new side of you! You don't smile anymore. You mope around the apartment like a ghost dragging chains. You don't bring any more cheerful little conquests home. You've changed, and I know why."

"Oh, you do?"

"Yes, I do!" I speak in bursts, my heart full of pain. "You're so weird! You're so distracted. Some nights you don't even come home. You have all the symptoms of infatuation. But maybe you're wrong, and it's not as serious as it seems." I cling to his own doubt-filled words I overheard in the park. He's the one who said he wasn't sure it was love, right? So I can afford to be frank. "In fact, I'm sure you're wrong. I'm certain of it. This is all just nonsense. This isn't like you, Luca. And you know what? You were right. You're too smart to let such a complication mislead you. Have you thought about the consequences? Having to make love to the same person every day . . . Doesn't that bother you? Change is the spice of life! So you should think about this, Luca. Yes, perhaps it's new for you. Are you really sure you know what love is?"

He regards me with a piercing stare. "Well, Carlotta," he finally says, coldly, "you've made yourself pretty fucking clear."

"Of course it's clear. Why would you leave? There's no reason to. We're fine. Come on . . . Where will you find another great friend like me? So I forbid you to leave, I forbid you to be in love, and I strongly encourage you to fill my apartment again with however many tramps you deem appropriate!"

"Well," he replies glacially, and goes away.

That was wicked of me. He wanted to confide in me and tell me all about his plight, and I wouldn't let him. But I wasn't being insincere. I really don't think he loves that elegant woman. He might like her . . . but doesn't he like me, too? If attention and tenderness mean love, then I'd say that Luca's loved me for months! So there's no way he can be in love with her. Period. Maybe he's attracted to her sophistication, or maybe he wants to change things up in the bedroom. That must be it.

Yes, he's put me through the wringer, but I don't want him to leave! If he tries to leave, I'll bind him to the bed with a pair of handcuffs and only unlock them when he needs to use the restroom. The fear of losing him is stronger than my survival instincts.

I don't understand how women from centuries ago, who stayed home and didn't work, who had all the time in the world to think, didn't drive themselves insane. What did Jane Austen do when she fell in love and couldn't watch stupid TV shows or gorge herself on snacks? How did she conceive of protagonists that are as witty and wise as Elizabeth Bennet and Anne Elliot; how come they aren't pissed off and chronically depressed? If I didn't have my work, between trashy TV and family-size bags of pretzels, I'd be a cross between Lord Byron and American Psycho.

I also have Rocky to distract me. It's really quite bothersome when he harasses me so much that I'm forced to stop brooding. This morning, for example, Rocky is angry with Romina, the actress who plays Laura. The poor thing has put on a few pounds, which, to Rocky, is equivalent to treason. Instead of threatening to report him to the union, she puts him in his place with some words of her own and condemns him to hell. Iriza and I, already onstage trying to implement a system to make the sets fold in on themselves without damaging them, find ourselves in the middle of the conflict. Franz tries to calm Rocky down, and Iriza watches him with love in her eyes. I'd like to grab Rocky by the balls and throw him right into the foyer. Iriza tries to distract me by asking me how the prop hunt is coming along.

"Great, I'm even staying within the budget," I say. "I'm meeting some guys in an hour who are going to sell me some other pieces of the collection."

"Can I come with you? Things are getting uncomfortable here," Iriza says. "When Rocky digs in his heels, he's so unbearable. He'll make Romina cry and force her to go on a diet. I think we'd better get out of here."

This house does not have flamingos or gnomes. It's actually a very elegant villa. This is unsurprising, seeing as you can't collect these kinds of toys if the only place you can afford to live is some shoddy tenement. I just hope the people are normal.

The door opens on a normal-looking mother dressed in jeans and a sweater. She's young and pretty, with a book in her hand. *The Hitchhiker's Guide to the Galaxy*. Cute.

"Jay and his friends are in the garage," she says. "It's just around the corner. I hope you brought earplugs."

"Earplugs?" Iriza and I ask at the same time.

She only smiles and closes the door after pointing us to the garage. Soon we understand what she meant. As we near the garage, we hear music. No, that's inaccurate, calling it music. It sounds like devil worship. The drums pound, the electric guitars groan, and a male voice sporadically yells a few words over the din.

As the leader of the expedition, I go first and peer cautiously into the garage. The door is up, and I get a whiff of the unmistakable aroma of marijuana. Four young guys are banging on their instruments; I must admit it seems more like the instruments are crying out from suffering than producing music. If I don't get this taken care of soon, we'll both be deaf. I march to the middle of the garage, right in front of the drummer, who appears to be a sixteen-year-old delinquent type with eyebrow piercings. But he doesn't notice me right away. The guitarist nudges the bass player, who kicks the drummer, who throws a stick at the keyboardist, who curses and rubs his head. This all takes a good five minutes. Finally, the racket stops.

"Um, hello." I greet them with a wave.

Iriza steps forward and simply says, "Hey."

The guitar player must be the *Hitchhiker* woman's son. He's cute, with long blond hair that's soaked in gel and probably hasn't been washed since the end of the last millennium.

"What do you want?" he asks, annoyed.

The bass player, a nerdy-looking teenager who you'd expect to be reciting theorems instead of smoking reefer, hurries to extinguish his cigarette. The keyboardist looks at me askew over the can of Sprite and the half-eaten Mars bar on his keyboard. I explain who we are, and the guitar player lights up.

"Oh, we spoke on the phone!" he exclaims. "Massimo, go get the cardboard box behind my sister's records."

Massimo rummages behind a stack of dusty LPs and pulls out a box sealed with scotch tape.

"My sister left for college. I don't know what's in the mess she left, and I need money. So I'm selling all her shit. She deserves it."

I join in purely for fun. "Well yeah, you get what's coming to you. Hey, can I see what all this shit consists of, exactly?"

The boy nods and allows me to open the box. When I see the contents, I'm caught between the urge to shriek with joy and pretend to be unimpressed. Almost everything we're looking for is in the box, including the Barbie doll dressed as Marilyn Monroe in *The Seven Year Itch*. I wonder how she got these!

"How much do you want for it?" I ask, trying to sound detached.

"I'd give it to you even if it were gold and diamonds," he says sarcastically. "You're doing me a favor. If only you knew what she's like."

"I'm getting an idea."

"Let's do it this way. I'll give you the whole lot at half price. Two hundred and fifty euro instead of five hundred . . . If you do me a favor."

I frown, worried that he's going to ask me to transport a few pounds of cannabis or show him my tits. If so, he'd better ask Iriza. Mine aren't worth the discount.

"We wrote a rockin' song. You've gotta hear it."

I'm instantly transported to a rainy winter Sunday long ago, when I was younger and I was forced to listen to Aunt Porzia singing show tunes.

The drummer kicks the snare. The keyboardist finishes off the Mars bar and the Sprite and belches. The bassist recovers his cigarette and stashes it behind one ear. The guitarist grabs a microphone, struggles with some kind of hard rock gesture, raises an arm, and makes a face like he was sniffing cat poop.

"Go!"

The name of the band is printed on the drum: *Fuck & Fuck*. The song is quite different from Aunt Porzia's show tunes, although the boy's voice does bear a resemblance to hers at times. The lyrics are very refined—a skillful repetition of the same two words that form the name of the band. And actually, there is art in their ability to differentiate between the various types of fuck yous, assigning different meaning to it every time. What a flattering song. It's all too much. I want them to stop singing. I want to smoke a joint. I can't read what Iriza wants to do. She's about to either be sick or burst into laughter. It's not every day that you're told such a thing for three minutes and fifty seconds straight, not including the instrumental solos. These are the kind of experiences that breed food for thought.

"Well?" the singer asks proudly when it's all over.

"Wonderful," I say. "You're destined to break out. Give this to your relatives for Christmas, and you'll end up rich. Actually, if you have a CD on hand, I'd like to buy it for my sister for her birthday. She's just like yours."

He doesn't have a CD, but he's very pleased with my comment. Two hundred and fifty euro later, I have the Barbies. We leave hastily before they ask us to stick around for another song. Just before we disappear from view, however, I turn around to the boys and call out.

"By the way . . . Fuck you! Right?"

All four boys give me a thumbs-up in approval.

Once we're far away, Iriza laughs to the point of convulsing. "Franz was right," she finally gasps.

"What do you mean?"

"He talks about you a lot. He says you're a total riot. He called you a phenomenon."

"From a sideshow, maybe."

"No, he only has great things to say about you. You're really funny. Nothing like that has ever happened to me."

"Prepare yourself, then, for a whole lot of madness."

"That's why he likes you. Being around you is . . . hilarious."

"He . . . likes me?" I ask, incredulous.

"Very much! Although he's never said anything about it. But I can tell. I see the way he looks at you. As soon as you walk into the room, his face lights up."

Well, now I'm uncomfortable. Even though she's smiling, Iriza looks so sad. She has clearly misinterpreted everything. I try to dispel the misunderstanding with a shrug.

"I just happen to always find myself in these ridiculous situations, probably because I already look like a clown. Look at me! I don't even need the wig or the fake nose. I'm just someone that Franz can laugh at."

Once I get home, I realize with horror that Luca seems to be moving out anyway. There's a bag on the floor of the foyer, and he's in the kitchen writing a note. I nearly trip over the bag, almost spilling the dolls from the box.

"Hey," he says. "I was just writing you a note. I'm leaving."

"Where are you going?" I ask, my voice quivering. If I have to, I'll wrap myself around his leg to keep him from leaving.

"Home. My mom is sick." He sounds worried. Now my desire to sequester him feels selfish.

"I'm sorry," I whisper. "I hope it's nothing serious."

"I hope so, too. She's in the hospital right now. They're running tests."

"It'll be okay." And I'm being sincere—I hope that the dear woman heals quickly so that the agony can be wiped off Luca's face.

"Okay, well, I'm off then. I don't know when I'll be back."

I feel broken, already lonely. He hasn't even moved a foot and the apartment feels like a tomb. I'm worried about him.

"Luca!" I say, just as he's closing the door. I yank it open. "Can I come with you?"

What a stupid question! Where did I come up with that? Did the marijuana fumes in the garage turn my neurons to mush? I want to take it all back when I see the stunned look on Luca's face.

"Okay."

"What? Did you just say okay?"

"Yeah, okay," he repeats. "But hurry up and grab your things. I want to get going."

I quickly gather some clean underwear, a toothbrush, and a pair of jeans and shove them all into a plastic bag. We head downstairs. It takes three tries to start Luca's old car.

I realize that I don't know where we're going or anything about his family. He answers my questions reluctantly; he's from Forte dei Marmi. It's a bit of a trek, a couple hours away, but it doesn't matter. I'd trek barefoot all the way to Peru just to be with him.

As we get closer to Forte dei Marmi, Luca grows increasingly nervous. The sun starts to set, and we can hear the crashing of the waves. I try to lighten the mood by telling him the story of Fuck & Fuck, and I'm thrilled when he bursts out laughing. We stop for gas, and after grabbing some sandwiches, we're back on our way. He laughs again when I turn around to find something in the backseat and his arm accidentally brushes against my ass. I'm feeling happy. After weeks of awkwardness, we are finally relaxed around each other. Everything is perfect inside this ancient, uncomfortable car.

It's nighttime when we arrive in Forte dei Marmi. During the last stretch, the car sputters and coughs like an asthmatic grandmother, and the radiator light comes on. There's a salty smell in the air here, and the temperature is mild. Country manors, hotels, and villas line the beach. A long jetty extends out into the sea. The moon is a wafer in the sky.

Suddenly, I see a gate, and a man peers inside our car. He's in uniform—a cop? After checking us out for a second, he apologizes and lets us go. We drive along a boulevard. Luca nervously drums the wheel. Finally, we pull up in front of a castle. Well, it's not really a castle, as there are no turrets and no moat full of crocodiles. But it's a giant stone villa with dozens of windows, endless foliage, and a fountain (that features neither Aphrodite nor a naked cherub).

"You . . . live . . . here?" I ask, very slowly.

"Not really. Last time I checked, I live with you in Rome."

"Yeah, I know, but I mean . . . This is your home?"

"Unfortunately, yes," he replies mysteriously.

We get out of the car, the gravel crunching beneath our feet. A street lamp, topiaries, and the house that seems to never end greet us. Luca grabs his bag; now I'm mortified that my things are in a plastic grocery bag.

A figure appears on the doorstep. It's a woman, but I don't think it's his mother. I need to calm down. It's not like I'm his girlfriend here to meet the family. I need to stop feeling so uncomfortable. After all, what can happen? They're not going to ask me to recite multiplication tables or to name all the kings of Rome or to calculate the area of a triangle! But I can sense that something is going to happen. For example, the woman on the doorstep could end up being Paola.

It's Paola.

I recognize her delicate attractiveness, her short hair, and her graceful manners. I shiver, about to fall over. Luca stops, kisses her on the cheek, and turns to me.

"Paola, this is Carlotta."

Paola stares at me. She has dark eyes. Her lips stretch into a smile.

"Carlotta, this is my sister, Paola."

What?

Sister?

Sister?

I repeat the same word in my head a dozen times. How is that possible? I've been tormented day and night over his . . . sister? I don't even understand. With a blank expression I extend my hand. Luca starts asking her about their mother. She's still in the hospital, but she's recovering. He asks about their father, but strangely, he calls him "your father." Paola tells him he's out of the country on business, but he'll be back tomorrow. Paola asks me if I'm tired and if I'd like to freshen up before dinner. Then she leads me to the top floor and tells the stern-looking housekeeper to make sure I have everything I need. Giving my plastic bag a disgusted look, the housekeeper escorts me to a huge room. It's so grand that even the toilet paper in the adjacent bathroom is luxurious. In my work suit I don't fit in. But I wash up and fix up my pale face in a mirror rimmed with crystal roses. Maybe this is why Luca never really talks about himself. I always thought he was a penniless writer-bartender in search of fortune and a place to live. Now I discover that he's heir to a throne he doesn't seem to want!

It's just the three of us for dinner. We eat right in the kitchen, around a marble island that's as big as my apartment. I don't know why, but I feel embarrassed. Despite my usual tendency to say stupid things, I am silent. I listen to them talk and absorb the affection between them, the kind that binds two people who grew up together. It's what's missing between me and Erika. But I'm not jealous. Instead I feel a combination of joy and nostalgia. Suddenly, Paola leaves the room and returns with a photo album. An inscription on the blue silk cover reads *My brother*.

"Put those horrors away! I command you!" Luca exclaims as he slices some bread. But he's smiling.

"No, Carlotta has to see how hideous you were as a child."

"Don't worry," I say. "If it's too shocking, I can reciprocate with photos of my Aunt Ermellina after a perm."

I'm actually not shocked at all. Luca was beautiful even as a child. I flip through the album as though it were a treasure chest. It shows his entire history: Luca as a child in his mother's arms, Luca at age six or so on a piebald pony, his arms around the pony's neck. He looks innocent and ecstatic; even the pony seems to be smiling. Luca as a teenager, already so tall that he towers over all his classmates in the class picture. He must have attended a private school, as they're all wearing uniforms and posed on a grand staircase. He's not laughing in this picture. His eyes betray some deep disappointment. Then I find pictures that seem to be from a photo shoot. He must be about twenty. Wearing designer jeans and an open shirt, he's striking a classic model pose with one hand in his pocket and the other in his hair. No smile, but a pout that conjures suggestive thoughts.

"You were a model?" I ask, surprised and kind of irritated because it's something he has in common with Erika. Luca rolls his eyes.

"I just did the one job, I swear. I tried it when I was nineteen. I was about to sign a contract with Elite. But after three months in that environment, I decided to go to Abruzzo to detox."

I want to hug him, but I refrain since Paola is staring at us. Actually, she's staring at me. I've caught her watching me with a smile on her face from time to time. Perhaps she finds me funny? That's my cross to bear. I'm the funny one. No one ever takes me seriously. But finding out about Luca's past makes my heart melt. I've discovered for sure that there's so much more to him than I already knew. I just don't know how I'm going to get over him. We spend the rest of the evening sharing stories and memories.

When we say good night in the doorway of my room, however, Luca brushes his lips against my forehead. He hugs me for a moment. I feel a minefield where my heart should be. He quickly steps back and looks at me with the eyes from his school picture, that same hard expression.

"Get some rest," he urges, and disappears along with his shadow.

THIRTEEN

Luca and Paola stay at the hospital until late afternoon. I eat lunch by myself while the housekeeper judges my table manners. Afterward, I take a walk through the garden. I can hear the sound of the ocean, but all I see is perfectly trimmed lawns, endless roses, and stone benches.

I hope Luca's mom is okay. I'm feeling protective of him, and it surprises me. I don't know what it means, but it adds another dimension to my feelings for him. I don't feel just passion for him. There's tenderness, something I wasn't prepared for. Love is such a mess! You think you're over it, but it's just a bottomless pit. I head back inside as the sun starts to set.

Paola tells me that their mother is back from the hospital. "Would you like to meet her before dinner? She can't come downstairs because she's still weak, but we talked about you, and she wants to meet you."

For some reason I feel embarrassed. I'm just a friend. And meeting Luca's mom shouldn't be a big deal. It's not like I'm meeting my future mother-in-law, right?

"Of course. I'd love to."

"My father will be at dinner," she adds, her voice turning shrill. "He and Luca don't exactly have the best relationship. So if it feels like an atomic bomb is about to explode, just pretend not to notice."

I think of my mother and Erika and their innate ability to make me feel like shit. "Don't worry, I know what that's like."

"Some of our family friends will be here, too," she goes on. "They don't see Luca very much, so when they found out he was here, they insisted on coming over."

"Oh . . ." I whisper. "I hope I'm not putting you out. You know, this was a spur-of-the-moment decision. I was still wearing my work clothes when I left! Back home, inviting family friends over means that sixty people will show up, half dressed in feathers and sequins, and when they get drunk, they try to involve the sober half in some absurd contest, like who can gargle longer."

I wonder what's wrong with me as all of that comes out. It's true, but did I really need to tell her?

"It's not a problem. But if it would make you feel better, I'd be happy to let you borrow one of my dresses."

"That'd be great, but your housekeeper will have to shorten it a bit."

Paola smiles and I feel foolish. We choose a simple turquoise sheath dress, and she helps me turn the empress's gown into a Smurf's frock by taking it in and shortening it. The fact that she indulges my nonsense is a sign of her kindness.

I don't see Luca until evening, and I can't deny that I'm nervous. I have a nagging feeling that his father won't like me. His mother, however, loves me. My heart pounds as I enter her room like a child who has been called to the principal's office. It's just the two of us. Her room is upholstered in delicate lilac silk. There is no evidence that a man sleeps here; she and her husband must occupy separate bedrooms. She is lying on a bench at the foot of the bed, wrapped in a green kimono that perfectly complements her pale complexion and long, graying hair. As soon as she sees me, she stands up and comes over.

"Oh, no, sit down. I'll come over there," I say gently. She looks like a classical dancer. Her steps are soft, her wrists are thin, and she's wearing no makeup. I ask her how she's feeling.

"I'm fine. It's nothing serious. I am often subject to these kinds of ailments, but my children are both so apprehensive . . ."

"Luca loves you very much, Mrs.—"

"Oh, call me Lorenza, dear."

"I'll try to remember that."

"You must love Luca very much, too."

"Well, sure—"

"This is the first time he's brought a girl home."

"But we . . . I mean . . . We're just friends."

She ignores my explanation as if it doesn't matter, and I'm starting to think that she's right—it doesn't. Friendship is even more rare than true romantic love, and it makes my presence in this house special. Lorenza gives me an exhausted smile before continuing.

"No, come to think of it, he did bring a rather odd young woman home once, but it was just to spite his father. He was eighteen. He couldn't even remember her name when she was here. He'll never forget your name, though, that's for sure. He couldn't stop talking about you at the hospital."

"Really?" I ask, turning red in spite of myself. Damn it.

"Yes, my dear. You just need to be patient and understanding with him. He has the potential to turn into Prince Charming, but he needs to see for himself that love exists. He didn't have a good example of that growing up, so that's why he might seem unfeeling."

I consider telling her again that we're just friends, that her speculations are all a misunderstanding, but I don't. Instead, I say, "I will be. I'll be patient and understanding. I'll love him forever."

Lorenza grasps my hand and gives me a look that's maternal and affectionate. Just then, Luca enters the room. I hope with all my heart that she doesn't say something like, "Your girlfriend is a wonderful girl, and she told me that she'll love you forever," which would smash me as flat as a rug. I jump to my feet as if thorns are pushing up through the bench.

"I have to finish getting ready," I say to her. "I'll see you at dinner?"

"No, I'll be eating in here. I'm not yet strong enough to make it up and down the stairs."

"Oh. Good night, then."

I lean in to kiss her cheek and leave her with her son. In an antique mirror in the hallway, I see the love written on my face. I wonder why on earth Luca can't see it when everyone else clearly can. I'm not just an open book: I'm a book with large-print text. I should have stayed home. I shouldn't have come here. This trip has been the final straw.

Luca's voice rings out suddenly. "Is everything okay?"

I gasp and realize that he's standing next to me. He hasn't shaved, and he's wearing a white shirt and faded jeans. I'm as sure that he deliberately chose his informal outfit as I'm sure his father is not going to like me.

"Everything's great. Your mom is really something."

"Did you tell her something funny?" Luca asks. "She kept laughing to herself, and she wouldn't tell me why."

Thank you, Lorenza, for keeping our little secret! "You know how it is," I say. "People laugh just looking at me because they can see how fun I am."

"Yes, that you are."

"And how are things with you?" I ask him.

"A fairy tale."

"You're not too thrilled about dinner, are you?"

"It's that obvious?"

"Kind of. But it's just one dinner, Luca. You'll feel better once it's over. Besides . . ."

"Besides what?"

"Besides . . . I'm here for you, right now and whenever you need me to be. Give me your hand. Just think of me as your mother for the night."

Luca smiles and looks at me through hair that droops over his eyes. The corner of his mouth raises in a strange smile.

"I could never think of you as my mother. Not tonight, not ever."

Family dinners at the Morli house are very different from those at the Lieti house. People don't swarm like an army of locusts. The aunts mind their own business. The young men don't wear lobster-colored jackets and cartoon character ties. Everything is understated and chic.

Yet my sense of inadequacy is the same. Luca's father is an austere and beautiful man. I imagine Luca will look just like him in thirty years. But he barely greets me and stares at me suspiciously. The family friends turn out to be three people. There's a tall and stern-looking middle-aged woman with a single string of black pearls around her neck. Her husband, who must be a military veteran, has tortoiseshell glasses, a goatee, and a chronic cough. Their daughter looks to be about my age. She is exotic-looking and busty, with dark hair, very little makeup, and almond-shaped eyes that make alarm bells ring in my head. Her name is Iolanda, and it's clear that she wants to eat Luca up. Even more alarming, it seems that everyone has given her their blessing to do so. Her mother keeps alluding to various things that her dear child can do, implying that she's superior to every other woman on the planet. I get the impression that Luca's father wouldn't mind such a union, either.

But Luca doesn't say a word. I've never seen him so silent and aloof. He doesn't speak for the entire dinner, even when his father reprimands him for his outfit. Meanwhile, Iolanda sizes me up from underneath her eyelashes, trying to decide whether she should consider me a threat.

"I don't understand what you do," she says suddenly. "Prop master? Is that a kind of ragman?"

Her mother jumps in, and her tone is not much friendlier. "I knew a Bulgarian woman who did something like that. She collected used things and resold them to street vendors."

This makes me blush. It's not that there's anything unseemly about handling junk or selling used things at flea markets. It's just that she so obviously said it to offend me. I want to come up with a witty retort to shoot her down, but this isn't my house, and I don't want to be rude here. Mr. Morli seems furious, too, but for an entirely different reason—he clearly views me as beneath both his table and his son. Paola opens her mouth to say something, but Luca cuts her off. He addresses Iolanda with a charming smile.

"What about you? Are you still screwing every eligible bachelor in sight?" He takes a sip of wine and basks in the silence that drops over the dining room. "Now, remind me again, why did that last nice young man leave you? Did he find out he was just one of hundreds?"

Iolanda stutters, flushed. Her mother's eyes widen, and she sways as if drunk. Her father smiles uncertainly, still coughing, but the real threat is Luca's father.

"Apologize to our guests immediately!" he orders.

"I don't think so," Luca replies, starting to lose his cool. "These people shouldn't even be here. Your wife was just released from the hospital, yet you host a dinner party like nothing has happened. You couldn't even be bothered to go up and check on her. You know what? I'm leaving. I'm over this shit."

He gets up, grabs my hand, and pulls me up and away from the table with him. Everyone stares at us, looking a bit green. I hear them start to buzz with shock as Paola follows us to the front door.

"Please, Luca . . .," she says.

"I can't, Paola. Apologize to Mom for me . . . But I really have to leave." She doesn't say anything, but two big tears catch in her eyelashes. As we drive off, I realize I'm still wearing Paola's dress.

Luca stares straight ahead, as if he were alone. From the look in his eyes, I sense that he's thinking about his past. He's running away, despite the limitations imposed by the precarious state of his car. Luca rolls down the window, letting in the salty night air as if that alone were enough to blow away the last hour. I lose track of the time and the number of curves we careen around—and the number of times nausea floods my stomach.

Suddenly, Luca looks over at me. "I'm sorry," he murmurs. "It's just that—"

"I know what it's like," I interrupt. "I've dealt with it for thirty years. I know exactly how much it hurts to realize that someone you share blood with doesn't accept you for who you are. And I know that your hatred for your father is just the rusty side of the coin . . . You love him in spite of everything and just want him to respect you. But that doesn't always happen, Luca. Families are only perfect in ads or '50s TV shows. In real life, they're just a bunch of messed up people, and we have to accept that we can't ask of others what they can't give us, whether it's because of who they are or what they've decided. They love us in their own way, I think, but it's no use damning them for it."

Luca turns to me, and although it's dark, I can see that he's giving me a smile that is more powerful than the sun. "You're very wise, little butterfly. But my father couldn't handle that both Paola and I left home as soon as we were adults, or that I'm still single, or that I've had a million jobs that he considers shameful, or that I'm chasing my dream of becoming a writer. He just thinks it's all bullshit. I feel sorry for my sister. She's always trying to make all the pieces fit, and she won't admit that some of them will never match up. I know that I should try my best not to provoke him, but sometimes I can't resist."

"Is that why you dressed like that tonight? Or why you brought home a weird girl when you were eighteen?"

"How do you know about that?" he asks. Calmer now, he's no longer taking every hairpin turn like a racecar driver.

"Your mother mentioned it to me." I summon the courage to ask him what's really on my mind. "Is that why you agreed to let me come with you? Did you know that your father wouldn't like me?"

He frowns. "Don't even joke about that. You're special. You're my best friend. Please forgive me for what happened tonight—and forgive my father's friends. They act like they're above everyone."

The phrase *you're my best friend* makes me feel like a tree trunk being chainsawed by a lumberjack. But still, it's something. "Don't worry," I say in a cheerful voice. "They kind of had a point. My job isn't exactly glamorous. Like, one time, for an ad for mozzarella cheese, I had to commission a craftsman to make a huge foam cow udder. Or another time, I had to carry a life-size cardboard replica of the statue of David to the theater on the subway. Do you think Iolanda would have appreciated that? By the way, is it true, what you said to her?"

He laughs. "I toned it down. I didn't want to upset her mother."

We talk about ourselves and our childhoods for a while. He tells me about the photo of him on the pony at the circus. I have a similar circus photo, but I'm posing—forced by my mother—next to a contortionist who's tied up like a sailor's knot, and sobbing. I've hated the circus ever since.

After a long time, we finally fall silent. He takes my hand and squeezes it, only releasing me when he needs to shift gears. I wish time would stop.

After two hours of driving, I can tell he's getting tired, so I suggest that we pull off the road. We find a hotel off the highway and take two adjacent rooms. It's getting late, so he says good night with a gentle kiss on my cheek.

The room is pretty bleak and cold; it makes me want to get out of here as soon as possible tomorrow. I wrap myself in a blanket. I know I won't be able to fall asleep anytime soon—the last twenty-four hours' most exciting highlights are replaying in my head, and headlights from cars outside stripe the room yellow. Then I hear a knock at the door. It's Luca, with a bottle of wine in his hand.

"Want to drink?" he asks. "I took it from the bar. I think it's pretty shitty, probably made with poisonous additives. It might kill us."

"Or it might just give us the shits. I'm in," I say. "How glamorous."

He comes in, sits down on the bed, and volunteers to take the first sip. "If I drop dead, don't drink this."

"If you drop dead, that's all the more reason to drink."

Two drops of bright purple liquid drip down his chin and onto his dirty shirt. He hands the bottle to me and wipes his lips with the back of his hand.

"In the words of a true sommelier . . . that's some shitty wine!" He laughs. We finish the entire bottle together, all the while giggling goofily. We're not that drunk, just happy, but we can tell what's about to happen. Suddenly, Luca turns on his side, his elbow propped on a pillow, and smiles at me. He's just been joking about how the mattress is as soft as a rock and the duvet as comfortable as sandpaper. And now he slowly strokes my arm with two fingers as if writing something. He starts at my wrist and trails his fingers up to my shoulder. A shiver runs down my spine. Maybe I should tell him to stop. But instead, I lock my mouth shut and throw away the key.

And then it happens. It starts out with an affectionate kiss that lingers, his lips glued to mine. Then his tongue searches inside my mouth. I open my eyes to make sure this is really happening. It really is Luca who is embracing me, who is on top of me. It isn't a joke anymore. My mother isn't eavesdropping down the hall. It's just us, the intermittent glow of headlights, and a hotel manager who won't even remember our faces. It's really happening.

His hands touch me, squeeze me, take me. He kisses me as I take my clothes off. He undresses, too, and I take in his gorgeous body incredulously. Is this how it is with every woman? Do his eyes always glow stormy green when he makes love? Is his mouth always this hot and impatient? And is this woman really me? Yes, it is. And I love him. I love everything about him. This miracle of muscle, lips, tongue, and fingertips crowds everything out of my mind but total happiness—I've never made love before now. But despite all of this, I feel chaste. He holds me close, stifling a scream in my hair. As we ride the wave together, I know that even if I were to die right this second, I will live forever. The sweat on our skin sticks us together. Luca smiles and says my name.

"Carlotta."

But happiness is so fleeting.

As soon as it's over, something breaks. He stares at the ceiling and swallows. We're silent. The moment is passing, the next one beginning, as I join the ranks of women prohibited from falling asleep on his shoulder. The polar frost chilling between us hurts my heart.

Then Luca jumps out of bed and does what I wish I could have done first. He throws his clothes back on without looking at me. Feeling more than naked—wounded, bleeding, dying—I cover myself with the blanket. I can't let myself cry. I knew this would happen. He finally turns to me with a guilty look.

"Damn it, Carlotta, I was so stupid!"

Not exactly what I was hoping for. Of course, I didn't expect a proposal right then and there, but still. A little harsh.

"We did it without a condom. Do you get that?" He paces around the room, rubbing his hands together as if cold. "Do you understand what I'm saying? You don't need to worry about diseases, because I get checked regularly, and I've always been careful. And I'm sure that's not something I have to worry about with you."

I nod, head spinning. However reasonable his concerns are, they make me nauseous.

"And what about . . . Well, is this one of those times of the month where you're . . ."

"No, no, don't worry."

"I swear, Carlotta. I'm mortified."

"Luca, come on. I'm sure there's nothing to worry about."

"Yeah, I know. But . . . Fuck! That shouldn't have happened! It was a mistake. We were drinking, I felt sad, and sadness and alcohol don't mix well."

Please, Luca, just leave, I beg him silently. Don't say another word or I will shatter into a million pieces.

"Carlotta, I just . . . I'd better get back to my room, okay?" He watches me like a hawk. Perhaps he's concerned about me.

"Yeah, go ahead. It's fine. No diseases and no babies!" I smile and make a funny face, trying to act like myself so he can leave guilt-free. He stops in the middle of the room and bites his lip. We're so far apart, after being so close, and now I don't know where we stand. I hate him and love him at the same time.

"Luca, don't take this so seriously. Nothing will change! It was just sex! Good sex, but nothing more." Still wrapped in the blanket on the bed, I force myself to smile.

"I . . . Yeah, you're right. You know, I thought that—"

"I wanted something more? Why would you think that?"

"Because you're you. Because I care about you. Because we're friends, and—"

"It's fine. Go back to your room. I wouldn't get any sleep anyway, if you were here—I'm used to sleeping alone."

Nodding, he leaves without another word. The headlights wash over me. I grab my pillow and bury my head in it as the sobs let loose. Before long, my sobs synchronize with the road noise. I wish someone would honor my pain by drawing the curtain. But it's just me and this scratchy blanket. So I have to do it myself.

FOURTEEN

On the trip home, I feel like a beat-up old car that's just been shit on by a whole flock of birds. Luca and I don't look at each other, and we don't talk. Instead, we contemplate the billboards and road signs we pass. I imagine that the Arctic Circle is warmer than the inside of this car.

I can't deny that I feel sick about it. Luca obviously can't handle being next to someone he slept with for this long. He doesn't even stop for bathroom breaks. He is pensive, chewing on the inside of his cheek, and every once in a while he takes a deep breath. As soon as we get home, Luca runs off to the bar—three hours before his shift starts. We're back in the Cold War. We've constructed an invisible Berlin Wall.

Our avoidance behavior lasts for a few days; then, one afternoon, he comes home with the results of his HIV test. He triumphantly exclaims that it's negative. I can't even look at him, but as he waves it around like a flag, I realize that it doesn't make any sense to keep going like this. I have to deal with it. I know what he thinks about sleeping with me from what he said that night. It was a mistake, an oversight, a blunder. All because of alcohol.

"So that's why you haven't spoken to me in days," I whisper.

"Well, you weren't exactly talkative."

"You're right. The silence helped me reflect. I was really confused," I say. "But now I feel sure that it was a mistake. It won't happen again. And I can tell that you feel bad, or that you're worried you disappointed me, or something, but don't worry. I have no hard feelings or delusions. We're adults. So let's move on and not talk about this anymore, okay?"

He seems to try to read my mind with an intense look. Then he runs his fingers through his hair and clears his throat.

"All right. Let's move on. I was stupid. But you learn from your mistakes, and it won't happen again. You can be sure of that."

I force myself to smile even though it hurts my jaw. I'm going to fix this grin on my face and keep it there as he goes back to his life. I try to save my pride and dignity by pretending that I don't care and that I'm okay with just being friends.

Yet I feel even sadder than before. I can't tell Lara or Giovanna anything, because I already know what they'd say. They'd blame everything on Luca. How could I argue with that? I can't tell them that I wasn't being reckless, that I was in love, or that I'd do it a thousand times over—even knowing how it'd turn out. They'd book me for the next available appointment with the local shrink. Or maybe they'd cry with me. I don't know. But I don't want anger or compassion from them. I just want silence.

Fortunately, work gets me out of the apartment—searching for furniture for the set and trying desperately to track down the last doll in the collection, only to realize that it can't be found.

One day, I help Iriza paint the backdrop at the theater. We work like crazy, and before long we're covered in paint splatters. I don't feel much like talking. Physical effort, concentration, and the cacophony of Rocky's voice all do me good. Iriza tries to ask me if everything's okay, and I flash her a smile to let her know that it is. But while I'm painting the portrait of Laura's father—who abandoned his wife and children with no warning, only a terse note reading *good-bye*—my strength vanishes. Men are like that, in fiction and in real life. They take you, use you, deceive you just long enough for you to bear their children, and then they vanish. Your children turn out strange, and people look down on you because you couldn't keep your marriage going. And yet you still keep their picture hanging over the fireplace.

I never cry in public if I can help it, especially if said public includes a pain in the ass like Rocky, and I struggle to stop myself. The tears well up, but I refuse to let them win. I've cried enough.

"I'm going to smoke a cigarette," I say to Iriza.

"You smoke?" she says.

"No, but I can always start."

I head outside; it's cold and windy. Why is the weather always like this when I'm sad? Is this nature's way of expressing solidarity with me? Is nature depressed by the state of my heart? If the sun were shining, the birds chirping, and the flowers blooming, would I be able to see the world in anything else but black and white? I lean on a wall. Someone walks by, and I ask him for a cigarette. He offers me one mechanically and gives me a light, as if used to the question. As he walks away, I take a drag and, as expected, choke and sputter.

A hand gently beats me on the back. It's Iriza.

"What's wrong?" she asks.

"Remember my theory about Penelope and Circe?" I say.

She smiles and nods.

"I tried to be a little bit like Circe, and I guess it didn't work."

"Romantic troubles?"

I sigh. "All I can do is think about him, but at best, he just thinks of me as a big mistake."

Before Iriza can say anything, someone cuts her off. It's Rose. She grabs the cigarette from my hand and smokes gleefully.

"What's going on, girls? What's the scoop? Are we talking about boys?"

The question comes out of my mouth before I know why I'm asking it. "Have you ever fallen in love?"

For a moment, Rose looks exactly like what she is: an old woman with heavy baggage that includes memories and the fear of death. She takes a long drag on the cigarette, which wrinkles her face like an accordion, and then speaks as the smoke filters through her nose and mouth.

"Yes, once. I was the costume designer for a big theater in Bari, and there was this beautiful actor who was Iago in *Othello*. He played the part of the traitor so perfectly. By the time I realized he wasn't performing at all, it was too late."

"Did he betray you?"

"He said all the things he had to say to get me into bed. Do yourselves a favor, ladies. Don't trust guys like Iago. Don't fall in love with them."

"Don't you have any good memories of him left?"

"Oh, sure. Rocky, my grandson."

She throws the cigarette on the ground and crushes it with the tip of an orthopedic shoe before heading back inside. Iriza and I don't say anything for a while. Maybe love is good to some people, but how many? And how long does that happiness last? Apparently for me, just long enough to have the best sex of my life. Love is destined to leave wounds and scars.

"Franz is going to ask you out," Iriza suddenly says, interrupting my thoughts.

"What?"

"He's not an Iago, trust me."

"Ask me out? What do you mean?"

"I told you that he likes you, didn't I?"

"But . . . but . . ."

I'm speechless. Iriza's smile seems totally natural, and I wonder if I was mistaken about her feelings for Franz. In any case, I don't want to be with him. Not just for me, and not just for Iriza, but also for Franz. Because my heart belongs to another.

"I'm absolutely sure that you're wrong," I say. "But if you're right, I hope he doesn't. I can't deal with it right now. I hope he asks out some other girl who is more deserving of him than I am."

"I hope he does, and I hope you say yes."

"Are you serious? I'm not the right woman for him!"

Iriza smiles slightly and shakes her head, her long red hair swaying. The freckles on her cheeks look like poppy seeds. "I know that, but he needs to figure it out for himself."

"So you want him to find out the hard way?"

"Yeah, something like that. You guys would have fun, but he'd understand that you're not a good match. There's nothing worse than fighting for a love that never has the chance to blossom. We tend to idealize the people who never get the opportunity to disappoint us. So if he asks you out, I hope you say yes. You have my blessing."

If I could close my eyes and press a reset button on my heart, banishing Luca to make room for Franz, I would be the happiest person in the world. But I just can't do it. There's another reason, apart from my feelings. While my period is usually very punctual, I seem to have missed it this month. When Luca asked me after we slept together if I was ovulating, I said no, but I lied. I lied on purpose. I wasn't ready to face the facts.

The pregnancy test I bought is still in my purse. I don't know why I haven't used it yet. Maybe it's because I'm not ready to find out. I know I should hope that this test comes out negative and thank my lucky stars if it does. Any normal woman in my position would—I'm almost thirty, my job pays me peanuts, I'm single, I slept with someone who took off exactly six minutes after he finished and has barely said one word to me since. But there must be something crazy in my DNA. The thought that new life might be growing inside me intoxicates me in a weird way. I wonder if it's maternal instinct or fear that this is my last batch of eggs before I hit menopause. Or just that I might be carrying

Luca's child. Ah, yes. Luca hates me, and I'm secretly hoping to have his baby. I'm insane.

Emma's birthday party is today. Giovanna said she couldn't come because of work, but I suspect she invented an excuse. Some people are afraid of spiders, snakes, or vacuum cleaners, but Giovanna—a very brave and determined woman—is terrified of little brats, especially in large numbers.

When I get to Lara's house, I'm greeted by a band of tiny scream-ing humans running amok; I instantly have chocolate stains all over my skirt. Emma hugs me, forcing me to stoop down to her height (which, to be honest, isn't that much lower than mine). She's thrilled with my present, a new book of fables and a makeup bag with raspberry lip gloss inside. I help Lara mind the little guests and keep them from launching cake into the walls with paper towel slings. Amid the chaos, I listen to Lara complain about how cruel her former husband is.

"He didn't even call to wish her a happy birthday!" she says in front of the other mothers, who listen enthusiastically. "He's probably in bed with some new perky-boobed whore. What a bastard."

"All men are. No exceptions," says one mother. She's a wiry woman with a stern face and hair the color of egg yolks. "After eight years of marriage, my ex decided that he prefers Brazilian asses! So why did he marry me? I've never had a Brazilian ass!"

"It's not about your ass," another mother says. She's petite and looks like a gnome. "It's the opposites theory. If you're tall, your hus-band will screw someone short. If you're a D cup, he'll find someone flat-chested. If you're a housewife, he'll worship a career woman. Men always want the exact opposite of what they have—so they can always say you weren't fulfilling their expectations."

"If you think that's the worst, then you've gotta listen to me," another woman says, sounding like she's dying to spill her juicy secret.

"After we were engaged for three years, lived together for two, and married for four, my husband suddenly discovered that he prefers men!"

I wonder if Lara only invited grumbling ex-wives who have been abandoned by scoundrels. I listen as they share horror stories of loneliness, one-night stands, and children who still wet the bed, imagining myself as a single mother of twin boys—with the hair on my legs starting to curl because I haven't had time to shave. Shit, I'm screwed. I'll have to quit my job, or worse, entrust my mother with my children. If it's a girl, my mother will make sure she's a tramp; if it's a boy, she'll turn him into a womanizer. My stomach will be forever soft, and I'll no longer be able to bend over to tie my shoes.

It's hopeless.

I get up, head spinning. It's time to end this torture. I grab my purse from its child-safe place on top of the fridge. Then I lock myself in the bathroom and pull out the device. This plastic blue-and-white wand will tell me if I'll be able to shave my legs or not for the next few years. I follow the directions. There isn't anything about how to tear your hair out if you don't get the response you want. Three minutes pass—I read the clear writing that has materialized like invisible ink. *Not pregnant.*

No tiny human in my belly. I don't know what to feel. Relief? Pain? I sit down on the toilet. Lara knocks on the door.

"Are you okay, Carlotta? You've been in there a long time! Did you fall in?"

I shove the test in my purse and go out, no longer in the mood to listen to the complaints of the mothers in the living room. I can understand the discomfort of living without a partner, but not the woes of raising children. I must look even weirder than usual, because Lara looks at me apprehensively. I smile. Life is good. I'm not pregnant. My stomach will stay flat. I won't have to anoint my stretch marks with oil, I won't have to buy underwear specially made for hippos, and I won't have to pee seven times a minute. It's all good. I feel free.

I stay a little longer. As Emma chases after a teasing boy, I'm almost tempted to pull her aside and tell her that men shouldn't be pursued. At least not so openly. You can suffer at the thought of losing them; you can wish for a one-night stand to get you pregnant; you can wear a groove into the floor as you pace, waiting for them to return; you can smell sweaters left behind on chairs; but you shouldn't chase them . . . You must be humble and disciplined. Take me, for example. I pretend to be strong, even though I've been thrown away like a used condom. I'm a real woman. I don't chase men.

I say good-bye to everyone and leave. It's a long journey home without a car, but the evening is mild. I'm wearing a cotton beret, a lightweight coat, a dress, and ankle boots . . . and I'm not pregnant. I must celebrate.

I enter the first bar I see—since I don't have any children to take care of at home, I can drink as much as I want. It's small and smoky inside, and most of the patrons have six piercings each and tank tops that emphasize their bodybuilder biceps. The few women here, gathered around the pool tables, are wearing shorts and studded vests. But I don't really care.

I order a drink from the bartender, who has very bushy eyebrows that I worry will fall off. A guy comes up to me while I'm nursing my drink. He has the leathery appearance of an old oak tree, and the inscription on his T-shirt is the antithesis of style: *I'm not a dick, but I can put one in you.* Impressive wordplay. He gives me a compliment, and then asks me what a girl like me is doing in a place like this. So I tell him the truth. I tell him that I'm celebrating the fact that I'm not pregnant. I tell him that the man I love slept with me a few nights ago, but now he hates me. I tell him that I don't really care what happens to me after I leave this bar. And I cry as I pour my heart out to him, a total stranger. When I'm finished, he looks at me right in the eye and gives me one piece of advice.

"Baby, that guy is not for you. You need to get rid of him, otherwise you'll be imprisoned forever."

I don't doubt that the biker prophet's advice has two meanings—the second being that he wouldn't mind taking Luca's place—but his advice resonates with me all the same. I grab a bus home, my breath reeking of gin and my head spinning. I'll sleep a little before I make a decision about Luca. But when I get home, I realize that sleep will have to wait.

Luca is home, and he's not alone. His coat and a woman's dress are strewn on the floor. I freeze, hearing voices from his room. What the fuck? Is he actually having sex? When I was this close to being the mother of his twin boys? I'm going to kill him. I try to count to ten, but I only get to three.

I fling his bedroom door open. He's lying on his back and she's lying on her side. They seem to be talking. He's granted her the luxury of conversation! My entrance startles both of them. The girl jumps out of bed immediately, stunned, but it takes Luca a moment to register what's going on, probably because he's still dulled from the languor of sex. Then he covers himself up—although I don't know why. Both women here have seen everything there is to see.

I take this moment to exclaim, "I just wanted to let you know that I'm not pregnant."

I leave the door open on purpose as I leave. Luca springs up, yanks on his boxers, and strides out to intercept me, disheveled and furious in a way that frightens me. The girl comes out, too, even though she's naked, covering her breasts with her hands.

"Carlotta! What are you talking about? Have you been drinking?" he asks me.

"Maybe, but that's none of your business. The real question is: Who the fuck is that?"

He gives me a disdainful look. "None of your business, either. I don't need your permission."

"Oh yes you do!" I shout. "I'm sick of the women you bring here, and I'm sick of sharing my apartment! You need to leave. Not tomorrow. Now. Get your stuff and your condom collection, and get out of my sight."

"You don't have to tell me twice!" He's shouting, too. "Do you think I enjoy living with a lunatic? You know what? You need a brain scan! One day you're all, like, 'sleep with whoever you want, it's not like we're dating, we're adults,' and now it's the opposite? What are you, some kind of schizo? Are you expecting a marriage proposal just because we slept together once?"

"Marriage? I'd rather go back to Tony. Do you really think I've spent the last few nights thinking only about Luca's tight little ass? Let me tell you something, my dear. You were nothing memorable!"

He laughs loudly. "Says the woman who's as frigid as an icicle! I really think that the other night was the first orgasm you've ever had." He's never been this cruel.

"This conversation is over," I declare. "Luca, I want you to go."

"You're damn right I'm going! I'm sick of you. You know what? You were terrible in bed. You were the worst sex I've ever had."

I think my vocal cords have imploded—I can't speak. Luca balls up his fists, staring at me. The girl snatches up her dress from the floor and disappears into the bathroom. I don't add anything else to this deafening, final silence and make my way to my room. My legs feel funny. I have to hug the door to keep from falling.

I lock myself inside and stand there, the doorknob pressing into my back, for what seems like forever. I listen to every single noise outside. Luca gets dressed, violently opens his closet, and throws his stuff into a bag. Then I hear the door slam.

He's gone. That's it. Now it's too late. I lose my balance and slump to the floor like a withered flower. I feel so awful that I can't even manage to cry.

FIFTEEN

Here I am, as charming as a chipped urinal, with bags under my eyes as dark as ripe eggplants. I've been cooped up for a week, and the tears still haven't dried up. I've eaten all the pitted olives and capers in the pantry. I've been sleeping in his room. I've kept the windows closed to trap his scent in here. Since Luca left, my mind has abandoned me. I don't even know what day it is. I have been wallowing.

Every time the phone rings, I hope it's him—but it never is. My mother called to ask if I prefer natural or synthetic diamonds, probably the worst phone call I could get from her right now. Lara called, concerned because she saw the empty pregnancy test box in her bathroom wastebasket. And Franz has called several times to find out how I'm doing and to urge me to come back to work. I've invented a thousand excuses to explain my absence. Opening night is approaching and being gone is unforgivable, but I just can't get up from the couch. A lot of people have called, but Luca is not one of them.

I should feel proud. I should take a shower, shave, and return to my normal life. But I succumb to humiliation. I was the worst sex he's ever had . . . I crawl to the toilet and vomit. As I'm rinsing my face, I hear the intercom buzz. It's Giovanna, but I don't want to see her. I pretend to be my housekeeper—not that I have one—and try to tell her I'm not at home.

But Giovanna laughs. "If you don't let me up right this second, I'm calling a shrink to come throw you in the loony bin."

As always, her strength prevails over my weakness. So I open the door. She's not alone. She's brought Bear! He jumps into my arms, and I topple over, overwhelmed by a mountain of fur and tongue. Giovanna pulls him away, and I see what Bear was really trying to get at: an empty bag of cheese crunchies stuck to my pants.

"Carlotta, what is going on?" Giovanna says. "You have every right to be upset, but there are ways of coping with it! Letting yourself turn into a heap of manure isn't doing anybody any good."

Bear goes wild over a tiny morsel on the floor that escaped my emotional binge-eating.

"How do I cope?" I throw myself down on the couch. "Should I set up a trap to catch him and bring him back? Please tell me how. The way I see it, the only satisfactory solution is to sit here until I shrivel and die like a . . . like a pistachio."

"Do you realize that you're on the brink of insanity?" Giovanna smiles at me as she scrutinizes me in all my postbreakup glory. She bends down next to my sprawled body and pats my leg. "I mean, do you even know what you're talking about? If you don't want to keep the baby, there's another way to go about it."

"Baby? What baby?" My mental state is so jumbled that I can't follow her argument.

"The baby, Carlotta! Wasn't that your pregnancy test that Lara found in the bathroom?"

"Oh, yeah, I get it now. The twins . . ." My face falls at the memory of the poor imaginary babies.

"What? Twins?" She sits down on the couch. A bag of potato chips, which I inflated and taped shut after consuming all the contents, pops underneath her. She jumps up, curses, and throws it in the trash before Bear can eat that, too.

"The children aren't here anymore. Don't worry."

"You already had an abortion?" This seems to upset her. Perhaps she was hoping to convince me to keep them.

"I mean that there never were any children. I'm not pregnant. I wasn't pregnant, and I never will be."

"I see," she says tenderly. "Do you know who would have been the father of these twins? Was it Tony? I know you aren't seeing him anymore, but he didn't tell me why."

"Better to respect his privacy," I whisper. "The almost-father of my children was Luca."

"What?" Giovanna's disbelief is truly flattering, really. "You and Luca slept together?"

"Yes." I don't want to think about it right now. I've replayed it in my head about three thousand six hundred times in the last few days. I'm entitled to a break every now and then. "Are you shocked because you don't understand how he could have possibly wanted to sleep with me?"

"No, silly. To be honest, I'm shocked that it hadn't happened before. I knew you would make the mistake of ignoring our advice—I've made plenty of mistakes, too, but you're different from me. You feel every emotion so intensely. I was worried. But now I can tell you what I think. Luca isn't Prince Charming. You deserve someone who has the courage to stay."

"We just couldn't agree on the timing . . ." I mumble. "He wanted once, I wanted forever. I wanted to *make love* forever. For me, it was never just sex. But it doesn't matter. I'm fine. He left with a girl with a great rack, but I'm fine."

"I can tell. You stink, your apartment is a mess, and your beautiful curls have turned into a bramble of thorns. And besides . . ." She pauses, clearly mulling something over. I gather from her tone that I'm not going to like it. Well, the time is right for the final blow. Just grab the fucking knife and stab me in the back already. "I didn't tell you that I saw him out with your sister."

"What?" I shoot up from the sofa like a bullet. "Erika? When?"

"I happened to see them at the bar where Luca works, and they left together. And once I saw them out on the street in the afternoon. I didn't want to tell you because I didn't want to hurt you."

"Hurt me? What? No, I'm thrilled!" I cry out, dancing around the room like a witch around a cauldron. I look down at the debris-littered carpet. Something buzzes inside me, some kind of alarm. Luca and Erika. I believed he was in love with Paola, and then I discovered she was his sister. So who was he talking about that day at the park? Could that unexpected love affair really be with Erika? I suddenly feel cold, and I know I'm about to throw up again.

I run to the bathroom and look in the mirror. I tell myself that I have to stop. I can't go on living in the dark, breathing the smell of his sheets. I'm not fifteen anymore. I'm not a teenager suffering from her first heartbreak. Well, that's not entirely true—this is my first heartbreak, but I'm an adult. I have to snap out of it. Life goes on, even without Luca. A man who, while claiming to care about me, treated me like crap. I admit that I couldn't expect him to love me, but he should have at least respected me. I can't let him win by letting myself disintegrate like this. I let the water run in the shower while I listen to Giovanna collect the rubble of my week of seclusion. Bear pesters her, trying to snatch residual crumbs. She yells a command at him in German that she learned from obedience school, but Bear must not speak German, because I hear him continue his search. I wash myself and shave. I feel human again.

Once I'm out of the shower, I see two new things in my living room. The first is my apartment itself. It's not clean, but it's clear of any remains of my squashed leftover snacks. The second is Franz. He's chatting with Giovanna as I emerge from the bathroom with my bathrobe untied. Bear sniffs insistently at his shoes. Jesus, she could have warned me! I cover myself up and glare at her, but she just winks.

"I'm leaving before this dog eats anything else," she says. "You're in good hands now."

"How are you?" Franz asks eagerly. She leaves us alone together, and as we sit on the sofa with our knees touching, I unexpectedly end up telling him everything.

Franz is so reassuring. Talking to him feels like a hot stone massage and a paraffin wax bath . . . But I feel nothing romantic. Why couldn't it be like this with Luca? Why did it feel like a tsunami hit me when I saw him in the doorway that summer day?

As I talk, Franz listens to me attentively. He even tells me some things about himself. "This last year has been painful for me, too," he says. "I separated from my wife. She went back to Germany and took our daughter with her. I really miss my little Annika."

We commiserate together. Franz is sweet. His eyes are heavenly, and he hides a tragic love story behind a never-ending smile. Then a noise startles us—the door flying open. It's my mother. I groan. She's probably delighted to find me half-naked and entertaining yet another young man. But didn't she give me back the key? I bet she has a drawer in her house with thirty copies of it. I'm going to have to change the lock.

"My darling!" she exclaims, waddling into the living room on a pair of sky-high stilettos. "I've been calling you for days! I thought you were dead. Ugh, what is that smell? Do you have a dead body in the closet? And what did you do to your hair? You look like a porcupine!"

"I'm alive, Mom . . . And didn't you know that corpse-scented fragrance is the new trend?"

I'm forced to introduce her to Franz. She shakes his hand and sizes him up. Franz, being the compassionate, sensitive person that he is, senses my embarrassment and leaves soon after. My mother doesn't even give him time to reach the ground floor before she starts.

"I preferred the first guy. Now *he* was a man. This guy's handsome, but he's not as macho."

"Don't you think that might be a good thing?"

"No! What nonsense," she exclaims, as if I had said something truly ridiculous. "Who wants to sleep with nice guys? Macho men are better in bed."

"I'd rather talk about something else. Can I ask what you're doing here?"

"I came to tell you about your birthday party. I've already invited all the relatives, and even that insipid little woman who's always clinging to your father."

"Coretta's nice."

"What kind of a name is Coretta, anyway?"

"I told you, I don't want a party," I say. "After last year's fiasco with the drunk ukulele player who started tap dancing on the piano, I don't trust your event-planning abilities. So prepare to have the party without the guest of honor, because I'm not coming. This is the last time I'm going to tell you that."

"So dramatic! Although I admit, you don't have all that much to celebrate," she says, chuckling. "After all, you're getting older, you don't have a husband, not to mention children, and your job is so absurd that I don't know how to explain it to my friends. But letting yourself go is just giving you wrinkles. Have you tried that new snail slime cream? They say it works miracles."

"You can give it to me at the birthday party that I'd rather die than attend. Now please go."

"You are ungrateful and rude," she says. "I'd better leave, otherwise I might get wrinkles."

"As far as I know, they're not contagious. But I do appreciate that you're leaving."

I'm almost tempted to ask about Erika as she's leaving, to try to uncover some trace of Luca in her answer, but I refrain. After all, if she knew something, she would overwhelm me with the news.

Once she's gone, I finally look around and register my defeat. Luca isn't coming back. I have to live without him. I have to bury him at the bottom of a drawer. I have to turn him into a memory, like Rose did with her Iago. But first, I have to find a way to kill him—figuratively, of course. A crazy idea hits me. I pull out paints and brushes from the closet. I go into Luca's room and climb onto the bed. The wall behind his headboard is large, smooth, and white. A perfect canvas.

I take off my robe and paint, working for hours in a flurry of brushes, hands, and anger. By the time I finish, it's almost nighttime, and I'm sweaty, dirty, and cold. It's as if all the anger has escaped from my heart and converted itself into a frenzy of creativity. I've captured my feelings in this wild picture and imprisoned them in the strong colors that saturate the wall. I hope Caravaggio won't hold it against me, but I've made my own version of *Judith Beheading Holofernes*. My Judith has curly hair, blue jeans, and two burning eyes. My Holofernes, a Luca look-alike, has one green eye and one black eye. He's sprawled on a bed, a sword impaling his chest. I don't really want him to die, of course. I just want him out of my life. It doesn't mean that I'm cured, but at least I'm trying.

Finally, I celebrate one last act of revolt. I crumple up his sheets in my arms and take them to the washing machine. Bye-bye, Luca Morli. There you go, in with the foam. I watch through the glass door as he churns and spins around. I think that I've just begun a new journey— one that will enable me one day to think of Luca without rancor.

SIXTEEN

I'm finally back at work. Being near Franz's calming presence gives me relief. Iriza doesn't seem to be bothered by our friendship. If she doesn't have a problem with it, then I don't see why I should hold back.

The set is really starting to come to life as rehearsals proceed. I often find myself helping out with the rehearsals, and despite the updates, the work still enchants me. Laura's character makes me feel nothing but tenderness. Every time I watch the scene where Jim, after seducing Laura, reveals that he's actually engaged, I am caught by surprise.

Time passes, but not quickly. Every morning I cross another day off the calendar, hoping that it's the day I will finally be freed from memories of Luca. I'll get there, whatever it takes. It doesn't matter that seeing the type of car he drives or a guy who looks like him paralyzes me. Just like it doesn't matter that *Star Wars* movie nights are painful for me because I have to hear the name Luke Skywalker. I can't let such trivial things demolish my willpower. I have to focus on what's important. Namely, that opening night is approaching, and I still haven't found the last Barbie doll, one that is as sought-after as someone on the FBI's most-wanted list.

As I sit down in the back row of the theater one day, Franz comes over to me.

"I may have some good news," he whispers in my ear.

"Has Rocky come down with laryngitis?"

"Even better. I found someone who might have the last Barbie we need."

"Are you serious?"

"Yeah, I did some thorough Internet research. You've been so sad, so I thought I'd try to at least solve this problem."

"How?"

"I found a forum for collectors of rare items. They were talking about an old man who lives in Pesaro who might have this legendary doll."

"He might? But is he selling it?"

"I don't know. He might not even exist. But we've got nothing to lose. What do you say, should we go?"

"Go where?"

"We're going to Pesaro! I'll take you. Are you free Sunday?"

I wonder if this is him asking me out, just like Iriza thought. But I don't think so. At least I hope not. So I nod. "I'm free on Sunday. Let's go."

I know I have to stop comparing everything and everyone to Luca, but I can't help but think that traveling with Franz is very different from traveling with Luca. Franz drives a really nice car that has air-conditioning, a fancy stereo, and comfortable seats.

He's polite and considerate. Every so often he asks me how I'm doing or if I need anything. The trip takes just over three hours, and we talk, listen to music, or sit in comfortable silence. Shortly after we pull off for lunch at a roadside travel stop, we come across a vendor selling strawberries. They're not the usual strawberries grown in greenhouses;

they're wild, small, and extra juicy. Franz buys a basket for each of us, and we eat them next to a fountain overlooking the sea.

Finally, we reach the mysterious doll owner's home. It's a charming stone house in a suburb near the hills, situated in the middle of a garden of sunflowers. But the house seems uninhabited. Everything is closed up and the shutters are drawn despite the afternoon sun. We knock, but no one answers, so we sit down on a bench next to the door.

"It doesn't seem like anyone lives here. Maybe he moved," Franz says regretfully.

"Maybe he doesn't even exist. Maybe he's just folklore, like the Loch Ness monster or UFOs."

"It's a real shame. That Barbie is so much rarer than I thought."

"'Rare' doesn't even begin to describe it. It's the very first Barbie doll ever released. Those dolls cast a spell on girls everywhere that's lasted over half a century."

We're silent for a moment. "In any case, it was a fun trip," Franz adds.

"It was a great trip. I haven't been that relaxed in . . . Well, I don't think I've ever been that relaxed!"

"Not even on vacation?"

"On family vacations when I was younger, we'd only ever spend time with hordes of relatives who would constantly talk over one another. And my mother would yell at me every five seconds."

"Was your mother really strict?"

"*Strict* isn't the right word. She was never obsessed with etiquette or manners; she thinks very differently from most mothers. She wanted me to be so much more . . . Hollywood . . . than I am. But she got her second chance with my sister."

"Hollywood?"

"Yeah, you know," I say, "she wanted me to compete in beauty pageants and always dress in the latest fashion so the other girls my age and their mothers would be jealous. She hoped I'd either land a job that was simple enough to explain to her friends or snag a wealthy husband instead and not have to work at all. I'm sure she never planned for me to be here at twenty-nine. Once you're past twenty-nine, you're automatically lumped into the 'hopeless' category."

"How very old-fashioned."

"Yeah, in some ways. Luckily, I had my dad to fill in the gaps. It just goes to show that you don't have to be a woman to be maternal. But that's enough about me. What were you like as a child? A blue-eyed prince waiting for his crown?"

Franz laughs and shakes his head. "No, I was a real terror as a child. I didn't become a prince until I grew up."

Now it's my turn to laugh. It's a beautiful day. The wind in the sunflowers is hypnotic. A bee buzzes around my face . . . and flies right into my hair. My curls trap it tight, and I hear it buzz desperately. Of course—classic Carlotta! This beautiful moment was too good to be true. I'm allergic to bees. If I get stung, I'll turn into an elephant woman and die right here. Franz will have to bury me among the sunflowers. (Although I suppose that wouldn't be too terrible.)

But Franz comes to my rescue. "Stay still," he tells me, and I trust him. I close my eyes and feel his fingers in my hair. The bee buzzes off. But Franz's hand doesn't leave my face; instead, he slides it down onto my cheek. I open my eyes; his face is right in front of mine. With those turquoise eyes, he really does resemble some kind of Germanic god. He clearly wants to kiss me. *Okay, let's do it*, I think. I don't care about Iriza, and I don't care about Luca. Plus, this guy's not half-bad. He smells good, and he looks like a good kisser. Do it, Carlotta! What are you waiting for?

Right as our lips are about to touch, the door of the house swings open. Franz and I jump apart. An elderly gentleman frowns at us.

"Come inside," he says.

For a moment, I feel like I'm in a horror movie. I can only hope Leatherface isn't hiding in here. But we soon discover that the man who stopped our kiss is precisely the man we were looking for. His skin is sunburnt, and his eyes are gray like slate. The interior of the house must have been beautiful once, but now it looks abandoned and so dusty that you could write out an entire Homer poem on the furniture with your finger. The man doesn't say anything, but he beckons us to follow him into another room.

Franz and I look at each other, puzzled. He doesn't look dangerous. I don't think he's concealing any weapons, and I'm sure Franz could take him out in a heartbeat if he ends up being a psychopath. When he opens the door, my heart stops. It's a little girl's room. It's neat, clean, and a little bit old-fashioned. It looks like something out of a TV show from the '80s. The entire room is pink, from the bedspread to the chandelier to the cabinet doors. And it's a shrine to Barbie's world. Barbie accessories are everywhere—on the shelves, the bedside table, the floor, the desk . . . Barbie's house, Barbie's horse, Barbie's dog, dozens of Barbie's dresses hanging on a tiny rack. There's even a Barbie tea parlor and a Barbie bathtub with soap bubbles. The Barbie dolls lying around don't seem to be particularly rare, and they've obviously been played with quite a bit.

Then, there, on the bed, I see the one I'm looking for. That mythical chimera. The first Barbie doll, in perfect condition, as if just removed from her box. She's sitting on a cushion, looking at us with eyes that I'm sure are the gateway to many secrets. This whole thing is just too much. I am afraid to touch her, for fear of breaking her.

"She loved that doll," the old man whispers to me. "She played with it like it was made of glass. She treated it with respect."

He ends up telling us the story behind all of this. Thirty years ago, his granddaughter was thirteen. She was developmentally delayed. While her body aged, her desires and faculties remained anchored at that age of innocence. Desperate and unprepared, her parents wanted to send her to a facility, but her grandfather insisted that she live with him. He cared for her here and made sure she was comfortable and happy.

Her life was filled with pure air, unconditional love, and a magical world of castles, stables, fancy cars, princess dresses, and dreams.

Years later, the girl became very ill, and the doctors said there was no hope. Her grandfather wanted to fulfill her greatest wish: to own the original Barbie doll. He bought a computer, hooked it up to the Internet, and finally tracked down a French collector who had this special doll. He sold all of the land he owned, except for the plot where he currently lives, to buy that doll. His granddaughter died a year later. It's the saddest story I've ever heard. I realize I've been crying silently while he talks. He reminds me of my father, which makes me cry even harder.

"Excuse me," I say, wiping away my tears.

"It's fine," he replies. "I heard what you said outside. You said something that struck me: 'You don't have to be a woman to be maternal.' I agree with that. And I know that Laura would have, too."

I can't believe what I just heard. His granddaughter's name was Laura, just like the protagonist in our production! I tell him this, as well as why we're really here.

"You can take it," he murmurs. "It's a gift. Provided that you take good care of her. I get the feeling that you understand, that your father must have been there when your mother wasn't."

Do I understand? Do I ever. I want to ask him to come back with us so he doesn't have to stay here alone while the dust gathers in all the rooms except this one. But I don't say anything, because I also know that you can't change the past. So we leave him there, in front of his house surrounded by sunflowers, waving good-bye.

It's now evening, and we've returned from our trip. I cradled the Barbie doll in my arms the entire ride back, alternately crying and napping. Franz must not think I'm a ray of sunshine after this. But there are more clouds inside my mind than I let on.

"I decided something," he tells me as he pulls up in front of my apartment. "I want to dedicate the show to that man's granddaughter. I'll write it on the playbill. What do you think?"

"That's a wonderful idea."

"I'll even reserve a front-row seat for him. I'll send him an invitation to come to Rome at our expense. But I don't think he'll come."

"I don't think so, either," I say. "But he'll hold onto it, and he'll tell Laura everything when they finally meet again."

Franz smiles gently. "Before, when he opened the door, we——"

"Yeah," I interrupt—we both know what we're talking about. The almost-kiss. "Maybe it just wasn't the right time yet," I whisper. "That's okay."

"So there will be a right time?"

"Maybe. I don't know." I smile sincerely.

"Do you want me to come in with you and make sure there's no bad guys hiding in your apartment?"

"Thanks, but no need. The bad guys know there's nothing to steal at my place."

"As you wish. Get some sleep. I'll see you at the theater."

He leans toward me and kisses me on the cheek. He waits for me to open the door before he drives off. A perfect gentleman. I climb the stairs tiredly. My eyes are puffy, and my heart is heavy from all the emotions of this strange day. I open the door and go inside. And then terror paralyzes me. I should have listened to Franz.

The hall light is on, and I know for sure it was off when I left this morning. Noises come from Luca's room. And then Luca himself appears in the doorway with his laptop under his arm. He's wearing jeans, a leather jacket, and Doc Martens with no laces. His hair is a little longer, and he's grown some facial hair. His expression is, simply put, hostile. I suddenly feel like a drug addict who's fallen off the wagon. How do you kill love? If there's a way, would someone just tell me what it is? Seeing him again is enough to make me feel like I'm finally able to breathe after holding my breath for so long.

"Beautiful fresco," he says venomously, alluding to my painting on the wall of what used to be his room. "It speaks volumes about what you think of me and of us. Better than a thousand words."

Anger bubbles up out of me. "What are you doing here?" I ask him, completely ignoring his words about the painting. It's my home, and I can paint whatever the hell I like.

"I came to get my laptop. I forgot it here. I buzzed the intercom, but you weren't here. Were you out for a walk?"

"I can go wherever I damn well please. Give me the keys."

Luca giggles and takes a few steps toward me. His boots squeak on the ceramic tile. I step back without knowing why.

"I saw you with the blond guy. Are you fucking him?"

I hate it when he's this crass, so I decide to fire back. "Do you have everything? I hope so, because I'm having the locks changed. If you try to come back, I'll call the cops."

In response, he takes a few more steps toward me. I'm basically trapped between him and the wall. Only Barbie is between us, still cradled in my arms.

"Are you sleeping with him?" Luca asks again. I feel strange, kind of like hot liquid wax. We are so close to each other that anyone observing us would think we were full of love, not hatred and resentment. I shove him back and walk away with force.

"Go away," I order him, shocked at how firm I sound. He shakes his head and scoffs, then runs a hand through his hair and pulls his keys from his pocket. He drops them on the counter dismissively and leaves, slamming the door so hard the walls shake.

I lock the door and pull the latch. I realize that I'm trembling. I slide to the ground and curl up in the fetal position. I hope I never have to see Luca again. I don't ask for much, so I'm asking for just this one little thing: that our paths divide so I can get back to my old self. I need to be the old Carlotta again. I don't know how much longer I can stand to be this weepy mess.

SEVENTEEN

Franz and I haven't had a chance to talk privately over the last few days, which is good, because I wouldn't know what to say to him. In my opinion, the interruption of our kiss was providential. The cosmic forces do not want us to be together. And neither do I. I'm sure Iriza doesn't either, although she continues to pretend that it doesn't bother her. She asks about our trip and merely shrugs when I tell her everything, including the almost-kiss.

"You're not mad?" I ask, surprised. "At me or him? You don't want to run me over with a tank engine?"

Iriza gives me a sad smile and a logical answer. "First of all, you didn't actually kiss. Second, it's not like he and I are even together. Besides, you can't make somebody love you."

"I know, but—"

"I can't pretend that I don't wish I were you. I can only hope that Franz develops feelings for me over time. But trying to force my life to go a certain way, just because I want it to . . . That's ridiculous. Whatever happens, happens. It's all up to destiny. Life has taught me that there are things you just have to learn to accept, and that makes you a better person."

I don't see any resignation in her eyes. Instead, she's warrior-like in her seemingly cold wisdom. I admire her. "You're right. But please know that nothing will ever happen between me and Franz. You can at least consider that obstacle circumvented."

Between conversations here and hard work there, the show finally arrives. On opening night, the theater is full, a turnout I didn't expect. Lara and Giovanna are here, along with Giovanna's new boyfriend, Roberto, who she says hasn't made a move on her yet. She thinks it's out of respect; I think he's gay.

The dolls are proudly displayed in a glass case. The actors are so pale in their makeup and costumes that they look like ghosts. Rocky is wearing his usual scarf and seven layers of black eyeliner. Rose attempts her usual ass-grab as Franz passes by and, as usual, he expertly scoots out of the way just in time. Nothing new here. I've grown fond of this madhouse. I'm afraid that I will miss it when it's all over.

During the show, the audience is attentive and interested. Apparently, they appreciate Rocky's update. I wander around backstage, listening to the lines that I've heard so many times that I know them by heart.

However, I sense something strange going on during intermission. Despite how smoothly everything is running, Rocky seems nervous. I have no intention of asking him what's wrong, so I try to avoid him by slipping into the dressing rooms and stumble on something quite unexpected. Romina, the actress who plays Laura, is in tears in one of the rooms while Rose attempts to console her. A young woman from the costume department is with them, and she obeys Rose like a soldier when she commands her to find Rocky. She returns with him moments later. I don't mean to eavesdrop at the door, but once you start, it's impossible to stop. Rose, who's usually so protective of Rocky, lashes out at him with bitterness I've never heard—as if he were the Big Bad Wolf just caught trying to devour Little Red Riding Hood.

"You will take responsibility for this, I swear to God," she says. "You will not abandon this girl and leave her to a life of ridicule. You will marry her, and our family will finally have a legitimate son after all these years. That's how it's going to be—I've decided."

Rocky tries to stammer out a protest, but his attempts are futile. Romina groans and yanks open the door. She doesn't even notice me standing outside as she rushes to the bathroom with a hand over her mouth. I hear her throwing up into the toilet. I guess Rocky knocked her up. I'm surprised that his swimmers were able to procreate, and I'm even more surprised that he's capable of making love to a woman. I've called Rocky a lot of names, but bastard hasn't been one of them—I really didn't believe he was the type of director who would take advantage of his actresses . . . Now I understand why Romina has gained weight! And the asshole had the nerve to admonish her for it in front of everyone.

Now the poor girl is crying her eyes out in the bathroom. I feel compelled to comfort her. After all, I just had a pregnancy scare myself, and I didn't have a grandmother like Rose forcing me to marry the villain of my story.

"I'm so nauseous," Romina murmurs, gripping the toilet bowl like a life raft on the open ocean. "I tried to hold it in during the first act, but I can't do it anymore."

"You can't do what?" I ask, vaguely alarmed.

"The rest of the show! I can't puke onstage."

"Of course you can't, but what can we do?" I'm asking myself more than her. "We don't have an understudy. We'll have to stop the show."

"Poor, darling man," Romina mumbles between dry heaves. "He's worked so hard on this."

It takes me a few moments to realize that the poor, darling man in question is Rocky. It's very difficult to imagine him as sweet and precious. Love is truly a mystery.

Rose comes into the bathroom, followed by Rocky, face contorted into a pout that resembles a chicken's backside.

"Don't worry, dear," she says, "Carlotta will step in for you."

Who is Carlotta? I wonder. Then it hits me. She means *me*.

"You've got to be fucking kidding me!" Rocky and I both yell simultaneously, me like Tarzan standing off with a group of poachers.

"There's no other way," Rose says. "Otherwise, we'd have to suspend the show and refund everyone's tickets. You know the lines by heart, my dear, and with all this makeup, no one will notice that you're a different actress."

"They'll notice, all right!" I shout. "I'm not an actress. What about my hair? Romina's hair is silky smooth, and mine looks like a rat's nest!"

"Trivial details. We'll figure it out," Rose insists. "It's not like you can really do that much to make this show worse."

Rose's comment so offends Rocky that he seems to forget all about her suggestion.

"I refuse," I exclaim. "Acting is beyond the scope of my contract."

But Granny just won't let this go. "To hell with your contract! Your friends are asking you to do this. A queasy expectant mother is asking you to do this. An old woman is asking you to do this. And when Franz finds out, he'll be asking you to do it, too, because I know he doesn't want to reimburse people for their tickets."

Damn, she's good.

"Absolutely not," says Rocky. Apparently finding out he's betrothed and a father is enough of a surprise for one night; he can't handle the idea of me acting in his show. "I won't have it. She's unfortunate-looking and dull. Just looking at her hair makes me sick. Her elocution skills are terrible. I will not allow you to ruin my work. You'll play that role over my dead body!"

After this string of compliments, someone speaks out vehemently: "Then prepare to die, asshole, because there's gonna be another Laura in the second act, and she'll knock your socks off."

I almost faint when I realize that voice is mine.

* * *

I'm ready. We solved the hair issue with a wig. I've got full stage makeup on. The dress fits me like a glove. I remember my lines . . . I think. Franz told me repeatedly that I don't have to do this, that we can postpone the performance, but I can't let Rocky get away with everything he just said. I am determined to show him I'm better than what he thinks of me.

As soon as the curtain rises, though, I curse myself for giving in to my pride. Couldn't I have just brushed off the insults and let bygones be bygones? But I can't let either Laura down—the character Laura that I love so much or the Laura whose name appears on the poster for the show. So I decide to throw myself into this performance, both for myself and for every woman out there who's in love with a man who ends up marrying someone else. I'm terrified, but here I go.

I am Laura as her mother forces her to wear a new dress in the hopes of catching the eye of their guest.

I am Laura as she trembles at the thought of being inadequate.

I am Laura as she curls up on the couch in front of her only friend, a laptop.

It comes naturally to me because I'm not acting. I'm being myself onstage. And everything happening onstage connects to my own life.

She loved him in high school.

He wouldn't even look her way.

She has no self-confidence.

He asks her to dance.

She shows him her collection.

He breaks the most important doll. It's an accident, but still.

Jim tells her, *"The different people are not like other people, but being different is nothing to be ashamed of. Because other people are not such wonderful people. They're one hundred times one thousand. You're one times one! They walk all over the earth. You just stay here. They're common as—weeds, but—you—well, you're—blue roses!"*

I almost cry as I dance with Jim, who I imagine to be Luca. I do cry as he kisses me. And when he reveals to me that he's engaged to be married, the tears come down my cheeks like waterfalls. No one expected this. Romina never cried in rehearsals. She looked sad and upset, but she didn't cry. I look like an orphan lost in the woods. But how can I hear him say, "Being in love has made a new man of me! The power of love is really pretty tremendous!" without thinking about how much I've changed? Or without asking myself what will become of me and where I will go from here?

Everything comes crashing down during the final scene—not just figuratively. I remain alone onstage, looking out into the audience, as the guy who plays Tom Wingfield tells me to turn off the light. I'm about to slowly press the switch, which will trigger the wings to fold in two after I leave the stage. But something catches my eye: Luca, in the front row. Despite my tendency these past few weeks to imagine him everywhere, this time I know I'm really seeing him. But this doesn't bother me quite as much as the fact that Erika is sitting next to him. What are they doing here? Why are they here together?

My thoughts jumble as I stare at them. I don't even notice the stagehands gesturing at me to get out of the way. I know I need to put one foot in front of the other and walk backstage, but at seeing them together, something inside shuts down. I can do nothing but stare. The backdrop falls and hits me in the head. I collapse to the floor. Now I see nothing.

I open my eyes to find myself in one of the dressing rooms. Lara, Giovanna, and Iriza are next to me. My head hurts. I'm having trouble extending my arm, as if I borrowed it from someone else and it's too big for my body. I curl my fingers, and I can feel them starting to swell already. Throbbing pain sears my whole arm.

"Fortunately, the backdrop is hollow," I hear Iriza say.

Giovanna places a bag of ice on my head. "How are you?" she asks.

"Let's get you to the emergency room right away," Lara whispers.

"Why didn't you move?" Iriza asks.

Lara and Giovanna look at each other, both grimacing. Their eyes do all the talking.

"You don't have to talk in sign language," I murmur. "I saw them together."

Lara's grimace turns furious. "We saw them, too. The nerve of them. They wanted to come see how you were doing. But I told your sister that if she even came near you, I'd kick her ass. The asshole, however, is waiting outside the dressing room."

"Luca is—"

"He's insisting that he has to talk to you. But if you let yourself—"

"I'm not going to see him. Not now, not ever," I say firmly.

My voice scares me. It's hard and sharp, which matches my mood exactly. He already hurt me so badly; I won't let him jerk me around anymore. What does he care about me for? He's got Erika now. The blow to my head seems to have turned on a lightbulb in my head. As painful as all of this is, I can see that I'm not at a crossroads. Instead, there's only one path to take, and there are no forks in the road.

"But you were so great," Iriza says. While she may not understand everything that's going on, she can tell that I'm upset about more than the head injury. "Your acting was incredible. Even Rocky went so far as to admit that you were tolerable. And I heard someone in the audience say that when you collapsed in the final scene, it was so realistic that you really seemed to be unconscious. You may want to consider a change in career."

"I don't think so. Wait, how are the Barbie dolls? Are they okay?"

"Don't worry. Everything's fine."

I breathe a sigh of relief. "Tell Rocky that I'm never doing this again. He's either going to have to get Romina a stash of antinausea drugs for the morning sickness or find a replacement. And Lara, if Luca's still around, I hereby authorize you to kick his ass. Although be careful, because he'll probably interpret it as flirting. Can we please go to the hospital now? I don't feel so good. But let's take the back exit. I don't want to run into anyone."

The emergency room doctor looks at me like I'm an asylum escapee. I don't blame her. My face is still caked with stage makeup and tears have plowed tracks down my cheeks. I feel dizzy, or drunk (although the only thing I've had to drink is a sip of juice that Lara forced me to suck through a straw). The hospital fixes me up a bed and admits me even though nothing is seriously wrong with me. In bed, I'm surrounded by a quadrangle of attention—Lara, Giovanna, and even Franz and Iriza, who insisted on tagging along. All this affection moves me. What more could I want? Well, for starters, I would have loved to have not noticed Luca and Erika. I wonder whose bright idea it was to come to the show.

I keep thinking about this even as the doctor examines me and asks me how I'm feeling. I respond mechanically until he asks about the play. Then I tell him that it was wonderful—even though the director's an asshole, the costume designer can't stop playing grab-ass with the executive producer, the lead actress had her head in a toilet half the night, and I came away with a head injury.

When the hospital releases me, Giovanna tries to persuade me to let her spend the night with me, but I want to be alone with my thoughts. I'm fine. I feel as fresh as a daisy. Or rather, a blue rose.

Franz insists on accompanying me home. He supports me as we walk to the front door of my apartment building. "Was that him?" he asks me as I dig in my purse for my keys.

"Who?"

"Was that the guy you're in love with? The one who wanted to get into the dressing room? I had to be stern with him. For a second, I thought he was gonna punch me."

"Yeah, that was him. In case you didn't notice, he was with another woman. To add insult to injury, she happens to be my sister."

"That complicates things, I suppose."

"I think it actually makes things easier. It's just as well. He doesn't give a shit about me. She can have him, for all I care!" I attempt a laugh, but it comes out as a neurotic guffaw.

"To be honest, he didn't really seem like he doesn't care. He was seriously worried about you."

"I'm sure he was worried about my health. He loves me in his own way. But there are other things that matter. Like how a person treats another person's heart, for example."

I realize something is wrong with the key as soon as I try to put it in the lock. I changed the lock so Luca couldn't show up unannounced again and must have grabbed the old key by mistake as I was leaving to go to the theater. Great. I'm locked out of my own home. I explain all this to Franz, but he doesn't seem to think it's as big a deal as I do.

"What's the problem? Just spend the night at my place, and we'll look for a locksmith tomorrow."

"What?"

"You know you're safe with me, right? Don't worry. I'm just offering you a roof and an aspirin."

"I just want to make it clear that—"

"You don't need to clarify anything, Carlotta."

Franz doesn't live very far away. His house is a charming cottage, neat and comfortable. There are just a few pieces of wooden furniture inside. He tries to make me take his room for the night, but I insist on sleeping on the sofa. I win the argument because I'm upset and exhausted, and my head is ringing like the Hunchback of Notre Dame has taken to it. Contradicting a person in this state would be rude, even if it is done out of kindness.

In the bathroom, I wash my face and look in the mirror. I'm very pale. Franz makes us dinner, pasta topped with a delicious pesto sauce and almonds. This guy is seriously marriage material. We talk about the show for a while. It went well, and people seemed to think that the actress change in the second act and the final blow to my head were all a part of Rocky's experimental theatrics.

"He really will need to find an actress to fill in for the role of Laura, though," I say firmly.

"I don't want to force you, but are you sure you don't want to do it?" Franz says. "Romina is in really bad shape." We laugh, thinking about Rocky's arranged marriage. His grandmother, very insistent that they be married before the baby comes, has already set the date. Her great-grandson must not be born out of wedlock. "You were way better than we expected," Franz goes on, "and it would only be for a few days, just until we can find another actress."

While I admit that my foray into acting was a bit more than I signed up for, doing it again is starting to seem feasible. Maybe it's the pain meds talking or maybe Franz's calming presence. But I can't help but think that maybe acting could be a kind of therapy, a way to heal and overcome the pain.

"All right, but only for a few days. And only because you asked me. But no more head injuries."

He smiles at me and offers me some fresh fruit. I'm chewing on a slice of apple that Franz pared with fatherly patience when he says something that surprises me.

"I really hate that guy."

"What guy?"

"The guy that's making you so gloomy."

I shrug. "What can you do? *C'est la vie*."

"You're right. *C'est la vie*. You can't always get what you want."

He looks at me, but I'd rather play dumb than follow his line of thought.

"Sure, take Iriza, for example," I say impulsively. "She hasn't gotten what she wants."

"What does she want?" Franz asks casually.

She might kill me, but I can't help it. "You."

He almost chokes on his apple.

"She hasn't said anything definite, but . . ." I pause. "Well, it seems like you might like her, too. If that's the case, please try not to hurt her. Don't tell her how you took pity on someone else who certainly doesn't deserve you."

I hope he understands what I'm trying to say.

When I tell him that I'm tired and need to rest, Franz nods and brings me a blanket. I turn on the television, and he turns off the lights.

"Thanks for everything," I whisper just before he disappears into his room.

So here I am, lying under a soft blanket, watching *Under Capricorn* with the volume on low, with a growing sense of insecurity that frightens me. There's no doubt in my mind that I'm doomed to become a barren spinster with nothing better to do than complain to the landlord about my neighbor's barking dogs. I will ignore any attractive men who may come my way (if they ever do again) simply because I once had the misfortune of loving one in a way that proved devastating. This pattern will continue as my hair turns white. And in eighty years, just like Rocky's grandmother, I'll try to recover my youth by attempting to hide my sad past behind a carefree facade.

As Ingrid Bergman spirals into an alcoholic depression, I think about Luca and how much water will have to flow under the bridge before I can forget.

EIGHTEEN

For the next two evenings I fill the role of Laura and dutifully kiss Jim onstage. Rocky seems more distraught as time goes on—he isn't wearing his kohl eyeliner, evidence enough—but I think it has more to do with Romina's newly acquired projectile-vomiting habit than the show.

Rose, however, has never been in a better mood. She's even forgotten about Franz's ass. Franz is suddenly very awkward around Iriza, although he tries to act normally. I don't understand how he never noticed Iriza's feelings for him. If it were me, I wouldn't have been so blinded by her facade of friendship.

One night, my father invites me to dinner. When I enter the restaurant, though, I realize I am not the only guest. Coretta and Erika are seated at the table with him, in the midst of conversation, and I'm tempted to run back outside and call him with a made-up excuse. But I can't do that to my dad. He was so excited on the phone, it reminded me of the childlike enthusiasm we shared when I was younger. So I gather my courage and head toward the table with a smile on my face that is meant only for him.

"My darling," he says, standing up and hugging me. Coretta shakes my hand, while Erika merely nods in my direction. For a while, we

Amabile Giusti

make small talk about my work, which Coretta is particularly interested in; the flowers that are blooming in the greenhouse; and the new kitten Coretta rescued one rainy night, who they named Anemone. As we order our food, I realize that Erika hasn't said much at all, and not one word to me—she won't even look me in the eye. She picks at her food and hasn't indulged at all in her favorite activity, provoking me. This is all very suspicious.

"Whatever became of that handsome young man who accompanied you to Beatrice's wedding?" my father says suddenly.

Erika and I both turn beet red. Her reaction comforts me—perhaps she's capable of feeling a shred of shame. But the question makes me nervous and annoyed. Even for Princess Bitchface, hooking up with your sister's ex-boyfriend right after they broke up isn't something to brag about. And okay, so we weren't *actually* together, but Erika doesn't know that . . . I hope. Although now I worry that Luca told her—maybe they even laughed about it together!

"It's a long story," I say, "but he wasn't anyone special." Now it's my turn to be the provocative one. "How about you, Erika? Are you seeing anyone?"

For the first time tonight, my sister looks at me, narrowing her eyes ever so briefly. I will never understand how her brain works. I'm the one who should be spiteful—she stole my man and humiliated me in public. She should be contrite and distraught, but instead, she's glaring at me! I would love nothing more than to grab her by the collar of her silk shirt, but my dad doesn't deserve such a scene. Besides, the only way to pull us off each other would be a spray from a fire hose.

"Yeah, I'm seeing someone. We're really happy together," she says finally.

"That's wonderful!" Dad says. "I'm so happy. Speaking of happy things, Coretta and I have good news to tell you."

They smile at each other knowingly. They're adorable together.

"We're getting married," Coretta says softly. "Your father and I are getting married!" As she says this, she demurely brings her left hand out from underneath the table and shows us a rose-gold ring shaped like a flower with tiny pavé diamond details. It's a beautiful and elegant ring. Coretta's cheeks turn a shade of coral. The joy I feel for them overshadows my anger. Even Erika appears pleased. I get up to hug and congratulate them, admiring the ring and asking all the right questions about the proposal.

After a minute, my dad pulls me aside and whispers in my ear. "You'll find love, too, honey. Don't worry. I had hoped it was that gentleman from the wedding, because he seemed to be truly taken with you . . . But it's okay. You'll find the right one for you. Don't give up. Remember, every experience is a gift, even the bad ones. My marriage to your mother brought me you. I'd do it all over again just to have you. You are, and always will be, my greatest love."

I put my head on his shoulder and let myself feel small and insecure for a moment, like a bird that hasn't yet learned to fly. If only I could tell him everything . . . But I can't. He's older now, his hair graying and his memory turning fragile, and I want to protect him from pain. I want him to be happy, especially now that he's found true love with Coretta, and to stay in his little bubble of flowers, leaves, roots, and the dirt under his fingernails. Thanks to my mother, he's already had his fair share of harsh reality. The least I can do is let him stay happy.

After dessert, we say good-bye. I'm the first to leave, and even though my dad tries to accompany me back to my apartment, I insist on walking home alone. I live close by, and it's a nice evening. As soon as I head out, I hear Erika behind me.

"Why don't you go out with that hot blond guy from the theater?" she calls. "The one who would bend over backward for you?" Of course she waits until now to bring this up. She had to put on the sweet little sister act in front of my dad and Coretta, but now she's showing her true colors.

"I could ask you the same question about the gentleman from the wedding," I hiss.

"Oh, you mean Luca?" she says. Her cocky attitude makes me want to slap her.

"I don't know, you tell me."

Her look rubs me raw. The tip of her tongue briefly touches her lower lip. "He's crazy about me, you know?"

I clench my fists inside my coat sleeves. "Well, this is a night full of congratulations all around. What great news."

"Do you have any good news to share?"

I could tell her the truth, about how I've spent a lot of time thinking about drowning myself in the river, about the pain that has shattered me like glass, but something inside makes me lie. I think it's my underlying need to prove to myself and to Luca that I don't care about him anymore.

"Actually, yeah. Franz and I are together. I didn't want to say anything because I didn't want to take any attention away from Dad and Coretta's announcement."

Erika squints. "So you *are* together?"

"Yup. He's the perfect guy. He is just so kind."

"Are you in love with him?"

I tighten the belt around my coat. "Since when do you care if I'm in love or not?" I ask casually. "Usually you couldn't care less. Or are you only asking because you want to make sure that it'll really hurt when you steal Franz from me?"

And with that, I turn around and leave, squaring my shoulders so I'll look confident and happy from behind. But my face betrays that I feel the exact opposite—more alone than ever.

One afternoon, Franz asks me to go with him to La Rinascente, an upscale department store, to buy a present for his daughter. He's going back to Germany in a few weeks to see her. He's as excited as a puppy as we navigate the department store. I discover that Franz is among the few men who don't seem to mind shopping trips. While he waits in line to buy a beautiful dollhouse that I would love to have myself, I go outside to window-shop. Suddenly, as I'm peering into the window of a shoe store, I notice a familiar shape in the reflection of the glass. Luca is behind me, standing at a flower kiosk displaying a sign that reads, *Roses for the One You Love.*

A burning sensation sizzles from my stomach to my heart. For such a big city, Rome can really be small when it wants to be. I stay put and spy on him in the reflection of the glass. He's scribbling on a delivery order card for a dozen roses. He looks self-conscious, like he's never done this before. And then he looks up and notices me. I think for a second I'll either faint or melt into the ground. But instead, I turn toward him without a hint of emotion. But my head is spinning so much that I feel like Dorothy whirling around in the tornado. I could pass right by him and ignore him, but I want to let him know that I'm over it.

"Hey!" I say exuberantly.

"Hey back," he says dryly.

Is that it? We just exchange niceties and go our respective ways, then don't see each other again for who knows how long? I get the impression that this is how it's going to be. Luca looks upset. Maybe he's feeling a little bit guilty for the way he treated me and for choosing to date my sister. He's lost weight. His features have hardened. His hair is longer, and there's a darkness in his eyes. Jesus, why do I feel like I want to comfort him? *Get a grip, Carlotta. He's not the victim here, you are!* I plaster a smile on my face and manage to ask him how he's doing.

"I'm fine," he replies, in a tone that's almost eerie. "How are you? Are you fully recovered from the theater incident?"

"Yeah, it was no big deal, thank God."

"Good. You seem really . . . calm."

"I just don't have too much to complain about these days."

"You were great in the play. I wasn't expecting that."

"Neither was I, but I wouldn't reprise my role even if I were up for a Tony Award. So what are you up to now? Are you still working at the bar?"

"Yeah. Every night."

"What about your book?"

"I finished it. I found an agent. He actually called it a masterpiece."

"That's great!" This time, my enthusiasm is sincere. I think he can sense this, because he relaxes. I've missed the smile that reaches his eyes. I've missed his full lips and his wavy hair. I smile back. "I'm so happy for you, Luca. I'm sure you'll find a publisher."

God, how I love him. I've been kidding myself. It's not over. I don't know what to do. I love him so much, it feels like there's a herd of horses in my stomach. He's so handsome. He runs his hands through his hair. Then, not knowing what to do with them, he shoves them in his pockets, only to pull them out and smooth his hair again.

"So everything's good with you," I continue.

"Yeah, everything's great."

"How's your mom?"

"Better. Much better."

"Good."

"Yeah."

I try to breathe new life into the conversation, throwing out, "You made a nice choice, by the way. Yellow roses are beautiful!"

"What? Oh, yeah, the flowers . . ." Now he seems awkward again. *Come on, Luca,* I think. *I know they're for Erika. Don't worry. I'll get over it, someday. Maybe then we can be friends again.*

"I gotta go. Franz is probably wondering where I went."

Luca flinches, then smiles at me dismissively.

"I'll see you around. Take care, Luca."

"All right. Take care, Carlotta."

I leave. I sense him standing motionless behind me, but I close my eyes and walk blindly for a few paces. My heart is pounding even under my eyelids. Franz catches up with me, a package tucked under his arm. It's way too small to be a dollhouse. He immediately notices my expression, then catches sight of Luca walking away.

"Everything okay?"

"Yeah, everything's fine. Where's Annika's present?"

"I'm having it sent to my house. I'm glad I'm driving to Germany, otherwise I wouldn't know how to get it there."

"She will love it. Any six-year-old girl would. She'll wish she could shrink down and live there herself. Shall we head back?"

In the car, my silence is palpable. Franz steals glances my way and tries to strike up conversations, but my answers are monosyllabic.

"I would love it if you came with me to Frankfurt," he murmurs.

"I'd like to go, too," I say. "I've wanted to see where *Heidi* took place since I was little. But I'm not a kid anymore. It wouldn't be fair."

"Fair for whom?"

"For everyone involved, Franz. For you, because I just see us as friends. For me, because I'm not the type of girl who gets over someone by getting under someone else. And for Iriza! It's already hard enough for her that I came here today to help you pick out Annika's present."

"But you and I—"

"I know, we're not a couple, we're not together, but it doesn't matter. What does matter is that I love her, even though I've only known her for a while, and that when you look at her, she lights up like Charlie seeing Willy Wonka's chocolate factory for the first time."

"You're wrong about that, you know."

"Men are so blind."

"So are women," he says enigmatically.

"What do you mean?"

"You'll see."

"What does that mean?"

His lack of response casts a shadow of doubt over me. Does that mean he has finally realized he actually does have feelings for Iriza? I hope with all my heart that he has.

Just as I'm about to get out of the car at my place, he stops me.

"I won't be there on your birthday, so I got you something."

He grabs the small package from the backseat of the car. I smile. What could he possibly have bought me at the department store? A doll, perhaps? I gleefully tear through the wrapping paper and find myself holding a strawberry-shaped purse, complete with a shoulder strap and a green magnetized clasp in the shape of the stem. It's adorable. It reminds me of something Luca once said about my appearance, but Franz doesn't deserve me thinking that. Neither does Luca.

"Thank you so much!" I exclaim. I imagine this is how Annika might feel when she sees her new dollhouse. I hug him. It's a platonic hug, but I know I will miss him while he's away. We've gotten so close the past few months. I wave as he drives off, the strawberry purse close to my chest and a twinkle of emotion in my eye. I can't wait to see him again.

Even though it's Saturday, I stay in tonight. I switch my answering machine on because I don't feel like talking to anyone, particularly my mother, who brought up the idea of a birthday party again recently. I ignored her. If she decides to throw me a party in spite of my protests, then she'll just have to do it without me. She can enjoy the ice sculptures, the coconut cake, and Aunt Porzia's famous anchovy puffs all by herself. Except she won't really be all by herself—the whole clan will no doubt be in attendance. Beatrice has given birth to twin boys, so she'll show up with the double stroller and attract all the attention. She has children to raise now, and in my family that makes a person worthy of respect. Since I have zero experience in that department, my birthday party wouldn't be about me at all; instead, the long, detailed story of Beatrice's labor—complete with a live demonstration of how loud she screamed and applause from the rest of the family—would be the center of attention. And like every year, I'd get drunk off of limoncello in a corner next to a pile of kitschy gifts while the relatives danced and the peacock-shaped ice sculptures melted.

So no birthday party for me, then. Turning thirty years old is hard enough as it is. I'm so glad I don't own a cell phone and changed the lock so my mother can't drop in here unannounced anymore. She can't reach me. I find myself perched on the couch, ready to consume an entire jar of Nutella, only to find that it expired two months ago. Oh well. If I get sick, no one will notice. They'll find me months later, shriveled up like a mummy.

I decide to get up and go into Luca's old room. I haven't been in there in weeks. The air smells musty. I sit down on the mattress and gaze at the painting on the wall between our rooms. And what a painting it is. It's huge. It takes up half the wall. I try to put myself in Luca's shoes the night he came back for his laptop and saw it. Now I notice how awful it looks. Judith looks pissed, and Holofernes looks like a sacrificial lamb. Why did I portray the characters like that? Instead of bringing justice, Luca's murder as Holofernes looks like a slaughter. What came over me? I wanted to paint the hatred that I was feeling. But maybe, despite all my efforts, I can't actually hate him. The biggest problem, I realize, isn't that I'm in love with him. People fall out of love every day, and it'll happen to me sooner or later (I hope). Love is like a trendy dress that will look outdated in just a year or two. The problem is that I love him in a different kind of way, too. I feel an affection toward him—and affection is like a classic, timeless outfit. This affection is what is preventing me from forgetting about him. That's the reason I painted Holofernes that way.

As I get up to leave his room, I notice that one of his desk drawers is slightly ajar, a white piece of paper sticking out of it. I open it to put the paper inside, and I freeze. It's Luca's entire novel, printed out in a stack in the drawer. He took his laptop with him but left a hard copy.

Did he mean to do this, or was it an oversight? I don't know, but I do know that my hands are trembling with excitement—I want to read it.

I lie down on my stomach on the bare mattress and dive through the pages. I read for hours on end, with no break. By the end, my eyes ache. I cross my arms and flop down on the bed, pondering it. I thought the main character was a little crazy, but she had a tragic past that made me cry as I read about it. I see pieces of myself in certain phrases that express her loneliness or reluctance to give her heart to another. When the love of her life is taken away from her, she turns into a ruthless, revenge-seeking assassin. Despite this, she's the type of woman I'd like to have as a friend. The erotic scenes are dense and detailed, with lots of moans and groans, but at the same time, they're incredibly . . . innocent. After fate crushes the heroine's dreams, the sex scenes are different. I'm astonished. Luca understands the difference—Luca knows what love is. So he must have realized somewhere along the line that two bodies coming together in love can exude purity, even though the mechanics are the same?

Reading this makes me love him even more. He shouldn't have let me see this side of him. Damn it, Luca. Trying to stop loving you is like trying to wrap my arms around the ocean.

NINETEEN

The play sells out for the next ten performances. The press gives it great reviews, especially after the authentic fainting on opening night. Next year, I hear, it'll go on tour around Italy. Rocky is even interviewed by a local TV station. He's wearing his scarf in the video clip, despite the heat of the day.

Today, however, is not warm at all. It doesn't feel like June at all. The sky is menacing, the air humid, and thunder rumbles in the distance. Despite the bad weather, I head to the theater to meet up with everyone to debrief.

The gang's almost all here, except for Franz, who left for Germany a few days ago. Even Romina's here. She finally stopped throwing up and has the tiniest baby bump. Rose looks after her like she's a precious child, escorting her everywhere and always keeping her within arm's reach.

"They're getting married in July," she tells us. "In a church! No civil union for these two. I'm thrilled. I don't know how long it's been since a member of our family has gotten married, let alone in the church. Rocky is very happy."

I think Rocky looks like he's ready to skip town and rebuild his life somewhere else. But perhaps he's just stressed because he has to eat real food now instead of his usual air-and-art diet. He says that he has a new project in mind: a reinterpretation of *Barefoot in the Park* by Neil Simon, set in a science-fiction future. I don't even want to imagine what that'll look like. He's telling us about the underground bunker where the newlyweds will live after the apocalypse, when he suddenly turns to me, where I'm sitting next to Iriza.

"You'll have to get busy finding those props," he says.

Rose erupts with loud laughter. "Admit it! She did a wonderful job. Just the other night, you told me that she managed to find you the entire Barbie doll collection you wanted, with a very tight budget. Our Carlotta is very smart."

Rocky looks like the announcer just declared a TKO, and he's the one down for the count. He makes a noncommittal noise under his breath. "She did okay for a Calabrian."

I guess I can't really expect anything more than that.

As we're chatting, the lights suddenly go out. A big clap of thunder shakes the foundation of the theater. My mind immediately jumps to the electric bill for the space—did we remember to pay it?—when I hear a buzz of voices in addition to the rain pounding on the roof. Soon after, a lit candle appears in the main aisle. I stand up, understanding it now. Today's the day. I'm thirty years old. Lara and Giovanna both called me quickly this morning, apologizing for not being able to stop by. Now I realize it was all a ploy. I had no idea they were planning a surprise party!

They're wheeling in, on a trolley, a three-layer cake covered in lavender icing and decorated with tiny sugar flowers. Millions of sparkling candles, or at least that's what it looks like to me, sit on top. The lights come back on again to a round of lively applause. I find myself at the center of a whirlwind of kisses, hugs, greetings, pats on the back, and presents. This is not nearly as tragic as some of the parties my mother has organized in the past, but I have to admit I hoped I would be able to fly under the radar on this one. I'm very grateful, though. It's always nice to know that you have real friends you can count on. Of course, Romina will still steal the show today because she's pregnant, but I'm happy. At least I don't have to pretend to be something I'm not, and no one will ask me about my job or whether I'm engaged yet. I blow out the candles and make a wish.

Giovanna comes over and whispers to me, "I'm sorry. I had to tell her. She bombarded me with phone calls."

I don't have enough time to figure out what she's talking about before my mother's shrill voice rings out. She makes her usual dramatic entrance, leaving more than a few people with their mouths agape. They must be wondering how this beautiful, elegant, tall woman could possibly have given birth to someone like me, who bears more resemblance to a monkey than to my own mother. Then they'll get a look at Aunt Porzia right after and see our unquestionable similarities. A man is with them who I've never seen before in my life. He looks about forty, on the lanky side, and mustached. I hope this is not another Catello repeat.

"Darling!" my mother exclaims as she air-kisses me, so as not to mess up her hair and makeup. Aunt Porzia grabs me and pinches my cheeks. The man shakes my hand. His grip is enough to crush my bones.

"This is Oreste," my mother gushes.

Oreste! The guy who sells panties! I had forgotten about him. I like him already, now that I know he's not here to seduce me on my birthday. He brings my knuckles to his lips and gives them a light kiss. Then he hands me a package gift-wrapped with a black lacy ribbon.

"It's a present for you!" my mother shrieks.

Apparently everyone else has nothing better to do than sit around and watch these events unfold. I unwrap the gift to find a thong that would make a prostitute blush.

"How subtle!" Rose blurts.

"What a chauvinistic, sexist gift," Lara says. "It's rather hideous, too. Not even a porn star would wear that."

Lara's comment doesn't appear to bother my mother whatsoever.

"In order to keep a man, you have to give him something nice to look at," she says. "You can't walk around dressed like a man and expect him to stay loyal. That's why husbands always run off with their secretaries!" She feigns innocence, even though she knows damn well that's what happened to Lara. Just as Lara and my mother are about to face off and Iriza is trying to calm everyone down by offering slices of cake, the curtain separating the foyer of the theater moves with a swish. I glance up . . . and wish I hadn't.

Erika and Luca are here together. Luca's hair is so wet that it looks like there are pearls at the ends of his locks, and his presence causes quite a stir. I get up, feeling like I've just had thirty cups of coffee. My hands and eyelids are twitching. My mother forgets about Lara, choosing instead to flatter Luca and cast admiring glances upon her favorite daughter. I've been reduced to a pile of crap once more. I mean, come on! I can barely handle the idea of them sleeping together. Showing up together on my birthday is just too much. What are they doing here? Who invited them?

I grab my coat and purse and find myself in the lobby before I've said good-bye to anyone. So what is this? The wish I made when I blew out the candles just five minutes ago was that I could be calm again, that my pain would heal, and this is how the birthday fairy treats me?

It's pouring outside. I don't think I'll have much luck getting a taxi. If I have to, I'll walk home. I'd rather risk getting pneumonia than stay here and watch the couple of the year reap their congratulations. Maybe Iriza can give me a ride home. I turn to go ask her when I see my little sister in the doorway, giving me a wry look.

"Leaving so soon?" she asks. It's not enough for her to take my man and share a laugh with him at my expense. She has to tease me, too. I nod but say nothing. "Why the long face, Carlotta? Isn't it your birthday?"

I stay silent, fuming.

"Here she is, the insatiable Carlotta Lieti!" she suddenly blurts out. "What are you doing, running away? You can't stand the idea that Erika, your mean, stupid sister, has something you want? Well, you know what? Rightly so. I have spent every moment of my twenty-five years wanting to be you. So now *you* can have a taste of what it feels like to be jealous of your sister."

"What? What the hell are you talking about? Are you insane?" I sputter.

"What can't you wrap your head around? That I brought this hot guy here with me, or that I said I wanted to be like you?"

"Obviously the latter. But it's gotta be your usual trick. You pretend to compliment me, but you're really trying to hurt me."

"Of course! I'm not just an illiterate slut, I'm also a total bitch. Erika Lieti, the brainless beauty," she snaps. "Did you ever think that maybe you were actually the wicked sister? Did you ever think that maybe I've always hated you because Dad likes you better? That maybe always having Mom and the aunts around might have been torture for me?"

"But—"

"You've always been too occupied with yourself, your books, Dad, and your fucking sarcasm to realize that the reason I left home when I was twenty was so I could get out from under your shadow! I needed to stop feeling so inferior to you. Your college degree, your feigned shyness, even your aversion to sex! I wish Dad would pay me half the attention he pays to you, even just for a second. I wanted to come get your advice before I lost my virginity all those years ago, but you looked at me like I was some bimbo . . . And now you have the nerve to criticize me for being with Luca? You really can't stand the idea that he could have feelings for me? Why is that? Do you just not think I deserve to be happy?"

What. The. Fuck.

Of all the strange things to happen today, I never saw this one coming. Erika's claim to envy *me*, the ugly sister with no boyfriend and no money, isn't just a surprise. It's an ambush. Is she serious? Or is this just her twisted way of getting me to stop hating her so she can feel better about taking Luca from me? I don't understand what's going on. Seeing her rage fueled by passion, sorrow, memories, and revenge . . . it hurts. And it angers me. At the same time that I want to just get out of here, I want to stay and work it out. The words catch in my throat. For a split second, I see her as she was when we were little, wearing Mom's clothes, lipstick smeared on her face. The same little girl tagging along wherever I went, unable to pronounce my name correctly.

Her disdainful laughter brings me back to reality; she's misinterpreted my silence. "Are you fresh out of your derisive little comments?"

I want to cry. All of the emotions of today, of yesterday, of the last thirty years crash together and surge up inside me. Instinctively, I take a step in her direction. I don't know if I want to make peace, continue the war, or make a run for it. Erika steps back as if I've slapped her. A hungry tiger would look more sympathetic right now.

"Don't you dare put on some pathetic little charade," she whispers. "And don't kid yourself. This isn't over."

And with that, she leaves the theater. My mouth hangs wide open. I sigh and shrug. This day has gone perfectly. I just found out my sister hates me even more than I thought she did, and for reasons that I'd never imagined.

I don't want to think about the one problem left to deal with— Luca and Erika staying together. I want to go home and shove Pringles in my face. But apparently the bell signaling the second round has already rung, because Luca's standing right where Erika just was.

"If you're looking for your woman, she just left," I tell him, shouldering my strawberry purse and trying to squeeze out the door.

"I'm looking for you," he says, his voice flat and emotionless. He blocks me from leaving.

"I don't know what you want, but I'm older now, and I need my rest. So I'm going to go home and try to forget about this awful birthday."

He grabs my arm. "We need to talk first."

"About what? Haven't you already said everything? What other wonderful things could you possibly tell the person who was the worst sex you've ever had?" I struggle against his grip, but Luca doesn't want to let me go. His eyes are burning with anger.

"What the hell is this, a sermon? Because you're so perfect? Maybe you've forgotten that you were the one who threw me out of that seedy motel. And you didn't exactly give my performance a rave review either! You're the one who wanted to forget that it ever happened. I would have liked to talk to you about what happened between us, but you just shut me up and turned me away. You made me feel like shit."

"*You* felt like shit?" I laugh. "I've got to be the hundredth girl you've slept with this year, at least."

"You're the most infuriating person I've ever met!" Luca fumes. "Just when I thought I knew you, it turns out I really didn't."

I escape him without replying and make it out the door. I'm drenched within three seconds of walking outside. But I don't care. I'd rather celebrate my birthday by being a murdered hitchhiker than stay in there a minute longer. Something is holding me back, however. I wince when I see it's Luca, also drenched from the rain. He's holding my hand.

"I haven't gotten laid in two months," he says grimly.

"Please apologize to your penis for me," I yell. "Will you let me go?"

"Go where? You're not walking in this. I don't have a car—I came here with your sister and she left. And we're not going to find a taxi anytime soon."

"I'm going to hitchhike, even if it kills me."

What is he doing? Is he . . . *smiling*? There's nothing to smile about. We're out here soaked to our underwear.

"What the fuck are you laughing at?"

"I'm laughing at you, silly."

"Has your impotence taken away your sanity?"

"That's entirely likely. I haven't felt sane in quite some time."

I wish he wouldn't look at me like that, like I'm some delicate feather. I wish he'd stop rubbing his thumb on my wrist. I wish he'd stop acting like it wasn't a big deal to show up here with my sister. He drags me under the shelter of a balcony, where the rain drips instead of pours.

"Luca . . . I don't understand what you want. You don't need my permission to be in love with my sister."

"I'm not in love with Erika."

"Don't lie. You're always out together. And the flowers? You've never given flowers to anyone. I knew right away they had to be for her."

"God, you're incredibly obtuse," Luca says. "First of all, Erika has been a pain in the ass. She's always coming into the bar where I work, and she follows me around constantly. I tried to be nice to her just because she's your sister. Secondly, I don't want Erika. I don't want her to be my girlfriend. I don't even want to sleep with her. She's too cold, always concerned with herself. She doesn't think about other people. She's like a statue. A beautiful one, yeah, but I only slept with her once. And third, the flowers weren't for her. They were . . . not important."

"Not important? It seems to me they were pretty important!"

"Shut up and listen. Let me get to the fourth point. I tried to call you to see if we could see each other, even if you were pissed at me, but you were never home. I always got your fucking voice mail. I'd rather smash my phone than talk to a recording. So then I came to your show, but I couldn't talk to you then. And believe it or not, Erika and I did not come together. We just happened to sit next to each other. So now I'm here. I just want to talk to you uninterrupted. Erika's the one who told me about the surprise party. And she asked you those questions about Franz for me, to see if you guys were together."

Words escape me. My sister's behavior shocks me. Everything I knew about Erika is upside down. She came to the theater—without knowing Luca was going to be there—to see *me*? She asked about Franz the other night at the restaurant for *Luca*?

"I wanted to talk to you in person, you know? Without that square getting in the way," he adds after a moment of silence.

"Who?"

"The blond guy. You're always together. Have you slept together?" he asks. His eyes are dark as iron coins. He stares at me with alarming intensity. I just don't understand. My stomach flip-flops.

"That's none of your business," I say without much conviction. My voice trembles a little, and I tremble a lot.

"But it is! I need you to tell me. Are you really together? Are you in love with him? If you are, just tell me to my face. If you love him, then . . . then . . . then I'll leave you in peace."

I stand there, completely dumbfounded. I don't know what to say. My heart pounds so hard it threatens to shatter my ribcage. Tears spring to Luca's eyes as he waits for my answer as if his life depended on my response.

"I haven't gotten laid in two months, not since that night at the motel," he says. "But you . . . That clearly hasn't been the case for you."

"You have a really short memory. Don't forget about the naked woman you brought into our home."

"I didn't do anything with her! I tried, of course; I'm a man. But nothing happened. I was confused, I felt desperate. You may as well have just cut my balls off, Carlotta."

I stare at him, shocked. I can't even breathe.

"Don't look at me like that," he continues. "For two months I tried to get laid but kept thinking about you instead. For two months I tried to see you, and when I finally did, I was faced with that creepy painting you did that told me exactly what you think of me!"

"Wh—what?" I stammer.

"Are you happy that you've reduced me to this? I've turned into someone who can't stop thinking about what you sound like when you're making love. I'm a fucking stalker, following you at the mall, pretending to buy flowers when you see me. I don't even know who I sent them to—I made up an address! So tell me, are you enjoying this?"

"No, I don't—"

"Carlotta, I don't know how much longer I can take this—this not knowing."

He brings me closer to him, hugging me.

"I don't understand."

"What's not clear to you? That I'm in love with you? That it was easy for me to believe that we were just friends until I saw you with another guy, and jealousy wreaked havoc on my insides? That I was so caught up at the motel that I forgot to use protection? I've never been that into someone before. I was afraid of you, of what I did, of how I feel, and of how I could have hurt you because I behaved like a foolish little boy. It's not true that you were the worst sex I ever had. I only said that to hurt you. Carlotta, could you please say something?"

It is not easy to formulate a response that resembles an actual word when all I want to do is let out a bestial scream of joy. I think my happiness is coming across as terror.

"Are you in love with Franz?" he asks.

I can't respond. I'm tongue-tied. He hugs me, and I'm afraid that it's good-bye. I need to tell him.

"Carlotta, you're the only person on this planet who couldn't see how I felt. I only slept with Erika because I was upset. I thought you were sleeping with Tony. I didn't do it to be with her, I did it to spite you. I was jealous, and I know it was wrong. I tried to write you a letter of apology, but I scrapped it. I couldn't find the right words. But if you give me a chance . . . If you let me show you . . ."

I'm sorry, what? Me? The girl with a face like a strawberry? The girl with the flat chest and porcupine hair? *I* should give *him* a chance? How did I end up with the power here?

I get up on the balls of my feet and trace a finger on his wet cheek. "Franz and I are just friends," I whisper. "Nothing has ever happened between us. I love you, you fool. I love you so much. I've loved you longer than you realize."

He smiles, and his expression jumps from astonishment to joy. He responds with a passionate kiss. His mouth tastes like rainwater, his tongue like dark chocolate. When we come up for air a moment or a century later, I note that it's still raining.

"I have an idea, my little butterfly. How about we go home and make love for three days straight?"

"That's not a terrible idea," I whisper. "But we're going to have to hitch a ride because neither of us has a car."

We laugh and kiss once more. I hear a noise behind us. There, under a bright pink umbrella, wearing a megawatt grin, is my mother. She holds a set of keys in her hand. I'm sure she's been standing there for a while, eavesdropping on every word of our conversation. Behind her, everyone from the theater is pressed against the glass, watching the spectacle that is my life. Rose gives me a thumbs-up. Iriza beams at me. Romina dabs at her eyes with a handkerchief. Lara glares at Luca, letting him know that she'll skin him alive if he makes one wrong move. Rocky looks like he's about to puke.

"Do you need a ride, my darlings?" my mother chirps. "Why don't you use Oreste's car? It's right over there." She points to an enormous blue Mercedes shining like a sapphire, parked at the curb. Luca takes the keys, but my mother isn't satisfied. Unexpectedly, she pulls something out of her pocket that I don't recognize right away.

"You forgot Oreste's present, honey. I'm sure it'll come in handy!"

My cheeks turn beet red with embarrassment. I'm about to say something, but Luca quickly grabs it and shoves it in his pocket.

"That's very thoughtful," he says. "It will certainly come in handy. I can't wait to tear it off of her."

I feel feverish. Even my mother, who has never heard the word *shame*, looks surprised. Then Luca leans forward and lowers his voice.

"I'll let it go this time, because he's letting us use his car. But if Oreste ever gives Carlotta a present like that again, I'll kick his ass."

No one has ever silenced my mother like that. Luca takes my hand and guides me to the car. We are so soaked that it's no longer worth trying to protect ourselves from the rain. We get into the car, laughing.

My mother's senses returned, she shouts after me, waving her umbrella. "Don't be dull, my darling Carlotta. Remember what I told you! Bad boys are always better in bed!"

EPILOGUE

My official initiation into my thirties has been nothing short of busy, considering what happened last night (twice) and then again this morning at dawn. Fireworks, with brief intervals to catch our breath. Now, as he sleeps, Luca seems so helpless. He's lying on his back with the sheets tangled around his waist. If I didn't know he was asleep, I'd say he looks posed. One arm is behind his head, the other at his side. His chest is bare, his hair in artistic disarray. But I know he's sleeping by his breathing, his soft features, and his relaxed muscles.

I get up to go to the bathroom, quickly throwing on a pair of his boxers with Kermit the Frog on the back. Luca stirs in his sleep. A little rest is in order after all that exercise.

In the mirror, I see a different person. I hate to admit it, but my mother was right. My skin is smooth, fresh, and radiant. I look ten years younger. The sex is good, but I think being in love makes it all the better. I love Luca, and Luca loves me, in all my weird glory. I feel stronger than I did yesterday, and tomorrow I'll feel stronger than I do today. The passage of time is nothing but a front for the timid and cowardly. Age is just a number. What counts is how you fill your years.

I've learned a lot from everyone over these past few months. Even my mother, in her own special way, taught me something: to not give up. I've developed a thick skin. In a sink-or-swim situation, I've learned to stay afloat. I think about Erika and all the things she said. She was so furious, but her eyes gave away her sadness. I stare into my own eyes in the mirror, thinking that I want to try to see her. I always assumed that our tattered relationship was her fault, but maybe I was to blame, too. I did to her what I did to Luca when he tried to open up to me: I assumed she was trying to insult me, and so I shut her down before she could hurt me. Of course, sarcasm can be a great defense mechanism, but sometimes you have to let yourself be vulnerable. I would give anything if it meant we could find our way back to being those two little girls who dreamed of being princesses someday. Maybe there's hope.

I smile at myself in the mirror, but then I remember something that makes me feel uneasy. I find myself in Luca's old room, standing on the mattress with a roller and a can of white paint. I'm not even dressed, but it has to be done. Judith and Holofernes gradually disappear under layers of white paint, their accusing, desperate eyes dissolving under the brushstrokes. The room feels lighter when I'm finished, and I'm pleased. There's a time for everything. I dealt with pain, and now I just want to be happy. I'll paint something new, perhaps a field of sunflowers.

I head into the kitchen, paint in my hair and on my hands, feeling ravenous. I open the fridge, only to discover the usual desolation. Apart from a jar of mayonnaise and an old banana, there's nothing to eat.

"I think we need to go grocery shopping," whispers a voice behind me. Luca hugs me from behind as his lips brush my ear, slide down my neck, and nip at my shoulder. His hands slip into Kermit the Frog's territory, and the butterflies in my stomach flutter their wings. A moan escapes me.

"I read your novel, you know," I whisper as he kisses me.

"I left it behind on purpose. Did you like it?"

"I like everything you do."

"Then let's go back to bed. I'll do *you* one more time."

He picks me up and brings me back to bed. There's nothing but love in his eyes.

I don't know what will happen tomorrow. All I know is that right now, I have everything I want in this bed, in these arms. Carlotta and Luca. The best of friends, ready for whatever the future holds.

ACKNOWLEDGMENTS

I met many wonderful people along this adventure, without whom I would be a sunflower deprived of sunlight. Thank you to Laura Ceccacci—you are so much more than an agent. You're a guardian angel and a wonderful friend. My gratitude comes from the heart and lands in your curls. I love you so much! Thank you to Cristina Caboni—I will never forget your encouragement and the confidence you've always had in me. You were the first to show me around in the middle of the storm. Thank you to Giulia Ichino for accepting this little wayfaring author. As soon as I heard your voice, I knew we were in for a beautiful journey together. Thank you to Laura Cerutti—you've been my rock in recent months. Thanks for your advice, your gentle wisdom, your crystalline laughter. Thanks to my family and close friends. Above all, a special thanks to Patrisha Mar—you're the reason that the Barbie dolls came into Carlotta's life. Because of you, I never felt alone, even in the darkest moments. Thanks to everyone who read the first version of this story—without your enthusiasm, affection, and support, I wouldn't be here. Finally, thank you to all the Carlottas in the world. I hope that this story is just crazy and romantic enough for you to dream and hope that the next toad you kiss may turn into a charming prince.

ABOUT THE AUTHOR

Photo © 2015

Amabile Giusti has lived in Calabria, Italy, her whole life. It's at the tip of the boot, nestled between the sea and the mountains, and close to an expanse of foliage that takes the shape of a seahorse when seen from above. While she has a degree in law, writing is her true passion. She's a great listener and doesn't talk much, but when she writes, she just can't stop . . . Ms. Giusti's other published works include *Non c'è niente che fa male così* (La Tartaruga, 2009) and, with Baldini & Castoldi, *Cuore Nero* (2011) and *Odyssea* (2013).

www.facebook.com/AmabileGiustiPaginaUfficiale
www.facebook.com/amabile.giusti

ABOUT THE TRANSLATOR

Photo © 2014 Lou McClellan (Thompson-McClellan)

Sarah Christine Varney is a translator of French, Spanish, Italian, and Portuguese. Her passion for languages began at a young age, when preparing for regional spelling bees took precedence over social activities. She holds a bachelor of arts degree in foreign languages from Scripps College and a master's degree in translation and interpreting from the University of Illinois at Urbana-Champaign. She is also passionate about the law; in addition to working full-time as a paralegal, she offers legal translation services as well. In her spare time, Ms. Varney enjoys literature, crossword puzzles, and foreign films. She currently resides in Kansas City, Missouri. This is her third published translation.